Please, God, let the guardrail stop her.

Slowing carefully as he approached the curve so as not to go off the road himself, he started around the bend.

No sign of the homicidal truck. And then he saw that the guardrail on this stretch of road was missing. A voice inside his skull started screaming, and the sound grew louder and louder as he stopped his truck. He jumped out before the wheels barely stopped turning. He raced over to the edge of the embankment and looked down in horror.

Long skid marks showed where her car had slid much of the way down a steep embankment. They stopped about three quarters of the way down and turned into big splat marks in the rocks. That was where her car had rolled. Heart in his throat, he traced them to the bottom of the ravine.

Anna's little red car was upside down, at least two hundred feet below.

His heart stopped. Literally stopped. He couldn't breathe, and a ten-ton weight crushed his chest.

* * *

Be sure to check out the rest of the Runaway Ranch miniseries later this year!

* * *

If you're on Twitter, tell us what you think of Harlequin Romantic Suspense! #harlequinromsuspense

Dear Reader,

I'm delighted that you've joined me this month for the launch of my new series about the Morgan clan of Runaway Ranch, Montana. The Morgan family has a long history of distinguished military service, and the latest batch of Morgan boys is no exception, until Brett Morgan's career goes up in smoke. Anna Larkin also left Sunny Creek in search of a dream and found only a horrible nightmare.

Now both of them have come home with their lives in tatters. Can they put their hearts back together and find a new life with each other in spite of past failures and the lingering secrets that follow them home?

Isn't that a question we all face when life throws us a curveball? How will we pick ourselves up and go on? In my humble experience, it's in our family we find our strength. It can be your blood family or intentional family, but they sustain us and lift us up when we're overwhelmed by life.

It's this love—this family—that the Morgan clan embodies, and why I'm so pleased to share their stories with you. So go pour yourself a beverage of your choice, curl up in a comfy spot and enjoy this book!

Warmly,

Cindy

NAVY SEAL'S DEADLY SECRET

Cindy Dees

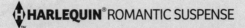

ISBN-13: 978-1-335-62639-4

Navy SEAL's Deadly Secret

Copyright © 2020 by Cynthia Dees

HARLEQUIN®
www.Harlequin.com

Printed in U.S.A.

New York Times and *USA TODAY* bestselling author **Cindy Dees** is the author of more than fifty novels. She draws upon her experience as a US Air Force pilot to write romantic suspense. She's a two-time winner of the prestigious RITA® Award for romance fiction, a two-time winner of the RT Reviewers' Choice Best Book Award for Romantic Suspense and an *RT Book Reviews* Career Achievement Award nominee. She loves to hear from readers at www.cindydees.com.

Books by Cindy Dees

Harlequin Romantic Suspense

Runaway Ranch

Navy SEAL's Deadly Secret

Mission Medusa

Special Forces: The Recruit
Special Forces: The Spy
Special Forces: The Operator

The Coltons of Roaring Springs

Colton Under Fire

Code: Warrior SEALs

Undercover with a SEAL
Her Secret Spy
Her Mission with a SEAL
Navy SEAL Cop

Soldier's Last Stand
The Spy's Secret Family
Captain's Call of Duty
Soldier's Rescue Mission
Her Hero After Dark
Breathless Encounter

Visit Cindy's Author Profile page at Harlequin.com for more titles.

Chapter 1

"Hoo baby, Anna. You've got a hot one at booth number nine!"

Anna Larkin glanced at the back of the diner and the lone man hunched in the last booth, looking intensely uncomfortable, as if he wanted to shrink into nothingness. As if he was attempting to be invisible, or at least to blend in with the locals.

Not happening. He was tall, broad-shouldered and gorgeous, with dark hair and eyes so blue she could see their color from the other end of Pittypat's Diner. Not the kind of guy who would ever blend in with the mere mortals of Sunny Creek, Montana.

He'd given it a good try, though. He wore a flannel shirt with the sleeves rolled up, and she would bet he was wearing jeans and cowboy boots under the scarred linoleum table.

"Well, go on," Patricia Moeller, the Pat of Pittypat's, urged her. "Say hello to the pretty man with no wedding ring."

Anna rolled her eyes at her boss. But she did tug down the hem of her T-shirt before she headed over with a glass of ice water.

Hoo baby didn't cover the half of it as she drew near her customer. His face was tanned, his features strong, his cheekbones chiseled out of Montana granite. She guessed him to be about thirty years old. A thin, red scar started near his ear and ran down into his shirt collar along the powerful neck of an athlete.

She studied him more closely. He looked familiar. But surely she would remember a face like that if she'd ever seen it before.

The old caution kicked in. She knew better than to fall for a pretty face. Much better. She'd suffered enough psychological wounds from the last pretty-faced man who crossed her path to make her skittish for a lifetime.

Maybe that was why she plunked this one's water down a little too hard, sloshing it onto the table and into his lap. He jumped, and their hands collided reaching for the paper napkin folded under his fork.

Hot. Hard. Strong. The sensations raced through her almost too fast to name. She jerked back, scalded. "I'm so sorry!" she stammered.

"It's just water. I won't melt," he said gruffly. He lifted the napkin out of her slack fingers and mopped at his crotch.

Realizing in horror that she was staring at his groin, she mumbled, "I'll, um, get you another glass of water."

"I'd rather have a cup of coffee."

"Right. Uh, how do you like it?"

His gaze snapped up to hers, startled and wary, as if some alarming innuendo was buried in her question. But then a faint smirk bent his lips. "I like it hot and sweet."

She stood there staring down at him like she'd lost her marbles until he murmured, "Coffee? May I have a cup?"

"Coffee. Right. Coming up." She whirled away, her face flaming in embarrassment. Good Lord. She'd been standing there, staring at him like a starstruck girl. And she was neither starstruck nor a girl anymore. She'd been both when she'd left Sunny Creek at the ripe old age of eighteen, but Eddie Billingham had stolen both her innocence and the stars from her eyes long ago.

"You okay?" Patricia asked her at the coffee station. "You look like you've seen a ghost."

"No ghosts in here," she retorted. Just ghosts in her head. The ghost of her innocent self. The ghost of her girlish hopes and dreams. The ghost of Eddie—

"I don't know," Patricia was saying. "Is that one of the Morgan boys? He looks mighty familiar."

Anna glanced over her shoulder at the customer and jumped to see him staring at her. Intently. She looked away hastily, staring unseeing at the coffeemaker. The Morgan family had four sons and two daughters, but they'd all moved away from Sunny Creek in the past decade. Last she'd heard, none of them showed any signs of returning.

Pattie continued, "He's got the look of a Morgan about him with that dark hair and those blue eyes. Good-looking like a Morgan, too."

"If you say so." She'd only had eyes for blond-haired, pale-blue-eyed Billie in high school. Stupid her. Anna poured a mug of coffee and piled a handful of sugar packets and containers of creamer on the saucer beside the mug. Determined not to spill hot coffee on her customer, she put the drink down carefully in front of him. "Can I get you a bite to eat?"

"Nah. Not hungry."

"Petunia baked this morning. Sure I can't get you a slice of her world-famous pumpkin chiffon pie?"

"No thanks."

The guy was showing no signs whatsoever of wanting to be social with her, and God knew, she didn't want to be social with him after making a complete fool of herself. She moved away, pausing at the next booth down to check on a retired couple passing through town in an RV. They asked for the check, which gave her an excuse to come back to this end of the dining room. She dropped off the bill and swung by the hunk's table.

"Need a refill on that coffee?" she asked.

"Nope. The deal was I had to drink one cup. No more."

What deal? She was tempted to ask him, but he forestalled her by frowning faintly at something over her shoulder. He muttered, "Someone just walked in and wants to be seated."

Far be it from her to look like she was hanging around his table trying to get his attention! She turned quickly and headed for the newcomer, yet another lone guy. Except this one looked to be in his early twenties. And if she didn't know better, she would say he was high. His entire demeanor was jittery. His hands were never still, and he tapped his booted heels incessantly. Like a flamenco dancer on crack.

God, she knew that look. Eddie used to get it when

he snorted crack to hype himself up before auditions…
and used his fists on her to come down from the hype
after auditions.

The guy pushed past Anna toward the counter and
the cash register, and she turned to ask him if he'd like
a booth, determined to be polite after being such a doo-
fus with her last single male customer.

Over the newcomer's shoulder, she spied her customer. He was frowning heavily, his gaze shifting back
and forth warily between her and the new guy. Trepidation leaped in her gut. The old panic that she would do
something wrong and provoke jealous violence flared,
making her insides quail.

Oh, wait. *Not Eddie.* She drew a breath of relief, tried
to exhale away the panic attack and turned to face Flamenco Heels.

She spied a flash of silver in his fist. *A knife.* Her
gazed riveted on the blade and time slowed around her
to a strange, silent blur while her mind kept churning
away.

Of course it was a knife. Karma was a bitch that way.

She watched the guy with the knife take a step toward her. Her entire world narrowed down to that lethal
bit of sharpened steel with her name on it. Of course it
was going to stab her in the belly. To gut her. Just like
she'd gutted Eddie.

The remembered feel of the blade slipping into her
husband's flesh, the slight resistance and then the slippery slide of it, the heat of blood gushing out onto her
fist, the metallic smell and taste of blood…

Relief flooded her, taking her by surprise, as the guy
took another slow-motion step toward her.

Thank God it was finally over. Justice had caught

up with her. There would be no more running from the truth. No more pretending she wasn't racked by guilt. No more fake smiles when people offered condolences.

She'd had no idea she was waiting for this—for the swift and certain retribution that was owed to her—until a punk with a knife charged her.

Her hands dropped to her sides. She stood up straight, threw her shoulders back and closed her eyes.

Peace. At last. A finish to the self-loathing and constant voice of judgment in her head.

Her body jerked backward without warning and she opened her eyes, startled.

Apparently, Flamenco Heels had stepped around behind her and thrown his arm around her neck, yanking her back against him. She staggered and choked as his arm dug into her airway.

She was no stranger to being choked and went limp in his arms, not fighting the unconsciousness to come. The kid turned, putting his back to the counter, dragging her with him.

She saw her customer surge up out of his booth, sending his coffee across his table in a spill of sable. Anna stared at him in dismay as he charged toward her. There was no need for him to put himself in harm's way! Not on her account. Particularly not since she'd been waiting for this ever since she got back to Sunny Creek. She'd known someone would come for her eventually. Eddie Billingham had always had plenty of hard-drinking friends and family in this town who were as violent as *he had been.*

She tried to shake her head at her customer. To warn him off. She managed only a frown, but hoped it was enough.

Nope.

He merely frowned back at her and kept on coming in a swift prowl that screamed of violence. And skill. He moved like some sort of trained killer.

"Give me all the cash in the register!" Flamenco Heels shouted in her ear. She was shoved forward violently and slammed into the edge of the counter.

Now. Kill me now, she begged the kid silently. *Before my customer gets here and stops you.*

The counter had slammed squarely into her solar plexus and knocked the wind plumb out of her. Gasping for air, she pushed upright just as something big and fast rushed past her. Spinning around to face her attacker, she was in time to see her customer smash into the would-be robber, shoulder first.

Both men crashed to the floor, the robber on the bottom taking the brunt of the impact.

The two men grappled, the kid's knife grasped in both of their fists. Her customer forced the punk's hand up over his head, but then the punk slugged her customer in the side with his free hand. Her customer grunted in pain, letting go of the kid's knife-wielding hand and rolling away sharply. She danced back out of the way of both men as they jumped to their feet.

Her customer slid in front of her, hooking his right arm around her waist and shoving her behind him. The robber jumped forward, knife first, and her customer reacted so fast Anna barely saw him move. His fist slammed down on the kid's elbow, and a terrible crunching sound of bone and tendon giving way accompanied the clatter of the knife on the floor. The punk screamed and collapsed around his ruined arm.

As the robber's face went down, her customer's knee

came up, connecting squarely with the kid's nose. Blood gushed from the robber's face, streaming down his chin onto his white T-shirt. He staggered back, holding his face.

"Take a knee," her customer said in a voice colder than arctic ice.

The robber was oblivious until her customer grabbed the kid's good arm and gave it an upward wrench. "Go. Down."

The robber dropped to his knees, and her customer maintained a grip on the guy's good arm, holding it twisted behind his back. The look in her customer's eyes was wild. Haunted even.

The front door burst open and she looked up sharply. The sheriff, Joe Westlake, charged in, hand on his holstered weapon. He took in the situation quickly, nodded at her customer standing over the bloody robber wannabe, and closed the snap holding the flap over his revolver.

"Helluva way to find out you're back," the sheriff boomed, pounding her customer fondly on the back.

Gradually, the trapped-animal terror in her customer's eyes faded. Caution replaced his panic. Belatedly, he mumbled, "Hey, Joe."

"Whatchya up to?"

"Doin' your job for you."

The sheriff laughed and cussed out her customer fondly, calling him Brett. Brett who?

Her brain clicked in recognition. Brett _Morgan_? Of the wealthy and powerful Morgan clan? Patricia had been right. All the Morgans were good-looking as sin, black Irish on their daddy's side and Norwegian on their mama's side, a big brawny bunch who owned and operated the Runaway Ranch. It sprawled north of town in the High Rockies beyond the Sunny Creek Valley. She'd never been out there, but she'd heard it was an impressive spread.

Relieved of the punk, her customer half straightened, favoring his side where he'd been punched. She lifted her hands to help him, but he subtly waved her off with the hand not pressed against his ribs.

"You okay?" he rasped.

"I'm fine. You?" she replied.

He straightened all the way, grimacing, and stared down at her, really looking at her. "Seriously. Are you all right?" he repeated.

"Yes."

He frowned, clearly not buying her answer. But then the sheriff loomed beside him, asking loud enough for everyone in the diner to hear, "Are you okay, Anna?"

She squirmed as all eyes in the diner turned on her. Lord, she hated all this attention. "I'm fine. Um, Brett Mor—" she stumbled over his name "—Morgan— rescued me."

"I'm going to need to interview you," Joe told her. "Can you swing by the station when you get off work today?"

Police. Questioning. Oh, God. The panic was back, clawing at the inside of her chest cavity. "What do you need from me?" she asked Westlake cautiously.

"I'll need a statement about what this punk said and did to you and what you saw in the fight."

"I would hardly call that a fight," she blurted. "It was a totally one-sided smackdown."

Her gaze lifted to the hooded stare of her customer,

and for the first time, a smile flitted across his face. Just for an instant. Then it was gone.

Petunia, Patricia's twin, emerged from her office, waving around a shotgun awkwardly enough that Anna briefly considered hitting the floor. Brett lunged forward and grabbed the ancient weapon by the barrel, pointing it up at the ceiling while he gently lifted the weapon out of the woman's hands.

Anna hurried over to the older woman and threw an arm around her shoulders. Petunia was shaking like a leaf. "Let me take you home, Miss Pitty."

"No, I'll be fine. I have to put the place back together and mop up that blood." The woman's legs started to give way, and Anna guided her quickly to a stool at the lunch counter.

The sheriff finished handcuffing the robber wannabe and headed for the door. "Brett, buddy. Can you take Petunia and Patricia to their place? They're looking a bit squeamish."

Patricia declared indignantly, "I'll have you know we don't get squeamish, Joseph Westlake. I remember when you fell off the roof of the hardware store and dislocated your shoulder. Who helped Mac MacGregor pop it back in and then fed you pie till you quit crying?"

Anna bit back a smile as the big, bad sheriff's ears turned red. A rusty sound vaguely akin to a laugh escaped Brett, and she stared at him in surprise. He didn't strike her as the kind of man who laughed often.

"Always were a jackass, Brett," the sheriff declared good-naturedly.

"Right back atchya, Joey."

The men traded good-natured insults as Brett escorted Petunia and Patricia out the door behind the sheriff and his prisoner. The door closed behind all of them, and suddenly the diner seemed hollow and empty.

An image of a knife flashed in her mind's eye. It started out as Flamenco Heels' knife but morphed into a bigger one. Clutched in her hand. Covered in blood. She shuddered all over at the gory memory. Would she never find a way to block out the image?

The remaining customers buzzed excitedly among themselves, cell phones out and texts flying. Anna winced. The gossip grapevine was one of the reasons she had run away from this town in the first place. And it was one of the main reasons why she'd dreaded coming back. What had she been thinking to come back here, anyway?

The adrenaline of the past few minutes drained away, and sudden exhaustion slammed into her. She trudged into the storeroom and filled the mop bucket, pushing it out to the dining room. Shuddering at the blood on the floor, seeing another, much larger pool of blood on a different cheap linoleum floor in her mind's eye, she hurried to erase the evidence of the crime. But which crime she was trying to erase—of that she wasn't sure.

A few swipes of the mop got rid of most of the robber's blood, but she had to get down on her hands and knees to reach under the counter to get the last of it. Nauseated, she ran a sponge under the counter, seeing another counter in a small, dingy kitchen.

Her finger touched something cold and hard. Metal. Startled, she peered under the pie display case. Something circular and round glinted under there, but it wasn't a coin. She used the mop handle to snag it and drag the object out.

It turned out to be a quarter-sized gold medal on a

thin gold chain. The piece was beautifully carved on one side, the figure of a man holding a sword high over the head of what looked like a dragon. Saint George, maybe? Wasn't he the guy who slayed dragons?

She turned the medal over. It was engraved with the words *B—Always come home safe—Love, Mom*."

B for *Brett*, maybe? Or did this belong to the robber? She tucked it in her pocket to take to the sheriff.

The rest of her shift was busy as locals flocked to the diner to hear the story of the robbery and check out the damage—which amounted to one smashed chair and the coat stand being knocked over. *Sheesh. Nosy much?*

She wanted nothing more than to go home to the tiny house she'd inherited when her mother died, curl up in a ball and sleep for about a month.

Instead, she smiled and pretended she wasn't shaken to her core, that the resurgent memories hadn't freaked her completely out, and served up pie and coffee in a continuous stream. She had never been so relieved to hang up her apron when the supper waitress, Wanda, showed up for her shift at 4:00 p.m.

It was just as well that she had agreed to visit the sheriff today. She was too wiped out, first by the robbery and then by the continuous flow of customers who'd kept her hopping, to make the drive over to Hillsdale to check out some used windows at a junk shop as she'd planned to after work.

She stepped into the combination police office and jail, acutely uncomfortable at the overpowering atmosphere of law and order. She'd never had a run-in with the law here in Sunny Creek, but the law was the law, no matter where she was. And she had no love for police. Not after the past few years.

"Thanks for coming down to the station, Anna," Joe Westlake said pleasantly enough.

She nodded, her throat too tight to speak. For crying out loud, she was the victim here. There was no need for her to feel like she'd just committed a murder. Still. Old habits died hard.

She perched on the edge of a chair beside the sheriff's desk while he tape-recorded her hesitant description of the robbery.

"Oh, I forgot," she said after he'd turned off the tape recorder. "Does this necklace belong to the robber? I found it on the floor when I was mopping up after the fight…er, robbery." She fished out the Saint George's medal and held it up.

"I recognize that!" Westlake exclaimed. "That's Brett's. His mom gave it to him just before he enlisted in the Navy. Want me to run it out to him?"

Her fist closed around the medal, warm from her pocket. "No, that's all right. I'll return it to him."

Now why on earth did she go and say that? She wanted nothing to do with men at all, let alone a good-looking one capable of hair-trigger violence and who made her belly flutter in ways it had no business whatsoever fluttering.

Chapter 2

Brett sank carefully into a crappy recliner that had been crappy thirty years ago, swearing under his breath at the knives of pain jabbing his side. The punk had punched him right over the spot where he'd broken a bunch of ribs in the explosion that ended his military career and erased his memory of the last hour of said career. An hour he would give anything—anything— to recover.

Dangling a bottle of beer in his fingers over the edge of the armrest, he closed his eyes. Immediately, the events in the diner started running through his mind. Oh, sure. He could remember every single second in the diner. But could he remember a damned thing about that mountain pass with his men? Hell, no.

He didn't even *want* to remember acting like a crazy man in Pittypat's. He'd decided not to intervene in the robbery. Truly. But then the strangest look had come across that waitress's face—certainty that she was going to die. Acceptance that her life was over. She was *way* too young to be killed. Just like his men had been. He hadn't been able to stop himself from trying to save her. He'd leaped to his feet and had to be some kind of hero. Damn, damn, damn, damn, damn.

Damn his old man for making him go to town. For making him interact with human beings at least once a month as the condition for letting Brett hole up in this old hunting cabin on the family ranch. This was what came of it. He ended up busting up some kid.

Hell, the kid was lucky Brett hadn't killed him. Lord knew, he'd been tempted. When he saw that punk slam the pretty waitress into the counter, something had snapped inside his head. The same something that was preventing him from remembering what happened on his last mission. It was that exact something that made him a menace to society and had sent him up here into the mountains to an isolated cabin to drink away his memories or die trying.

A furry head bumped his free hand, sliding under his palm until it rested on a soft back. "Hey, Reggie," Brett muttered.

The black Lab took another slow step forward, bringing Brett's hand to rest at the base of his tail. Brett obligingly scratched the dog's back over the spot where the dog's pelvis had been broken and subsequently repaired, leaving him with a permanent limp. They made a perfect pair. Both broken. Both alone in the world.

"You're a good boy, aren't you?" The dog's tail thumped against the side of the recliner.

"At least I don't have to go back to town for another

month," he told the dog. "Until then, it's you and me, buddy. The rest of the world can go straight to hell."

Brett took a long slug from his beer, not particularly enjoying the taste. But a man could drink only so much whiskey before he needed a change of pace. Beer didn't provide as fast or sharp an escape from reality as hard liquor, but it got the job done eventually.

He'd downed the rest of his beer and must have dozed off because he jolted awake to a short, sharp bark of warning from Reggie.

Brett bolted from the chair and into the shadows beside the front window, hiding behind the cream-and-brown plaid curtains. His palm itched to feel the cold steel of a weapon. But his father—wisely—had removed all firearms from the cabin. Not that he needed a gun to be lethal, of course. Hell, he didn't even need a knife. His bare hands would do the trick. Brett peered through the filthy window, his gaze predatory, seeking the slightest movement of an incoming threat.

There. A vehicle was coming slowly up the gravel switchback trail that served as a road to this place. It was one of those prissy little hybrid cars, all ecological self-righteousness and no muscle. Who in the hell was driving one of those up here? Nobody with a lick of sense came up into the high mountains without four-wheel drive and a set of chains in the back of their vehicle. The weather was unpredictable as hell, and snow was known to fall up here on the Fourth of July.

It might be sunny now, but in ten minutes, a line of storms could blow in over the mountain peaks at his back and drop a deluge of rain that turned the road into a sheet of slick mud or blow in a blizzard that made the mountain entirely impassable for days or weeks.

Apparently, his would-be visitor knew none of that because the little car continued chugging up the track toward him. More irritated than interested, he waited to see who would climb out of the car. The vehicle stopped beside his muddy pickup truck and the door opened.

The waitress from Pittypat's? He hadn't seen that one coming. What the hell did she want? To spill another drink on him?

Which was, of course, an uncharitable thought. He had long experience with women being flummoxed by his good looks, and she was far from the first waitress to dump a drink on him. At least she hadn't insisted on mopping his lap for him like most of the others had.

She marched determinedly on the steppingstones across the patch of wildflowers and moss that served as a front yard and up the porch steps. Her feet hardly echoed on the old wood, though. Tiny little thing, she was.

Should he pretend not to be home? He'd already done his minimum human interaction for this month. He didn't have to talk with her. No. He wouldn't answer the door.

She knocked on the aged-wood panel hesitantly.

She didn't want to be here either, huh? Then what brought her all the way out here in the middle of nowhere?

Maybe he should find out. He didn't have to let her in, after all. He moved over to the door and opened it just as she raised her hand to knock again. Her hand fell forward awkwardly into thin air, and she looked startled. Her big brown eyes were wide and wary, like a doe's, as she stared at him.

"Um, hi," she said breathlessly. Was that the eight-thousand-foot altitude or his stealing her breath away? Not that he cared, of course.

"Can I help you?" he asked gruffly. Lord. When was the last time he talked with a woman? Before his last tour in Afghanistan. That would make it almost two years. He was out of practice.

"I wanted to thank you for saving me from that guy earlier." She sounded like she'd rehearsed that line all the way up here.

His first impulse was to shrug it away. He ought to be thanking her for not freaking out completely while he pounded the punk into hamburger. But he could hear his mother threatening to tan his hide if he wasn't polite in response to his visitor. And nobody messed with Miranda Morgan. He ended up mumbling, "No problem."

"I think you dropped something during the fight. I found this when I was cleaning up afterward." She fumbled in her pocket and pulled out a pile of gold chain and his Saint George's medal. "Is this yours?"

He nodded tersely. "A gift. From my mother."

She smiled, and her pretty face transformed in an instant to fantastically beautiful. He stared, stunned. Her smile burned as bright as the sun. Hell, he could feel its warmth on his skin. It didn't last long, though, and was quickly replaced by a tiny frown between her gently curving brows. She murmured, back to being shy and uncomfortable, "The ring holding the chain to the clasp broke, but I fixed it for you."

Startled, he mumbled his thanks without meeting her cinnamon gaze.

She held it out to him and he took it, his fingertips brushing against hers. The girl froze, her face turning into a careful mask. But her eyes. Good grief, her eyes. He'd seen that haunted look in the eyes of women in the worst war zones on Earth. Women who'd seen more suffering and lost more loved ones than any human soul could bear without breaking. He shook off the memory of the horrors that had made those women into ghastly specters of their former selves in time to see the wait-ress shiver like a dead man had just touched her. *Da hell?* He studied her more closely.

He'd checked her out in the diner, of course. After all, he wasn't dead yet. He'd registered the gold-streaked chestnut hair, light brown eyes and great legs encased in tight denim. She looked athletic, rather than skinny, although she barely topped five foot four. He could imagine those juicy legs wrapped around his hips—

Ix-nay on the exy-say thoughts.

He slipped the necklace over his head and tucked the medal inside the collar of his shirt. He was surprised by the sigh of relief that slipped out of him. That medal had been to hell and back with him. It had protected him through four combat tours and brought him home in one piece, if not exactly unharmed.

"Is your side okay?" she blurted awkwardly. "That kid didn't hurt you did he?"

He snorted in disdain. "Not hardly. It would take a hell of lot more skilled fighter than that to challenge me." He hadn't been a forward operator in the U.S. Army Rangers for nothing. Hell, he'd gone hand to hand against Taliban fighters who were whipcord hard and fighting for their lives. Now *they* were a challenge.

"Glad to hear it," she murmured. Yet another awkward silence fell between them, and he wasn't inclined in the least to help out his visitor. The sooner she caught a clue and went away, the better.

"My name's Anna, by the way. Anna Larkin."

The name was familiar. She'd been a year behind him in high school. Hadn't she run away from home right after graduation senior year to pursue an acting career in Hollywood or something? "Did you ever go to California?" he shocked himself by asking.

The strangest thing happened. Her entire demeanor changed, and she folded in on herself, literally hugging her waist with her arms and doubling over a little as if he'd kicked her in the gut. All the light went out of her eyes, and lines of grief etched themselves around her eyes. Geez oh Pete! What did he say?

"Yeah," she mumbled. "I made it to California."

But she was back here, now. From that, he assumed the Hollywood dream hadn't gone as she'd hoped. Too bad. She seemed like a nice person. He asked, "Didn't Eddie Billingham go with you?" Eddie had been in his class in high school, and Brett had always found him arrogant and self-centered. Of course, it hadn't helped keep Eddie's ego in check that every girl in school seemed willing to sleep with him at the snap of his fingers.

Anna shook her head, not as if to say no, but as if to ward off the question. Huh. Bad blood between her and Eddie, maybe?

"Well, thanks for fixing my necklace and coming all the way out here to return it," he tried, hoping she would catch the hint and vamoose.

She nodded and took a step back from him. She backed away from him quickly, her hands up defensively. What in the hell had he said to flip her out like that?

"Watch out!" he cried hoarsely. But too late. She stepped backward off the edge of the porch, missing the step with her foot and tumbling backward, arms flailing.

He lunged forward and made a grab at her, but missed. She went down, rolling heels over head and landing in a crumpled heap at the foot of the porch steps. He raced after her, dropping to his knees beside her.

Explosion. Screaming. Blood. His guys. Oh, God. His guys. Death. Loss. Agony.

He fought to breathe, fought the panic. Clawed his way back from the abyss inch by black, painful inch. He didn't know how long it took, but he finally blinked his eyes hard, clearing the last remnants of hell from his mind's eye, replacing them with a pretty young woman sprawled, unconscious on the ground.

Crap. Anna was out cold. He reached quickly for her throat, relieved beyond belief to feel a strong, steady pulse beating beneath her fragile, transparent skin. His fingers trailed down the slender column of her neck, reveling in the silken softness, so foreign to his hard-edged world.

He jerked his fingertips away from her neck and swore luridly. What the hell was he doing? He was damaged goods. Worthless to any woman.

Carefully, he slipped his hand under her head and felt her scalp for bumps or blood. Nothing. His palm slid ever so gently down the back of her neck, counting vertebrae and checking for any protrusions or swelling to indicate a neck injury. Nothing.

Very gently, he ran his thumbs outward from the hollow of her throat, tracing the line of her collarbones. So delicate. So feminine. And thankfully, intact. He swept his hands down her rib cage next, shocked at how much of them his hands spanned. She really was a tiny little thing. Her T-shirt was soft and worn beneath his hands and felt like…home.

He could tell by looking that her legs were lying at the correct angles. She might have wrenched a knee or ankle, but nothing was obviously broken. He sat back on his heels, frowning. She was going to get cold fast lying on the ground like this, though.

He slipped his arms underneath her shoulders and knees, and awkwardly climbed to his feet. Aw, hell. His ribs protested violently, and he gritted his teeth against the fiery agony shooting through his side. He staggered up the front steps with her and laid her down on the dry wood porch.

She started to stir and he jumped back from her as if she would bite him, hating himself for the impulse. Since when had he become afraid of small, unconscious women who meant him no harm? Was he that screwed up in the head? He was a warrior, for crying out loud. He'd stared down death and laughed in its face more times than he cared to count.

And yet, here he was, hiding from humanity. Hiding from himself. From his own memories. He backed another step away from Anna as she reached for her head and felt it gingerly. She opened her eyes, frowning faintly until she caught sight of him.

"Oh dear," she sighed. "I am a bit of a klutz, aren't I?"

He felt no need to restate the obvious. Of course she was a klutz. A rather adorable one, in fact.

She sat up and reached for the porch post. He offered his hand down to her. She looked startled, nervous even. But she laid her hand in his. It was soft. Fine boned. As delicate as the rest of her. And cold, too. He gave a gentle tug and she popped up to her feet. He watched, his gut turbulent as she dusted off her rear end. Her very nice rear end. Cupped temptingly in those skinny jeans. *Off-limits. Dangerous.*

"You'd best come inside," he said gruffly. "Warm up and make sure you don't have a concussion or something."

She stared up at him as if she didn't comprehend his words. She mumbled, "Feels like weather moving in. I'd better get off the mountain before it hits."

"Are you sure? You hit your head hard enough to knock you out. You should stay a little while. Just to be safe—"

She cut him off. "Thanks. But I'll be okay."

One part of his mind chanted silently to her, *Go away. Go away. Go away.* But another part of it whispered, *Don't go. Don't go. Don't go.* He wasn't going to beg. And it was her life, after all. Still, he wished she would stay long enough to make sure she wasn't seriously hurt.

She'd gotten that look in her eyes again. The haunted one that screamed of mistreatment and abuse at the hands of a man.

He crossed his arms over his chest, anchoring his hands to stop them from reaching out and forcing her to stay. He wasn't about to force any woman to do anything she didn't want to. Especially when it put that awful hurt look in her eyes.

He watched helplessly as she turned and navigated the porch steps facing forward this time, with better success than before.

She glanced over her shoulder at him as she opened her car door, her eyes wide with fear. As much as he hated the idea of a woman being afraid of him, maybe if she was scared of him, she would leave him the hell alone.

Except something painful twisted deep in his gut as he stood there, unmoving, and watched her drive away. Lonely. He was lonely.

Which was no less than he'd earned.

It was better this way. He didn't deserve to be part of the human race.

Chapter 3

She'd made it back to the sprawling stone-and-log mansion that had literally stolen her breath when she'd passed it on her way up to Brett Morgan's place when it started to sleet. She barely spared a glance for the massive dwelling now. She had to get down to a lower altitude and warmer temperatures that would turn this wintry precipitation back into relatively harmless rain. Her lightweight car wasn't the least bit suited for the high Rockies.

She couldn't stop picturing the man she'd left behind, brooding on his mountain. There was something... wounded...about him.

God knew, she'd never been able to resist hard-luck cases. She had taken in cats and dogs and wild animals—and humans—in need of healing for pretty much her entire life. There was no reason to believe that impulse would stop just because she had come home to Sunny Creek or because she was wounded herself.

Dark was falling by the time she pulled into the driveway of her bungalow—a renovation project in progress. She hadn't grown up here; her mother had inherited the run-down house from a crazy great-uncle after Anna left town.

She could picture the finished craftsman cottage in her mind's eye, but whether she would ever actually transform the decrepit structure before her into that homey, welcoming vision was anyone's guess.

But hey. The new roof didn't leak. And good Lord willing, the furnace she'd spent the past two weeks rebuilding would turn on tonight. Winter was coming, sweeping down out of the high reaches to consume the narrow valley that the Sunny Creek and town by the same name huddled in.

As she hustled inside her house on a gust of bitter wind, a few snowflakes flew past her nose. Yep. The cold was already cutting painfully through her California-conditioned body.

She called Vinny Benson, owner of the junk shop in Hillsdale, as soon as she shrugged out of her coat, scarf, sweater, and mittens. "Hey, Vinny. It's your favorite impoverished house renovator."

"Hey, baby. You coming to see me tonight? The windows I got are sweet. Original weighted mechanisms and everything. Dimensions are exactly what you need."

"I'm sure I'm going to buy them, but I got hung up at the diner today and can't make it over tonight. Looks like some weather's blowing in anyway. I can't risk the trip over the McMinn Pass."

"It's not snowing up in the pass, yet. Come on over to Hillsdale anyway. If you get snowed in, you can always shack up with me."

A chill chattered down her spine. That was the sort of thing a teenaged Eddie would have said. Vinny was endlessly hitting on her, but so far, was harmless. So far. Not that she trusted any man to stay harmless for long. She had no intention of getting snowed in with him or anyone else. She took a deep breath and forced herself not to tell him what she really thought of him and all men. "I can head over there first thing in the morning to buy the windows. Just hold them for me, please." She grimaced and amended, "Pretty please?"

She despised flirting with men, but if it got her the wooden replacement windows for her living room that she'd been hunting for desperately since she bought this house, she would find a way to stand it.

Vinny tried to extract a dinner date out of her in exchange for holding the stupid windows, but she made a lame excuse about having to work and dodged that bullet. Finally, he agreed to just hold the windows for her.

That unpleasant fire put out, she moved through the kitchen into the bungalow's main room, a combination dining-living area. Might as well sand a little paneling tonight. The exercise would help keep her warm in the drafty house. Until those new windows were installed, she was resigned to more or less camping inside her home.

She set her phone on top of a cheap speaker and blasted beach music as she sighed, picked up a piece of sandpaper and went to work on the wooden wainscoting. At the current rate of progress, she figured she would complete refinishing the walls in approximately a million years.

It would go a ton faster with a power sander, but she was trying to save every penny and put all her money back into the materials she needed to restore the home. Elbow grease was free, and she had plenty of that. Besides, the mindlessly repetitive work of sanding wood lulled her brain into a state of thoughtless boredom in which she could actually, oh, sleep from time to time. And the physical labor tired her out enough that, on a good night, she wasn't beset by nightmares that had her awake and screaming in the wee hours.

Sometimes, the enormity of the project she'd taken on got to her, though, and tonight was one of those times. In lieu of crying, she opted to sing along with a classic Beach Boys tune and dance around the spacious living room. It would be a gracious room if she ever managed to make it habitable for humans. Maybe someday she would finally put this house and her life back together. Someday. But not this day.

Brett heated up a can of baked beans and poured them over a couple of slices of toast. He was just sitting down to eat the makeshift grub when headlights flashed through the window. Reggie growled beside him.

"Now who's come to bug us?" he grumbled at the dog.

Reggie merely glared at the front door and growled again, low in his throat.

A door slammed outside, and a familiar voice called, "Brett? You home?"

Oh dear Jesus. His mother. The original Morgan hurricane. No way in hell would she go away quietly after a few not-so-subtle hints like Anna Larkin had. And he couldn't very well pretend not to be here. Miranda would have to walk right past his truck, parked out front as proud as you please, to get to the front porch. Swearing under his breath, he opened the door.

"Of course I'm home, Mother. My truck's parked out front and the lights are on in the cabin."

"I heard there was some excitement down at Pittypat's today. Are you okay, sweetie?"

He ground his molars together at being called sweetie. He was a freaking commando, for crying out loud, and had killed dozens, or maybe hundreds, of hostiles over the years. Only Miranda Morgan had the gall to call him something so childish and insulting.

"I'm fine. Thanks for coming up to check on me."

She stomped up the steps like a freight train gathering momentum. Nope. Not gonna take the hint to go away. Dammit. She barreled inside the tiny cabin, filling it up with her huge personality. "This place is a dump. You really should have let me redecorate it before you moved in here," she announced.

"It's fine for me. I don't need anything fancy. Just a roof over my head and a dry place to lie down at night." What he did most nights didn't actually qualify as sleep, truth be told. He tossed and turned in between nightmares that woke him sweating in cold terror, most nights.

"Is that what you're eating for supper?" she demanded. "Come down to the main house and let Willa cook you a proper supper."

"Willa Mathers? Hank's daughter?"

"Correct. She helps me out around the house and does some bookkeeping and filing for your father when she's not studying. She's going to school, you know. Working on a PhD in counseling or something."

Good for her. Daughter of the ranch's longtime foreman, he remembered Willa as a skinny kid with long black braids and a magic touch with horses.

"Seriously, Brett. I'm not letting you sit up here starving yourself to death."

"Do I look like I'm starving?"

"All this time you're spending alone isn't good for you. Come down to the house and eat supper with us every day."

Brett's voice went flat. "No."

He was *not* putting himself in the way of his father on a daily basis. No way. John Morgan was a born-again son of a bitch, and he could do without his father's judgment and condescending crap, thank you very much. Just because his father was a decorated war hero didn't mean his sons had to be the same.

Hell, he didn't know if he was a hero or a traitor, anyway, after that last mission. If only he could remember—

"You sound as stubborn your father when you talk like that."

His gaze narrowed to a cold stare. He would take that as a compliment, this time. "Don't push me, Mom. I'm only here until I figure out what I'm doing next. If you can't leave me alone like you agreed to, just say the word, and I'm gone."

Miranda scowled back at him, no less stubborn than him or his father. Silence stretched between them as Brett refused to be the one to give in, and Miranda did the same. Even Reggie felt the tension, for the dog eventually whimpered and came over to bump Brett's hand. The mutt seemed to be looking for reassurance more than a scratch, so Brett let his hand rest on the dog's back.

"Fine. Be like that," Miranda huffed.

He didn't deign to speak or to let her off the hook.

She flopped down on the ratty sofa and threw up her hands. "So what happened at Pittypat's? Joe called to tell me you broke a guy's nose and arm."

He ground out, "The *guy* was a punk who tried to rob the place. I stopped him."

"By half killing him?"

"Trust me. If I had tried to kill him, he would be dead."

Miranda rolled her eyes, not fazed by the remark. But then, John Morgan was an ex-Green Beret who'd killed his fair share of Vietcong.

Brett picked up a knife and fork and dug into his meal, such as it was. He didn't invite her up here, and he felt no obligation to entertain her.

"What about the waitress? Joe said she got roughed up but you saved her."

He shrugged, but his shoulders felt unaccountably tight. It still pissed him off that the punk had slammed her into the counter like that. The fear in her eyes—he would be dreaming about that in his nightmares for days to come. And that other thing in her eyes... He could swear it had been a death wish. What the hell was that all about? "What about her?"

"Is she okay?" Miranda asked in exasperation.

"Of course. I saved her."

"What's her name?"

He didn't want to share her name with anyone. He wanted to hold it close within himself. A secret. His secret. But Miranda was, well, Miranda. Sometimes it just wasn't worth fighting her. He mumbled, "Larkin. Anna Larkin."

"Didn't she go to Hollywood a while back or something ridiculous like that?"

His gut clenched at Anna being labeled ridiculous, which was weird. He hardly knew her. It was none of his business what the locals thought of her. He shrugged. "How the hell would I know what she did? I've been overseas for ten years."

Miranda tapped a front tooth with a short, neat fingernail. "I think she went west with a boy. Her mother was fit to be tied. Disowned her."

Indeed? That sucked. Although, right about now, he wouldn't mind being disowned by his own intrusive, pushy mother. He ate in silence, not tasting a bite of his beans and toast.

"Is she all right?" Miranda startled him by asking.

"Who? Anna Larkin?"

"Of course Anna Larkin. Was she hurt today? Was she struck? Did she fall? Hit her head?"

An image of her pitching off his porch earlier leaped to mind, and he winced at the memory of her hitting her head on the ground. He really wished she would've stuck around for a little while so he could've been sure she was okay. But it wasn't like he could have bodily dragged her into his cabin and held her against her will.

"I wonder if she's been to a doctor. She could have a concussion or broken ribs or something."

"She would know if she had broken ribs," he replied drily. Lord knew, he still felt his when he exerted himself too hard, four months after he'd broken them. Of course, he'd gotten off easy. Four of his men had died.

Apparently his scowl of self-loathing finally did the

trick and convinced Miranda that he had no desire whatsoever to be social with her tonight.

"Don't stay up here too long, Brett. You need people around you. Your family loves you." She came over to force an unwanted hug on him, which he tolerated uncomfortably.

She left, and he listened to her truck retreat down the mountain. Blessed silence settled around him once more. He didn't deserve a family. And certainly not one that loved him.

Grimly, he gave the leftover beans to Reggie, who lapped them up eagerly and finished with a loud smack of his lips. Dogs surely had the right of it. Live completely in the moment, no past, no future. Just the simple pleasures of right now.

He turned on the television for background noise but didn't bother to watch whatever flashed across the screen. Instead, a memory of Anna Larkin's sweet face came to him. Her smile. Her embarrassment when she'd spilled water on him. Her terror when that kid slammed her into the counter…and her bizarre disappointment when he'd come charging to her rescue like some damned knight in shining armor. Who the hell was he kidding? He was nobody's good guy.

He was the jerk who'd let her go away without finding out if she had a concussion.

He downed a couple of beers but didn't much feel like getting drunk tonight. Which was a first for him since he'd come home. Maybe all the excitement had taken more out of him than he'd realized. He should call it a night early and get some sleep. Except when he eyed the bed through the open bedroom door, fear came calling, ugly and insidious, crawling inside his gut and gnawing at his insides until he doubled over in pain.

The walls began to close in on him, and his breathing accelerated until he might as well have been running for his life.

And that was exactly what he did. He bolted outside, unable to stand being confined any longer. Reggie had already settled down on his fleece bed in front of the wood-burning stove for the night, so he didn't go back for the dog.

He climbed into his truck and pointed the heavy vehicle down the mountain without any destination in mind. Maybe he should check out the Sapphire Club. It was a strip joint that had opened up on the edge of Sunny Creek sometime since he'd joined the Army. But he had no appetite for crowds and smoke and drunks, and instead pulled over by a curb in the ramshackle part of Sunny Creek down by where the old lumber mill used to be. The neighborhood had gotten significantly more ramshackle since he left a decade ago, and a bunch of the houses were boarded up and had waist-high lawns of weeds.

He pulled out his cell phone and did a quick internet search on one Anna Larkin of Sunny Creek, Montana. Nothing. Crap. She must not have been back in town long. He debated starting a rumor, but ultimately risked calling Joe Westlake.

"Hey, Joe, It's Brett Morgan. Can you tell me where Anna Larkin lives? I want to stop by and thank her for returning my Saint George's medal to me."

"Yeah, sure." Joe rattled off the address. "She's single, by the way."

"Eff off, Joe," Brett bit out. He hung up on his cousin's laughter.

He drove past her place with the idea of just taking a quick look. Making sure she was okay.

How his truck ended up parked at the curb in front of her house, he had no clue. And how his door opened and his boots crunched down into the frosty grass, he couldn't say. He really shouldn't be heading up the cracked sidewalk to the wreck of a house in front of him. A pile of torn-out drywall at the end of the driveway announced that construction was ongoing inside the bungalow. That, and light showing around the cracks in the plywood covering the front windows announced that someone was home.

Turn around. Go back to the truck. Get the hell out of here. Run!

And yet, his feet kept moving, one reluctant step at a time. What was he doing? The rational side of his brain answered that he was only checking on her health, doing what he should have in the first place. The other side of his brain, the skeptical side that knew his BS for what it was, informed him he was lying to himself.

He watched in disbelief as his fist knocked on the wooden door frame.

Please, God, don't let her answer the door, he begged her.

Light footsteps sounded behind the panel, coming close.

So much for God giving a crap about him.

The door opened, and there she was, outlined in light spilling from behind her, strains of bad disco music blaring in the background. Her hair fell in two messy braids over her shoulders, and her shirt was covered in fine brown dust.

"Oh! It's you! What are you doing here?" she asked.

That was a hell of a good question. "You hit your head earlier," he mumbled. "At my place." Damned if he didn't feel like scuffing a toe against the doorjamb. He refrained, however, mumbling, "Wanted to make sure you don't have a concussion."

She stared at him like he'd grown a second head.

"Should've done it before," he muttered lamely. He risked a glance up from his scuffed boot toes and was blown away by how clear and soft her brown eyes were, even when filled with skepticism. And fear. He swore at himself. Coming here had been the mother of all dumb ideas.

He was careful to make no sudden moves, to keep his hands at his sides, to do nothing to spook her further. He even leaned back, even though his impulse was to move closer to her, to provide the bulk of his body to protect her from whatever was scaring her so badly. Thing was, he suspected he was the thing scaring her.

Up close, her skin looked like the finest velvet, impossibly smooth, dewy and flawless. He felt like a scarred old relic in comparison with her.

"How does one check for a concussion?" she inquired.

What? Oh. Right. His totally transparent excuse for stopping by to see her. "Pupils," he choked out. Crap, he couldn't even find the simplest words. Language had all but deserted him. "Uneven dilation," he managed.

When he didn't say any more, she finally asked, "Are mine even?"

He glanced up unwillingly once more. "Can't tell. Too dark."

"Oh." She stared back at him, looking as confused as he felt.

"Porch light?" he managed.

"Not working yet," she replied. "It has to be rewired. I, um, haven't gotten around to that."

It was his turn to mumble, "Oh."

"Come inside?" she offered reluctantly. "There's light in the living room."

"Uh, sure." Geez. He hadn't been this awkward around a girl even when he was sixteen and picking up Suzy Niblock for his very first date.

His gaze drifted to that pert derriere of hers as she led him over to a work light pointing at a stretch of partially sanded wood wainscoting. Actual sweat broke out on his brow as he watched her rear end twitch temptingly. *Day-um.* He exhaled carefully. She might be diminutive, but she had one fine body.

How long had it been since he'd been with a woman? He couldn't remember the last time, truth be told. It wasn't that he was a monk by any stretch. He just hadn't been anywhere near any women other than female soldiers who were strictly off-limits in, well, forever.

Abruptly, his hands itched with the remembered feel of soft curves, smooth skin, and the yielding strength of the female body. He remembered the scent of a woman, sweet and lightly musky, each one slightly different. The taste of clean, fresh flesh, the warmth of a woman's arms around him, the delight of a woman's mouth opening beneath his—

The memories flooded back so fast and hard, slamming into him like a physical blow, that he stumbled behind Anna and had to catch himself with a hand against the wall.

How could he have forgotten all of that stuff?

Anna stopped abruptly in what looked like a dining room and turned to face him, tipping up her face expectantly to the light. The curve of her cheek was worthy of a Rembrandt painting, plump like a child's and angular like a woman's. How was that possible?

"Well?" she demanded.

"Uh, well what?" he mumbled.

"Are my pupils all right?"

He frowned and looked into her eyes. They were cinnamon hued, the color of a chestnut horse in sunshine, with streaks of gold running through them. Her lashes were dark and long, fanning across her cheeks as lightly as strands of silk.

Pupils. Compare diameters. Even or uneven. Cripes. His entire brain had just melted and drained out his ear. One look into her big, innocent eyes, and he was toast. Belatedly, he held up a hand in front of her face, blocking the direct light.

She froze at the abrupt movement of his hand, and he did the same. Where was the threat? When one of his teammates went completely still like that, it meant a dire threat was far too close to all of them. Without moving his head, he let his gaze range around the room. Everything was still, and only the sounds of a vintage disco dance tune broke the silence.

He looked back at her questioningly. What had her so on edge? Only peripherally did he register that, on cue, the black disks of her pupils had grown to encompass the lighter brown of her irises. He took his hand away, and her pupils contracted quickly.

"Um, yeah. Your eyes look okay," he murmured. "Do you have a headache?"

"Yes, but it's from all the sanding I have to do and not from my tumble off your porch."

He frowned at the wood paneling as high as his chest and extending the entire length of the long wall, not to mention the intricate molding outlining it. "You're planning to refinish all of that by hand?" he asked dubiously.

"Power sanders are expensive, and I'll probably never use one again after I finish renovating this place."

His frown deepened. "You're fixing this house up all by yourself?"

Her spine went straight and rigid. "Yes. I am. Have you got a problem with that?"

"No. Not at all. I'm just impressed that you took on such a big job by yourself."

She shrugged. "I inherited the place. Which is to say I didn't volunteer for this. And my needs aren't great— a roof, a bed, a place to cook my meals."

He tilted his head, studying her more closely. Men in his line of work were trained observers, and he used those skills now. She wasn't lying to him. She truly didn't want anything beyond the basics. And she craved safety, if he wasn't reading her wrong.

"You still got any family in Sunny Creek?" he asked.

"No. My mother died about six months ago. She was the last of my family."

She was alone, then. Lucky dog. "I'm sorry for your loss."

"I hadn't seen her in a long time. We had a falling-out about—" She broke off. "Well, a falling-out."

Awkward silence fell between them, and he didn't

have a clue what to say next. Thankfully, she broke the silence. "I appreciate you stopping by to check on me."

Humor pricked at him. She was getting rid of him the same way he'd gotten rid of her earlier. Turnabout was fair play, he supposed. Admiration for her spunk passed through him. Not too many women in Sunny Creek would be in this big a hurry to kick one of the Morgan boys out of their house. Of course, it was no less than he deserved. Not only was he unworthy to breathe the same air as someone like her, but he'd also been a jerk to her earlier.

He nodded as much to himself as to her, and spun on the heel of his cowboy boot. He muttered over his shoulder, "I'll show myself out. Good luck with your sanding."

Anna stood in the middle of her dining room, breathing hard. She couldn't tell if it was fear or something else stealing the oxygen from her lungs. It had been nice of Brett to stop by and check on her. She wasn't sure what to do with nice, however. It made her nervous. Jumpy. Mistrustful. Did he have an agenda of some kind?

But what could he possibly want from her? He came from a rich, powerful family, and she was a broke waitress.

Her better self kicked in. The entire world wasn't made up of men like Eddie. Decent men no doubt existed out there. She shouldn't read too much into Brett's visit. Maybe the man truly was just making sure she was all right. Which was kind. Thoughtful. Totally nonthreatening.

She had to admit that man was beautiful. His eyes,

when he'd stared into hers, had been so blue it almost hurt to look at them. And that jaw. Wowsers. His hair was a shade shaggy, just messy enough that she'd actually felt an urge to reach up and push it off his forehead.

Which was insane. She never wanted to touch another man as long as she lived. And she sure as shooting didn't want a man to touch her. She'd barely managed not to flinch when he reached up toward her face.

Restless and disturbed by Brett Morgan's visit, and by his overwhelmingly male presence invading the sanctuary of her home, she threw down the sandpaper and headed for the big, old cast-iron soaking tub that had been the very first thing she restored to its former glory when she moved into this place.

She filled the big tub with hot water and eased into the steaming bath, which was almost too hot to stand. Perfect. She leaned her head back and let the bath do its magic, unwinding the tension of the entire day, starting with the robbery and ending with her late-night visitor.

Strange man, Brett Morgan. Not much for talking. Not much for social interaction of any kind, in fact. How was it that a man as beautiful as he was seemed so totally ill at ease with women? From what she remembered of him in high school, he'd always had girls hanging all over him. She also remembered him laughing a lot and being plenty gregarious. How had he turned into the awkward, taciturn man in her dining room tonight?

It was a mystery. And God knew, she was a sucker for a good puzzle.

Except he was not her problem. She had enough of those in her life without some hard-luck cowboy messing with her head.

Eddie had been nearly as pretty as Brett, but he'd

been completely self-centered. It was all about his desires, his pleasure. She had always been merely a means to his ends. But Brett—the way he'd stared so deeply into her eyes, the way his nostrils had flared when he'd stepped close to her—struck her as the sort of man who would take an interest in pleasuring the women in his bed.

She knew the sex with Eddie hadn't been a shining example of how it could be. Problem was, if she was going to experience decent sex at some point in her life, that would entail an actual relationship with another man besides her ex-husband. No way sex was worth that. Brett Morgan might be nice to look at, maybe even to fantasize about, but that was as far as that was ever going to go.

She closed her eyes, careful not to let herself drift off to sleep and drown, which would be just her luck. To heck with pleasure. If only there was a way to wrest some peace from the wreckage of her life.

It had been a huge mistake to come back to Sunny Creek. Her need for self-destruction ran a lot deeper than she'd realized until today—when she actually was relieved to face death. Until Brett Morgan apparently appointed himself her guardian angel.

How was she supposed to pay for her sins with him on the job?

Chapter 4

She dreamed of Eddie. Or to be precise, of his ghost. He haunted her dreams most nights, terrifying her and accusing her, never letting her forget, never letting her move on. Not that she deserved to move on. She was already in hell. A hell of Eddie's making that was never going to let her go.

She woke up breathing hard, as if she'd been running for her life. Which she was in a way. No matter how far she ran, she would never escape Eddie. Not now. Not ever.

While she lay huddled under the covers trying to catch her breath, she heard the new furnace working hard. But the tip of her nose felt like an ice cube. Until she got something more permanent than plywood and duct tape to seal the window openings, she supposed no furnace could possibly keep up with subfreezing temperatures outside. Urgency to solve the window problem was the only thing that got her out of bed this morning and rushing into jeans, a T-shirt, sweatshirt, thick socks, and sheepskin-lined boots.

She was huddling over a mug of hot coffee, stealing its warmth with her red, chilled fingers and willing away the unpleasant memory of Eddie, when a knock on the front door startled her into nearly dumping the scalding drink on herself. Who on earth was banging on her door like they wanted to knock it in?

"I'm coming!" she shouted. She paused with her hand on the door handle. "Who's there?"

"Brett. Brett Morgan."

Her stomach leaped in anticipation, then fell back in dismay.

She threw the front door open, and a burst of frigid wind gusted around her, making her shiver violently. The shape of a man wearing a cowboy hat was silhouetted against the bright white of the year's first snow turning the weeds in her front yard into a blanket of white.

"Brett? What do you want?"

He looked intensely uncomfortable, but a determined look filled his eyes and made his jaw hard. He ground out, "I'd like to come inside and quit blowing all the cold air in Montana into your living room."

"Oh." Dumbfounded, she stepped back. He swept past her, his sheepskin rancher's jacket big and cozy looking, filled to bursting with muscles and more muscles. What on earth had brought him back here at the crack of dawn? It was barely 8:00 a.m. Hardly a civilized time of day for an unannounced visit! He was darned lucky the cold had already woken her up.

"Are you here to check my pupils again?" she tried.

"No. I brought you something."

A gift? From Brett Morgan? What on earth? He held out a plastic grocery bag, and she took it, startled at how heavy it was. She peered inside.

A rotary power sander.

"It's old, but I cleaned and greased the motor last night, and I stopped by the hardware store this morning and picked up new sanding disks for it."

"I can't accept this—" she started.

He cut her off briskly. "Then consider it a loan. Do you know how to use it? If you lean on it too hard, you'll leave swirl marks in the wood. Start light with the pressure and gradually press down harder—" He broke off and reached for the bag he'd just handed her. "Here. Let me show you."

"I can figure it out—"

He wasn't listening. He slung down a coiled orange extension cord that he'd been carrying over his right shoulder. "You attach the disks like this…"

In minor shock, she watched as he showed her how to operate the sander. He put the thing in her hands and guided the sander to a broad expanse of paneling. He flipped the switch, and the machine jumped in her hand. Hastily, he put his big, warm hands over hers, steadying the bucking sander. Not satisfied with that arrangement apparently, he stepped behind her and reached around her to put his hands over hers once more.

Her brain went completely blank as his arms surrounded her, and the heat of his body permeated her clothing all down her back. For a millisecond, she enjoyed the sensation of being held and protected. But then fear reared its ugly head, making her go stiff.

Oblivious to her distress, Brett guided the sander across the wall, and the old finish melted away from the wood like butter, leaving fresh, bright walnut exposed, its natural tones a mix of blond and brown. As if *that* was what she was concentrating on at the moment.

Man. Muscle. Heat. The simultaneous push and pull of attraction and repulsion all but paralyzed her. She could do this. He didn't mean anything by it. He was just showing her how to sand a wall. *Concentrate on the good parts.* Like the scent of pine trees and mountain air rising from his clothes. It was as if the Rocky Mountains themselves had swept into her living room. She always had loved the mountains.

Brett's hands pushed hers back across the wood in a gentle, even swath, magically clearing away another broad strip of old varnish and grime.

"Ohmigod," she breathed. This thing was going to save her hundreds of hours of tiring, dusty, muscle-aching sanding.

"You'll still have to do a little hand sanding to get into the crevices of the molding," he murmured in her ear. His deep voice vibrated down her spine, terminating somewhere near her toes in a little shiver of delight. Ha! No fear that time!

"This is fantastic," she breathed. She wasn't sure she was talking about the power sander or about being surrounded by his heat and muscles.

He stepped back, and something deep inside her wailed at his absence. She hushed that needy part of herself sternly and concentrated fiercely on sliding the sander evenly and smoothly over the aged wood in front of her.

"Christ, it's cold in here. Is your furnace on the fritz?"

She stood back from the wall and switched off the sander. "Actually, I just installed a new furnace last week. It's the windows that are the problem."

"Or the lack thereof," he muttered.

"I was supposed to go pick up some windows in Hillsdale yesterday, but I had to go to the police station instead."

Brett winced. "Sorry about that."

"You didn't try to rob the diner."

He shrugged but didn't look convinced. Was he the kind of person who took responsibility for things that weren't his fault? Well, wouldn't that be a total reversal from Eddie who never once in his life had been responsible for anything bad that ever happened to him. He'd always had an excuse or a scapegoat other than himself.

In the latter years, that scapegoat had almost always been her. It was her fault his acting career hadn't taken off. Her insistence on him getting a job that forced him to miss the best auditions. Her selfish need for a place to live that cost him acting job after acting job. Frankly, she wasn't sure he'd ever had any talent in the first place.

"…my truck to pick up your windows?" Brett was saying.

"I beg your pardon?"

"My truck. Do you want to borrow it?"

"Oh! Uh, no. I wouldn't know how to drive a truck."

He snorted. "You're from Montana and don't know how to drive a truck? What are you? A city slicker?"

"I grew up in Sunny Creek, not on some dude ranch."

"Fine. I'll drive. Where are these windows of yours?" Brett asked briskly.

"You don't need to help with my windows. I can fit two at a time in my car."

"That tin can you drive barely qualifies as a car."

"Don't be dissing my car, Mr. Cow Pie Kicker."

"I don't kick cow pies. We use helicopters to move the cattle on our spread."

She blinked, startled. "Really?"

"Yeah. Runaway Ranch uses the latest in ranching techniques. Our yield per acre of beef is tops in the nation."

"Um, congratulations?"

He shrugged. "Not my circus, not my monkeys. My old man and the ranch hands do all the work."

"Why are you living on the ranch, then, if you don't work on it?" she asked curiously.

Brett's gaze went as hard and cold as the sapphires the mountains around Sunny Creek were known for. Huh. She'd hit a nerve, apparently. He strode to the front door, picked her parka off the coat rack and stood there, holding it out expectantly. "You coming?" he asked.

She started forward automatically, conditioned by years with Eddie to jump to that tone of voice. But then she realized what she'd done and stopped in her tracks a few feet out of reach of Brett. "I don't take orders from anyone," she declared strongly.

He studied her far too intently for far too long before saying mildly, "Okay. Please let me help you pick up your new windows so you don't freeze to death in this shack."

"It's not a shack!" she exclaimed indignantly.

"What would you call it?"

She looked around at the plastic tarps, paint cans, sawhorses and general chaos. "It's a work in progress."

Brett grinned briefly. "An optimist, are you?"

"Not hardly."

"Had me fooled."

She shrugged into her coat, which he held out for her, and he lifted it onto her shoulders. If she wasn't mistaken, his hands lingered for an instant on her shoulders. Not as if he was trying to put any kind of a move on her. More as if he was remembering what it felt like to touch a woman. And then his hands were gone, and she was left frowning to herself. Surely a man like him got all the female companionship he could possibly want.

She slipped as her sheepskin boots, which were cute, warm and left over from happier times, hit the thin layer of fresh snow. Brett's hand shot out fast to steady her, and she flinched hard as his hand swung toward her. As soon as she was safely upright again, he pulled his hand away from her.

Rats. He was studying her like a bug under a microscope. Thankfully, he made no comment as he opened the passenger door of his truck and helped her climb up into the big truck. Again, his hand pulled back immediately.

"You need better boots," he commented as he slid behind the wheel.

"I know. I've been so busy trying to make the house weatherproof before winter that I haven't had time to go shopping for any." And she wasn't about to tell him that the hundred bucks she would spend on a decent pair of winter boots could better be used to by a few rolls of insulation for the attic.

"Where are these windows of yours?" he asked.

"Hillsdale. Benson's."

"The junk shop?" Brett asked.

"It's an antiques store and salvage yard," she corrected.

"Right. A junk shop."

She rolled her eyes and didn't bother arguing. If she'd learned nothing else from Eddie, it was that men were pigheaded and completely unwilling to listen to reason.

Brett was a good driver, handling the truck with confidence and just the right amount of caution on the wet roads. He was silent, and she was content to let the silence be.

The drive to Hillsdale took about a half hour, and she gradually relaxed into the warmth and quiet. Brett seemed to know where he was going when they reached Hillsdale, so she sat back and let him drive, enjoying being chauffeured for a change.

"Here we are," Brett murmured as he pulled into the parking lot beside the salvage yard.

She fumbled at the door lock, and before she could get the thing opened, Brett had come around to her side of the truck and opened the door for her. He held out an expectant hand and she stared at it doubtfully. Men's hands and she didn't have a great track record together. His palm was calloused and hard. That hand had seen plenty of hard work in its day.

"How'd you get that scar across your wrist?" she asked.

"Knife."

She flinched. She couldn't help it. God, she hated knives.

"Caught one in combat. It wasn't that bad a cut," he

said quickly. Crud. He must've seen her reaction to his mention of knives.

She headed into the store, which was cluttered with all manner of antiques, knickknacks, and—face it—junk. "Morning, Vinny!" she called.

"Anna!" a voice called from the back of the mess. "How's the prettiest girl this side of the Rockies—" The voice broke off as Vinny stepped out of a back room and spied her and Brett.

"I'm fine. Do you still have those windows you said you would hold for me?"

"They're back here. Follow me."

She wound along a narrow path through the mountains of junk toward his voice. Brett seemed bemused, staring around like he'd entered an alien world. To a man like him, this place probably was alien.

Vinny led her to a half-dozen window frames stacked in a pile to one side of a warehouse-sized space. "You wanna measure these again?" he asked her.

"If you say these'll fit my window frames, I believe you," she answered.

Vinny smiled intimately and sidled closer to her. "Would I lie to you? You're far too pretty for that."

He was so awkward she felt sorry for him. It was sweet of him to flirt with her, but she was damaged goods.

He touched her arm lightly, innocently pointing out where to go, but she couldn't stop the shiver that passed through her. Vinny steered her to one side of the warehouse, and she braced herself out of long habit. The windows. She needed the windows.

Without warning, a big shadow loomed beside her and a heavy arm landed across her shoulders. *Brett.*

"Hey, darlin'. You about ready to start loading up those windows of yours? I have plans for us today, and I want to get this errand over with." Innuendo lay thick in his voice.

She stared up at him, shocked. What was he doing?

Vinny took a quick step back, scowling up at Brett, who exuded something very male and very dangerous at the moment.

Oh.

One guardian angel to the rescue.

She leaned into Brett's side and played along. "Can I call on all those big, strong muscles of yours to help me load my windows into your truck?"

Brett grinned down at her. "Only if you'll give me a back rub later for my troubles."

"Sure," she choked out.

That did it. Vinny turned away, his face red, and stomped to the front counter to ring up the sale. Brett's grin turned lopsided as she slipped out from under his arm.

It took Brett only about two minutes to load all six windows in his truck, layering them with cardboard boxes folded flat to act as shock absorbers and protect the original, heavy glass.

They'd started driving back toward Sunny Creek when Brett asked abruptly, "Why don't you like men touching you?"

Oh, Lord. Did he have to be quite so observant?
"What are you talking about?"

He glanced across the cab at her. "You flinched when Vinny touched you."

"I didn't flinch when you touched me," she retorted.

"You went stiff as a board."

She shrugged. It wasn't like she owed him any explanations. Brett let the subject drop, for which she was deeply grateful.

When they got back to her place, Brett offloaded the windows with quick ease, carrying them into her house and depositing four of them in front of her living and dining room windows and one in the kitchen.

"Where do you want this last window?" he called as he came in through the front door.

"I'll take it."

"I'm already carrying it," he retorted. "Just tell me where to put it."

Men. So bossy. A girl couldn't tell one anything. "My bedroom," she huffed.

He barged into her inner sanctum and stopped cold as he stepped across the threshold. Fine. So she liked white lace and pink bows. Shoot her. She was, in fact, a girl. She glared at him defiantly as he emerged from her frilly bedroom, and wisely made no comment.

"Do you have the tools to install the windows?" he asked.

"I think so."

"Let's get them into the frames so this place can be properly heated."

"I can do it myself," she declared.

"I'm sure you can," he replied evenly. "But it'll go faster if we work together."

He was not wrong about that. She wrestled with the dilemma of accepting the help or going it alone and getting away from his disturbing presence. He took the decision away from her when he ripped down the plywood covering one of the living room windows and a blast of freezing air slammed into her.

Pesky guardian angel!

Brett lifted the window into the frame and looked over his shoulder at her expectantly. "You gonna nail it in place or not?"

Jerk. But a helpful jerk, she mentally conceded.

She had to give Vinny credit. The window was a perfect fit and took practically no shimming or shaving to fit into the slot intended for it. While Brett hammered in the last nails holding it in place, she caulked around it, sealing the opening securely for the first time since she'd lived here.

They unboarded the window openings and installed the remaining windows, working mostly in silence. With each one, her furnace caught up a bit more in its efforts to heat the house. Natural light streamed in for the first time since she'd lived here, and the cave-like gloom retreated. Her spirits lifted along with the temperature.

This house might turn into a livable home, yet. "Thank you so much for your help, Brett. You made that go a ton faster. I owe you huge. Let me pay you."

He pulled back sharply, looking offended. "Since when don't neighbors help each other out?"

Ah, yes. The credo of small towns. Spy on thy neighbor, gossip about thy neighbor, but help thy neighbor when they need it. "At least let me take you out to dinner or something."

Brett stared at her doubtfully.

"Say yes," she urged him. "Otherwise, I'll feel guilty for taking advantage of you."

His frown deepened. Rats. He was going to say no, and she really was going to feel bad about letting him work all morning on her house. "Fine," he bit out.

Oh, God. Now she was the one with suddenly cold feet. Frostbit. Heck, frozen solid.

A date with Brett Morgan? Cripes. What on earth had she just done?

Chapter 5

How in the hell had he let Anna Larkin talk him into a freaking date? He stood in front of his closet, debating which of his extremely limited supply of decent shirts to wear tonight.

It didn't mean anything. He had no intention of getting involved with her. She'd neatly maneuvered him into letting her thank him for helping install her windows. That was all. But hell's bells, he'd polished his cowboy boots for this date of theirs.

He fingered his fresh-shaven jaw and the haircut that he'd gotten down at the barbershop in Sunny Creek before he'd headed back up to his cabin. Why had he felt compelled to get a damned haircut for her? After all, Anna was fully as skittish as he was about relationship stuff. She'd practically had a stroke when he set foot in her bedroom this morning.

Reggie leaned against his thigh affectionately, and he reached down to scratch the dog's head. "What am I doing, buddy? I know better than to get involved with anyone right now. I'm a mess."

Worse, the shrinks at the VA hospital hadn't been able to give him any time frame in which his nightmares might subside or his memory return. Maybe never. They hoped a change in scenery from a hospital room would help the process, but so far, being back on Runaway Ranch hadn't done anything but make him stir-crazy.

He was an idiot to let Anna talk him into this dinner thing. Public places made him sweat bullets, and the whole notion of being social with anyone panicked him. Although this morning with Anna hadn't been so bad. Maybe because he sensed that she was as reluctant to deal with other human beings as he was. Hell of a pair they made.

Reggie barked from the living room.

"You're better than a doorbell, Reg," Brett commented as he headed for the door. Said doorbell thumped his tail on the floor happily. Brett pulled out a new rawhide bone for the Lab as Anna's ridiculous little car huffed up to his cabin. Grabbing a coat, he headed outside quickly, lest she try to kill herself on his porch steps again.

Fine crystals of snow were drifting down as he stepped out into the soft darkness. Anna had just gotten out of her car and turned to face him as he jogged down the steps.

"Hey," she murmured shyly.

"Hey," he muttered back.

"Looks like more snow tonight," she commented awkwardly.

"It's supposed to get colder," he replied equally awkwardly. "Why don't we take my truck just to be safe?"

"But then my car will be stuck up here."

"I can give you a tow down the mountain."

"That sounds like a lot of trouble," she said doubtfully.

He shrugged. "It's better than you ending up in a ravine and freezing to death."

"Well, when you put it that way…"

He moved to the passenger door of his truck and held it open silently, waiting. She took a step toward him. Another. His heart rate leaped. She was as skittish as a deer, and he stood perfectly still lest he scare her off. Step by step she approached him, and he took deep satisfaction in her hesitant trust.

Smiling a little, he backed up the truck, turned it around and headed down the mountain. They came out of the high valley above the main ranch complex, and the huge stone-and-log mansion his mother had insisted on building a few years back came into sight, a warm, golden jewel glowing against the snow.

"Your family's home is magnificent," Anna commented.

"I guess. It's a house."

"But not a home?" she asked astutely.

"My family's complicated."

She tensed beside him, and he glanced over at her curiously.

"Don't get me wrong," he added. "We get along for the most part. We Morgans are just a noisy, rowdy bunch."

"Sounds awful."

He shrugged. "It was fun growing up here."

She didn't speak, so he asked, "Did you like growing up in Sunny Creek?"

"I had nothing against the town."

But her childhood hadn't been happy. Was that why she was so jumpy about men?

Silence fell in the cab of the truck as he turned out of the ranch and onto the main road.

"Why the Army?" she queried, surprising him.

"Mom, apple pie, and patriotism, I suppose."

"What did you do in the Army?"

His knuckles tightened on the steering wheel. "Kill people," he bit out.

She stared at him, wide-eyed. *Welcome to the monster I really am,* he thought bitterly.

"Want me to take you back to your car?" he asked tightly.

A heartbeat's hesitation, then, "No." Another hesitation. "I trust you."

Aw, honey. That's a mistake. He wished it wasn't so, but he didn't even trust himself.

He and his team had been ordered to patrol that stretch of terrorist-infested road. It was their duty to make sure convoys could pass through the area without getting shot to hell and back. But something had gone terribly wrong. That had been no simple improvised explosive device that blew up, killing four of his guys. What the hell had he missed? Had there been intel he'd failed to read? A report by a local liaison that should've warned him to expect more than crude IEDs?

If only he could remember exactly what happened. But the ambush was a blank in his mind. The shrinks said it was obscured by battle stress. That maybe someday he would remember it all. Or not.

Everyone hoped that coming home would relax him enough to cut the memory loose. A military board of inquiry was waiting for his testimony—but they wouldn't wait forever to hear his side of the story. Eventually, they would run out of patience and charge him with dereliction of duty.

He realized he was jerking the steering wheel roughly, barreling along the main road toward town. He took his foot off the accelerator and slowed to a saner pace. It was harder to force his fists to ease up their death grip on the steering wheel.

"Where would you like to eat?" he managed to grind out past his clenched teeth.

"Not Sunny Creek," she blurted. "There's a new Italian place in Hillsdale. Want to try that?"

"Sure." Not Sunny Creek, huh? Was she afraid to be seen with him? Not that he was complaining. Lord knew he wasn't interested in feeding the local gossip mill.

"What brought you back home to Montana?" he asked curiously.

"I have no idea what I was thinking when I came back here."

Despair laced her voice, reminding him sharply of that moment in the diner when she'd seemed to long for death. Obviously, she and Eddie had split up. He would have to ask his mother for details. She knew everything about everybody in town.

Anna was silent, pensive even, for most of the drive to Hillsdale. But as he ushered her into a blessedly dark little dive of a restaurant, she smiled bravely at him across the candle in the middle of the table.

"You okay?" he asked quietly.

She blinked like she was startled. "I am, actually. You?"

He considered. "I guess I am." Color him surprised. Since when had he gotten comfortable with her? Maybe when it had dawned on him that she didn't want a darned thing from him.

The food was average, but given that he didn't have to cook it, clean up after it and, furthermore, it was the first chicken parmesan he'd had in years, he enjoyed the meal far more than he'd expected to. He and Anna chatted about harmless topics—movies he'd missed in the past few years of being deployed, how bad he thought the coming winter would be this year, where kids they went to high school with had ended up. She conspicuously avoided discussing the fate of her husband.

Something odd happened somewhere along the way. He relaxed a little.

He caught himself just looking at her. The curve of her cheek, the lines of her nose and jaw, the way her eyes glowed in the soft candlelight—she was the stuff of paintings by the great masters. As he refilled her wineglass a few times, she relaxed as well, and her eyes lost that pinched, scared look they usually had.

She wasn't exactly ready to throw herself at him, but she finally seemed like she wasn't on the verge of bolting from him at a moment's notice. It was a definite improvement.

He risked saying, "Tell me about California."

Her entire being went still. Crap. Too soon.

But then she surprised him by saying, "Eddie wanted to be a movie star, and he convinced me to run away to Hollywood with him."

"Did you want to be an actress, too?" Brett asked curiously.

"That was the plan. But as it turned out, someone had to pay the bills and put food on the table. Eddie needed acting classes and fitness training and tanning salons. And there was always an audition to go to. So I ended up getting a job and giving up on my dreams."

Something sad bubbled up in his gut. Nobody should have to give up on their dreams for someone else.

"And Eddie?" He asked the question mostly to keep her talking. He wasn't prepared for the ravaged look that entered her eyes.

"Eddie never broke into the business. He got a few jobs here and there. Finally resorted to making porn films." She added tonelessly, "He started drinking. Doing drugs. Lost his looks. And it was over for him."

"Is that when you split up?"

She looked down into her lap and mumbled, "No."

Good Lord. A wealth of pain was contained in that single syllable. *No.* She hadn't left when Eddie self-destructed. What the hell happened to her in the mean time?

If he was the least bit social with any of his old friends, he would probably know this story already. But as it was, he'd stayed away from everyone who might have shared the local gossip with him since he'd come home.

"Enough about me," Anna murmured. "Tell me more about you. Where were you stationed in the Army?"

"All over. I spent most of my career overseas."

"War zones?" she asked soberly.

"Yup."

She, too, seemed to sense that he was leaving a great

deal unspoken. She shifted topics slightly. "Are you glad to be home?"

Huh. He hadn't really stopped to think of it in those terms. He wasn't exactly glad he'd made it home. There would have been more honor in dying with his teammates. He answered bitterly, "If I have to recuperate, I suppose here's as good a place as any to do it."

"Recuperate from what? Were you wounded?"

His jaw tightened. Not all wounds were visible. Besides, he wasn't as much wounded as he was broken.

Thankfully, their waitress came over just then to ask them if they'd saved room for dessert. He sipped a cup of coffee while Anna worked her way through a giant piece of chocolate cake. She looked like a kid in a candy shop, savoring every bite, and licking the frosting off every tine of her fork.

Watching the tip of her tongue stroke down the length of the fork made his man parts stir alarmingly.

"Wanna try some?" she asked him.

Hell, yeah, he wanted to taste that pink little tongue and have it stroke him, doing all kinds of clever things to his flesh—

"Uh. Sure," he mumbled. She pushed the plate his way, and he took a bite. As chocolate, rich and dark, exploded on his tongue, guilt exploded in his gut. Here he was, out with a pretty girl, having a nice dinner and enjoying chocolate cake, while his guys were dead and buried.

The drive back to the ranch was silent. Snowflakes splatted against the windshield and the wipers thunked back and forth clearing their wet corpses.

They were almost back to his place when Anna asked quietly, "Were they bad? The war zones?"

He turned into the driveway, passing under the big iron arch announcing that this was the Runaway Ranch. The name fit him, all right. He was running away from everything and everyone.

He answered grimly, "Most of the time it was boring and exhausting. But yeah. It was bad sometimes." Which was as close as he'd come to talking about his experience with anyone besides a shrink since he'd gotten back to the States. And those shrinks had the official files and already knew what had happened to his unit.

"I'm sorry."

He glanced over at her. "You've got nothing to be sorry for. You didn't send me over there."

"I'm an American citizen. You fought for all of us."

He shrugged. "I volunteered."

"Why did you really join the Army?"

He scowled at the main house glowing like a great shining pile of false welcome and steered his truck around it. "It was the fastest way to get as far as possible from this place."

"What's so bad about it?" she asked, sounding surprised. "It's a beautiful place. The land is gorgeous, and the mountains are amazing."

"A place doesn't make a home. The people in it do that."

He felt her staring at him, but he kept his gaze locked on the dirt road passing through his headlights.

"Your family wasn't…happy?" she asked in a small voice.

"In our own way, I suppose we were."

"My parents divorced when I was little. I don't remember much about their marriage except a lot of shouting."

"My parents' battles are epic," he volunteered.

"Really? I mean, I've met your dad. I could see him being a little, uh…"

"*Pigheaded* is the word you're looking for," Brett supplied.

He felt her smile as much as caught sight of it in his peripheral vision.

"Have you ever met my mother?" he asked.

"No."

"She's a force of nature. Only a woman of her fortitude could stand my old man for any length of time. In spite of all his bluster, Miranda actually rules the roost in the Morgan clan."

"Wow. She must be a strong woman to corral you and all your brothers."

"Have you met the twins? They're the biggest terrors of all."

"Your sisters were a few years behind me in school," Anna replied. "I didn't really know them."

He shook his head ruefully. "They're trouble. And together, they're hell on wheels."

"Where are they now?"

"Kristin's in New York. Owns a tattoo studio. Emmaline's in Charleston, South Carolina. Interior designer. Two human beings couldn't be more different from each other."

"Wow. I guess. What about your brothers?"

"They've scattered. Wes is burning a fast track through the Pentagon. Caleb's still flying jets in the Air Force, and Jackson's playing doctor somewhere in Africa."

"Africa?" she exclaimed.

"He always was the family hippie. He's working for

some charity. I imagine he's giving babies immunizations and singing folk songs with the villagers."

"Your mom must miss all of you."

He made a sound of disbelief. "She loves this ranch more than she ever loved any of us."

"It's not entirely bad to love your home and put down deep roots," Anna said reasonably.

"Then why did you take off for the West Coast the second you could?" he shot back.

He parked the truck in front of his house and turned in his seat to wait for her answer.

"I was young. I wanted…more."

"Did you find it?" he asked soberly.

Her gaze faltered and fell away. She stared unseeingly out the front window at the snow, falling in a ghostly blanket. She found something in California, all right. Something that put a haunted look in her eyes and stole away her ability to speak.

"Thanks again for helping me pick up and install my windows," she murmured.

Not going to talk about her private nightmares, was she? He could respect that. He had plenty he didn't want to talk about, too.

She mumbled a hasty good-night and climbed out of the truck before he could get out and make his way around to her door. He watched, bemused, from the seat of his truck as she practically ran to her own car and leaped inside. What had he done to scare her like that? Hell, he hadn't even tried to hold her hand, let alone put a move on her.

Not that he wouldn't be happy to lay a seduction on her if he thought it would work. She was a fine-looking woman. Better than fine. Hot. Sweat inducing.

He climbed out of his truck thoughtfully. Maybe if he was lucky he would dream about her tonight instead of explosions and blood and death.

Chapter 6

Life at the diner was almost back to normal by Friday, and Anna was glad for it. If she had to tell the story one more time of being rescued by Brett Morgan, she was going to scream. Not that she wasn't grateful to him, but she *hated* being the center of attention.

Pitty was pushing a plate of flapjacks across the short-order delivery counter when the older woman whistled under her breath and muttered, "Well, look at that. Her Majesty has come down from on high to grace us with her presence."

Anna picked up the plate and turned to see what had provoked that remark. Ohmigosh. Miranda Morgan. The regal, five-foot-ten frame and snow-white hair were unmistakable. As were the vivid blue Morgan eyes.

Patricia rushed over to make nice with Miranda and show her to a booth, but Miranda more or less ignored the woman and headed straight for Anna with a deter-mined look on her face. *Oh crap.*

"Miss Larkin?" Miranda asked.

"Um, yes. That's me. Can I, um, show you to a booth?"

"I'm not here to eat. I'm here to invite you to a party. A barbecue at Runaway Ranch tomorrow. It'll be ca-sual. Family and friends. You'll come, yes?"

"Uh—"

"I insist."

Sheesh. Talk about getting run over by a freight train. "Tomorrow?" she echoed, feeling a little slow on the uptake.

"Yes, tomorrow. Meat will come out of the smoker at about four o'clock. Can I count on you to be there? People will start arriving around noon to watch foot-ball games."

Anna frowned, searching for a delicate way to ask a question. She couldn't find a way and ended up blurt-ing out, "Why me?"

After all, she barely knew any of the Morgans, and goodness knew she didn't run in the same social cir-cles they did. She didn't run in any social circle, truth be told. She knew as well as anybody that she was a pariah to Eddie's friends and family, who were plenti-ful in this town.

"I'm inviting you because you are the only human being my son Brett has voluntarily had any contact with since he came home from the Army."

The only one? Really? What did that mean? She real-ized Miranda was staring at her expectantly. "Oh. Um. It's kind of you to think of me."

Miranda's patrician features crumpled momentarily.

Her voice low, the older woman said, "Please come. I'm losing my baby."

Shock slammed into Anna. What was wrong with Brett? Sure, he'd seemed a little withdrawn, maybe a little antisocial even, but he'd been nothing but kind and considerate to her. What was going on with him that could terrify this terrifying woman?

A surge of sympathy for Brett's mother had her reaching for the woman's hands and murmuring, "Of course I'll be there. Can I get you a cup of tea?"

Miranda's spine stiffened proudly. But she murmured, "I would like that."

Anna led her to a booth and practically ran to get Miranda a pot of hot water and the good jasmine tea from Patricia's desk in the office. She carried the lot to the booth, desperately careful not to spill the boiling water on Brett's mother.

"Sit with me," Miranda ordered.

Anna glanced around the diner. Both of her customers had full cups of coffee and were digging into plates of food. She had a minute to spare. She slid into the booth across from Miranda, vividly aware of the woman's expensive silk blouse and perfect makeup. Not a hair was out of place in the elegant waves of snowy white on the woman's head.

"Tell me about yourself," Miranda said firmly.

Trepidation made Anna's voice wobblier than she would have liked. "I'm originally from Sunny Creek but left after high school to pursue other opportunities. I've recently returned and am renovating a house."

"Are you back to stay?"

"I don't know. I guess so. I don't have any immediate plans to leave."

"Good," Miranda replied. "I gather you're single?"

Anna restrained an urge to hide her left hand, bare of a wedding ring, under the table. "Correct."

"I need you to know a few things about my son if you're going to be spending time with him."

Anna blinked, shocked. Her spend time with Brett Morgan? Like, dating him? That seemed like a bit of a reach. They'd installed some windows and had one thank-you dinner. That did not a relationship make. In fact, he hadn't called her all week. She hadn't even had a text out of him since their date, which wasn't really a date at all.

His complete radio silence since then had sent the message loud and clear that he wasn't interested in her romantically. At all. She opened her mouth to say so to Miranda, but the woman talked over her.

"His mental state is fragile right now. But he's a strong man. He's had a terrible shock, but he'll get over it. If he'll talk to you, by all means, spend as much time with him as you can. He has completely cut himself off from the human race, and anything you can do to bring him back to it will be deeply appreciated. Deeply." The woman paused significantly. "We Morgans take care of our own."

Anna chose her words carefully. "Your son is a fine man. He rescued me from a robber and was kind and thoughtful afterward."

Miranda reached across the table and squeezed Anna's hand briefly. If Anna wasn't mistaken, that was gratitude shining in the older woman's cobalt gaze. "I'll see you tomorrow, then."

Miranda stood up quickly, tossed a twenty-dollar

bill on the table and swept out of the diner, while Anna stared at her retreating back.

What on earth did one wear to a casual barbecue at a magnificent mansion? What constituted casual in the world of the wealthy, powerful Morgans?

She was still pondering that question the next day, standing in front of her closet in dismay. She couldn't afford to go out and buy a new outfit. Although she wouldn't have bought new clothes anyway. She was who she was. Simple Anna Larkin, waitress at Pittypat's. And she wasn't about to start putting on airs for anyone.

She settled on jeans and a pastel plaid blouse over a pink tank top. It was probably some etiquette faux pas to wear Easter colors as Thanksgiving approached, but she liked the shirt and the way it complemented her fair complexion. Miranda said it was casual, so casual the woman would get. If she was completely underdressed, she could always make her excuses and duck out early.

Anna groaned when she turned into the driveway at the ranch. At least fifty cars were parked between the mansion and the first big barn behind the house. Just family and friends, huh? Half of western Montana and all of Sunny Creek must be here.

Dread settled in the pit of her stomach, and she suddenly felt an acute need for an antacid tablet or ten. She seriously considered turning her car around and leaving, but a cowboy had caught sight of her and was waving her forward into a parking spot. Not to mention she suspected Miranda Morgan would take a piece of her hide if she failed to show up today.

Feet dragging, she trudged to the house on a crushed gravel walkway. It was a sunny day and above freezing, and the early snow had melted, leaving behind the last remnants of green grass and a lot of mud.

She slipped into the house, which was full of noise and people, making herself as unobtrusive as possible. A few people she didn't recognize said desultory hellos to her, and she headed for the giant kitchen where a drink station was set up. She filled a glass with sweet tea and then wandered the main floor of the mansion in amazement.

It looked like a hotel lodge, with three-story-high vaulted ceilings held up by giant, carved wooden beams. A huge chandelier made of antlers hung down in front of a floor-to-ceiling stone fireplace with a roaring blaze on its massive hearth. It was every inch a Western showpiece, elegant and casual, welcoming and intimidating as hell. A lot like its mistress, in fact.

Anna had always felt like a fish out of water in California, but she felt like a fish trying to climb a tree in this place. She might be a Montana girl born and bred, but this… This was a whole different world.

"Anna, there you are!"

Miranda. Crap. Mentally wincing, Anna pasted on a smile and turned to greet her hostess. "Your home is stunning, Mrs. Morgan. It ought to be in magazines."

"It has been featured in several. Have you seen Brett? I made him promise to make an appearance today."

"No, ma'am, I haven't seen him."

"If he doesn't show up shortly, I'm driving up to that decrepit shack he insists on hiding in and dragging him down here myself," Miranda declared.

"I'm sure he'll be here soon," Anna replied, feeling deep sympathy for any kid who had to grow up under this woman's iron thumb.

"Have you met my husband?" Miranda asked.

"Um, not officially—"

"Come with me," Miranda interrupted. "John wants to meet the girl who managed to lure Brett out of his cave."

"I'm not sure I would describe it that way. It was more chance than anything else—"

Miranda waved over a big, imposing man who looked to be a well-preserved sixty years or so old. He had a full head of iron-gray hair cut short on the sides, and was a solid six foot four, broad shouldered and still muscular, even if he did have a bit of a belly these days. Her initial impression was of a walking, talking, real-life John Wayne.

"John Morgan. Pleased to meet you. Anna is it?"

"Yes, sir. Anna Larkin."

"Knew your dad. Went to Vietnam with him. Good man. Too bad things didn't work out for him and your mother."

Anna stared. Nobody in Sunny Creek talked about her father in anything other than hushed tones of scandal. He'd left her mother when Anna was only about five years old. "What was he like?" she blurted.

John Morgan speared her with gray eyes that stripped her bare. "He was the kind of man who had your back. Loyal. Didn't rat a guy out if a rule got bent or broken here and there. Hell of a shot, too. He was a sniper, you know."

"Really?" That was the first she'd heard of it.

"I've got some pictures from 'Nam around here somewhere. If you'd like me to dig 'em up—"

Miranda interrupted. "Not today. We're having a

party, and you're not boring our guests with reminiscences of the good old days in Vietnam."

Anna looked at John Morgan regretfully, and he winked at her. "Another time, Anna. You come visit any time, and I'll show you the stuff from our unit."

"That would be amazing," she replied. Who'd have guessed her father was ever something other than a deadbeat? Did his experience in Vietnam explain why he'd left his family? Had being a sniper messed with his head? How could it not?

"Piece of work, isn't he?" a male voice murmured in her ear.

She jumped and looked up at Brett, who stood behind her, watching his father dispassionately. "Both of your parents are rather...dynamic...people."

"If you mean pushy and overbearing, you would be correct," he commented in amusement.

She smiled and shrugged. "Your words. Not mine."

"They're forces of nature, those two. You ought to see them fight. It's like watching Titans do battle. I swear I hear thunder and lightning when they lock horns."

"No, thank you. I'm not a fan of conflict." The words were out of her mouth before she stopped to consider them.

"Why's that?" Brett asked.

"I just don't like fighting."

"Can I get you a refill on your tea?"

She gave him her glass and watched him wind his way through the crowd. He had a knack for making himself invisible to the people around him. He was incredibly adroit at avoiding conversations with people.

Either that, or he was just being rude to everyone he passed by.

He came back with her sweet tea and muttered, "You look nearly as uncomfortable as I feel. Wanna get out of here?"

"Your mother will kill you if you leave her party early."

"I'll take my chances with her. And I'm not leaving until I get some of Hank Mathers's barbecue anyway. The man can smoke meat until it falls apart on your fork. C'mon."

She followed Brett outside, vividly aware of Miranda's gaze from across the great room. Nope. Nothing got past that woman.

Brett led her toward the sprawling barn behind the house. Two long rows of horse stalls joined by a feed room in the middle formed an H that housed upward of forty horses.

"These are my mother's pride and joy," Brett murmured.

Anna peered into the first stall and spied a beautiful quarter horse mare with heavily muscled shoulders and haunches, but with a swanlike neck and beautiful face. Big, brown eyes turned her way. "My God, she's beautiful," Anna breathed.

"You have an eye for a good horse," Brett commented. "She's a Supreme Champion. Reining National Champion horse and mama to my mother's favorite up-and-coming stud colt. Wanna see him?"

"Absolutely," Anna said eagerly.

They walked to the other end of the stable to a big, double stall. Inside a young stallion, maybe three years old, paced restlessly. He was a bright chestnut with a white blaze from forehead to nostrils, and four white socks that highlighted his flashy movement.

"Aren't you a handsome devil?" Anna crooned. The colt came over, sniffed at her through the bars, then snorted and threw his head. "And you know it, too," she added, smiling.

"His name is Runaway Skipper. We call him Skip."

"He looks like he wants to stretch his legs," she commented.

"He hates being confined. But there's some winter weather forecast for tonight, so he's stuck in here," Brett replied. He reached for a rope halter and lead rope hanging on a hook on the door. "But we can let him take a spin around the indoor riding arena."

Anna backed up as Brett haltered the eager horse and led him out of the stall. "Oh, Brett. He's magnificent."

"Mother has high hopes for him. He should take her breeding program to the next level."

Anna wasn't sure what levels were left to climb. Skip was darned near perfect as far as she could tell. She walked alongside Brett as he led the stallion through a big, sliding door into a cavernous riding arena that was at least the size of a football field.

Brett unclipped the lead rope and Skip took off, tearing down the arena and kicking up his heels. Anna laughed in delight. "Look at him move! Such freedom in his shoulders. Such power in his hindquarters."

Brett grinned. "Do you ride?"

"I did a lifetime ago. Before I left for California."

"You should come out here and ride. God knows, there are plenty of horses in need of it. Miranda has two full-time girls who do nothing but clean stalls and groom and ride her babies."

"That's a kind offer, but I couldn't. These are really expensive horses—"

"Every horse still has to be a horse, no matter how expensive it might be. They're beautifully trained, and they like to go out on the trails around the ranch. Come ride. Promise you will."

"I can't—"

Brett laid a finger on her lips, startling her into silence. "I'll go with you if that makes you feel better. Next warm day we get, you're going riding with me."

She stared up at him equal parts hopeful and wary. What if he didn't keep his promise? If she got her hopes up but then was disappointed, it would hurt so much worse. She'd missed riding almost more than anything else when she left Montana.

"It's a deal, then," he declared.

"You're as big a freight train as your mother."

"I beg your pardon?"

She planted her fists on her hips. "You and your mother. You just roll right over anyone who gets in your path."

Brett laughed ruefully. "I confess that you're correct."

"For the record, it's exasperating to us normal mortals," she declared.

He grinned. "Yes, but we're both so charismatic and charming that you'll forgive us."

She rolled her eyes at him but was distracted by Skip trotting up to them, nostrils flared, neck arched and prancing like a foal. "That horse thinks as highly of himself as you do," she accused.

Brett laughed again. "I can live with the comparison. How 'bout you, old boy?"

Skip tossed his head, spun and took off running again.

"Men. All the same," she observed drily.

They watched Skip rip and tear until the colt finally wound down and started nosing around for treats out of Brett's pocket. They put Skip away and Anna promised the colt she would bring him a carrot the next time she came to visit.

"You'll spoil him," Brett commented as they headed back toward the house.

"And what's wrong with that? He's special and he knows it."

Brett went silent at that, and Anna wondered what nerve she'd struck. For a few minutes in the barn, Brett had been warm and outgoing and friendly. Or maybe it was the prospect of going back into the party that silenced him so abruptly.

She murmured as he reached for the door, "I'm planning to eat fast and then leave, but it's no reflection on you. Frankly, your parents scare me." She added, "And I'm not fond of crowds."

"That makes two of us," he murmured back. "We eat, and then we bug out. Deal?"

"Deal."

The smoked meat and vinegary-sweet barbecue sauce baked into it were fully as tender and tasty as Miranda had promised. Huge pots of baked beans and potato salad and charred garlic bread rounded out the meal.

She and Brett sat on the edge of the huge stone hearth to eat, balancing their plates on their knees. The fire at her back slowly roasted her, but it was the warmest she'd felt in weeks. She prayed her California-thinned blood would adapt to Montana soon because she was tired of feeling like a popsicle all the time.

Brett was more withdrawn in the house than in the barn, but he answered her questions pleasantly enough as she asked about various features of the house and guests whom she didn't recognize. He even volunteered a few anecdotes about some of the more colorful guests that made her laugh.

All the while, she was acutely aware of Miranda watching the two of them. Oh, Brett's mother was subtle about it, but the woman always managed to be facing them while in conversation with other people, and her sharp blue gaze shot to Brett any time he even shifted weight.

Talking with Brett was like balancing on the edge of a razor. They managed to keep a conversation going, but were always in danger of falling into awkward silence. She sensed that Brett liked talking with her, but that he often had no idea what to say. She knew the feeling. After the traumas in her life, making small talk just didn't seem important.

Under other circumstances, Anna might have found Miranda's interest in her full-grown son stifling. But she could respect a mother's concern. If only her own mother had shown the same interest in her, maybe she wouldn't have run away with Eddie and effectively ruined her own life.

Anna ate too much and groaned as Brett lifted her empty plate off her knees. He asked, "Want some coffee or a beer?"

"No, thank you."

Brett moved away and she let out the breath she'd been holding. A need to escape the confines of this house and the people in it overcame her and she headed toward the rear exit of the house.

She'd almost reached the double French doors to the wide, stone veranda when a hand grabbed her upper arm none too gently and spun her around. She opened her mouth to tell Brett to take it easy but her throat muscles froze in the act of speaking as she saw who was holding onto her so roughly.

"Jimbo Billingham," she said reluctantly. "I never thought I'd see you again."

"What? You mean after you got away with murdering my brother?" he snarled.

Chapter 7

Brett returned to the living room, eager to spend more time alone with Anna away from this noisy crowd and the oppressive attention of his parents. He knew John and Miranda were worried about him, but for crying out loud, he was almost thirty years old and had been a commando for a decade. He wasn't their little boy anymore, and he could bloody well take care of himself.

Hearth empty.

Where did she go? He scanned the great room quickly and spied a tiny silhouette across the room with a man looming close—very close—behind her. Not sure it was her, he started across the room, angling to one side to get a better view of the woman.

He caught a glimpse of her face.

Christ. That was Anna all right, and she looked like she'd seen a ghost. And not in a good way. He could see how pale she was from here, a good fifty feet away. He lengthened his stride, aggressively pushing past everyone in his way. Alarm bells clanged wildly in his head. Something was very, very wrong. She looked scared out of her mind.

As he approached with cat-like speed and predatory intent, he saw that the man was hanging on to her, lifting her left shoulder practically to her ear with that grip on her upper arm. And the bastard just shook her a little.

Brett lunged then, accelerating to a full sprint. In the blink of an eye, he came up behind the man and had him around the neck in a grip that would cut off all air to the guy's brain in a matter of seconds. Brett snarled, "Let her go or die."

The man fought—or tried to—but Brett wasn't a highly experienced Special Forces operative for nothing. He knew every move the bastard would try to slip from the arm around his neck, and he knew every countermove. Hell, he'd used every countermove on more hostiles than he cared to count in no-kidding, life-or-death fights.

The guy's hand fell away from Anna's arm and she staggered back, looking so terrified she might faint. A need to go to her, to comfort her, warred with his desire to kill the bastard who'd laid a hand on her and scared her so bad.

"Let him go," Anna gasped. "You're killing him."

The asshole would be turning a rather impressive shade of purple right about now, a few seconds before he passed out.

"Please," she begged.

Brett let the guy go but gave him a hard shove that

ensured the guy would be off balance and unable to turn around and launch a counterattack on him right away.

"Brett! What on earth?" Miranda exclaimed from just behind him.

Anna took a few more steps back, staring in horror at the guy he'd nearly strangled and then up at him. Abrupt remorse speared into Brett. Perhaps nearly killing a guest at one of his parents' barbecues wasn't entirely socially acceptable. Dammit. A great feeling of being a total outsider—hell, an intruder—washed over him.

The guy he'd just attacked finally straightened and turned around, gasping for air. Jimbo Billingham? Why in the hell did he scare Anna half out of her mind like that? What did he say to her?

Jimbo started to sputter, swearing and threatening to sue the whole damn Morgan clan.

Whatever. Brett spun away from the guy and came up short, swearing to himself. Everyone in the whole damned room was staring at him. He turned once more and raced out the French doors, desperate to get away from all those accusing stares.

He'd *known* better than to try to be around human beings.

He all but ran for his truck, and it wasn't until he reached for the door handle that he heard the footsteps behind him. If that son of a bitch wanted a fight, by God, he'd get one out here. He turned aggressively—

Anna.

"What do you want?" he bit out.

"Same thing you do. To get away from Jimbo Billingham and all those staring people."

"Get in."

He didn't wait for her or hold her door for her. His

panic was too great for such niceties. She climbed in as he started the engine and had barely slammed her door closed before he stepped on the gas. Gravel spurted loudly from under his tires as he pointed the truck up into the mountains. Into the refuge of their cold, impersonal embrace.

Anna was silent for the whole ride up the mountain. Which was just as well. He was too freaked out to engage in polite chitchat. God. He'd almost killed Jimbo. For holding Anna's arm. His reaction had been out of all proportion to that of a sane man in control of himself.

It wasn't until he'd stepped into the cabin that he looked at Anna cowering just inside the door and asked harshly, "What did Jimbo do that scared you so badly?"

"Uh, nothing. He just came up behind me and startled me."

She was lying.

"Anna, I'm trained to observe how people answer questions, their conscious and unconscious body language signals, the words they choose, inflections in their voices. I'm told it makes me a pain in the ass to be around, and multiple women have assured me it makes me impossible to have a relationship with."

She stared at him a long time. Eventually, she mumbled, "Oh."

"Let's try that again. What did Jimmy do that scared you so bad? You looked ready to faint."

"He really did startle me."

Okay, that was truth, but not the whole truth. "And?" he prompted gently.

She sighed. "And he doesn't like me."

"It looked to me like he hates your guts. Enough to harm you," Brett commented.

"You wouldn't be wrong."

Brett stared at her. He hadn't been expecting her to say that. "Why?"

"He blames me for Eddie's death."

"Eddie's dead?" Brett exclaimed.

Anna's entire face became a mask of—something. Not grief exactly. Horrible memories, maybe. Her shoulders slumped, and tears slipped down her face.

Aw, hell. Not tears. They were kryptonite to him. He took the two strides that brought him to her and gathered her into his arms.

She burrowed against his chest as if in search of comfort. Or maybe hiding from something. God, she was hard to read. It felt strange to be cried on like this. It had been a long time since a woman had looked to him for any kind of solace. He wasn't exactly a comforting kind of guy. His life had made him hard. Calculating. He'd long ago locked away anything resembling real feelings and thrown away the key. Feelings were weaknesses in his line of work.

Anna's shoulders shook as she cried silently against his chest. But then she took several deep breaths and her spine stiffened as she tangibly pulled herself together. He let her go when she stepped away from him, but his arms felt strangely empty without her warmth and softness in them.

Whoa. He didn't actually like holding a crying female, did he? Surely not.

He tore a paper towel off the roll on his kitchen counter. It was as close as he came to a tissue in his Spartan cabin.

She mopped her face and he took the crumpled paper towel silently, tossing it into the trash can beside the kitchen sink. While he was there, he filled a glass of water and carried it over to her.

Anna smiled wetly at the proffered water. As she took it, she murmured, "The first thing I learned as a babysitter is that a kid can't cry and drink water at the same time."

He sat down cautiously on the sofa beside her, studying her face. She seemed calmer now. Apparently, her cry had been cathartic.

"I'm sorry about that," she mumbled. "He took me by surprise. I didn't know he would be there, today."

"Why doesn't Jimbo like you?"

"He and his family blame me for Eddie not succeeding in Hollywood."

Brett frowned. "How could you torpedo his career? You didn't call Hollywood producers and spread lies about him, did you?"

She sighed. "He failed because he was lazy and spoiled. He thought that because he was handsome, fame and fortune would fall into his lap. Honestly, he just wasn't that good an actor."

"Why does Jimbo blame you, then?"

Her face closed down like Fort Knox locking its vaults against an attempted theft. Dammit, he'd stepped into another minefield. He was trying to make things better, not worse! Tears began to flow again, and he scooted over and gathered her into his arms.

Desperation began to build in his chest as she continued to cry silently. She made no sound at all. It was as if she was holding everything inside so tightly that only her tears were able to escape the stranglehold she had on her emotions.

Military shrinks hadn't been bombarding him for the

last few months for nothing. He might not know much, but he did know that suppressing everything was bad. Really bad. He didn't stop to think about it. He just did the only thing he could think of to get her to let go of that brutally tight control. He kissed her.

It was a dumb idea. But then her sweet, soft lips touched his, and all thoughts of being an amateur psychologist fled his mind. He didn't move. Didn't want to frighten her. His lips caressed hers lightly, a simple brush of warmth. An invitation, nothing more. His body was available to her if she wanted it.

Anna hesitated for a moment, and then it was as if a dam broke and a wall of emotions burst out of her. She surged upward in his embrace, her arms going around his neck, and holy cow, did she ever accept his invitation. She kissed him desperately. Her mouth was awkward against his, but he didn't mind. He tilted his head a little to better align their mouths, and he opened for her eager little tongue, which darted across his lips skittishly.

He returned the favor slowly and thoroughly, tasting her warmth, sipping at the sweet barbecue taste lingering like a savory treat. His tongue moved easily into her mouth, and she met him there tentatively. As tempted as he was to devour her, he held back, letting her set the pace.

She kissed him with her whole body, her hips surging against his belly, her small, resilient breasts pressing against his chest. Her arms tightened around his neck, clinging to him as if he were her lifeline to something precious that she'd lost and only just now found.

He knew the feeling. How long had it been since he'd held the warmth of a woman in his arms, felt her curves against his body, savored the excited passion of a first kiss? His brain was so befuddled with the reality of this woman in his arms he couldn't summon any memory at all of any previous women.

Anna's hands started to fumble at his shirt buttons, and cold reality intruded upon his fog of delight. "Um, Anna?" he mumbled against her mouth.

"Huh?" she panted. Her lips slid across his jaw and she kissed his neck, nipping at his shoulder as she pushed the collar of his shirt aside.

Sweet baby Jesus. His groin reacted so violently he groaned aloud. "We've got all the time in the world, darlin'. And I don't want to be accused of taking advantage of you in the first rush of pleasure."

"So what do you want to do?" she mumbled against his neck. "Stop kissing and read the telephone book until I have second thoughts?"

He laughed reluctantly. "Don't get me wrong. You're incredibly attractive. And I'm incredibly interested. But you've had a shock. You're upset. I don't want to be the schmuck who took advantage of you in a vulnerable emotional place."

"Got it. Now kiss me."

Her abrupt capitulation was giving him mental whiplash. "Are you sure you want this? You've seemed... reluctant...in the past."

"I'm not dead yet," she mumbled.

He turned over possible contexts for that comment. She'd felt dead before, maybe? Or passion had only recently woken within her? Or maybe she just didn't want to let this chance pass her by before she died—

"Please, Brett. For once I'm not overthinking this."

Well, okay, then. "You don't have to ask me twice."

He turned her in his arms, pressing her down into the crappy cushions. If she wanted to kiss, then by golly, kiss her he would. He took control of things then, cupping her head in his hand as he made slow, sweet love to her mouth.

His tongue plunged into her dark warmth, withdrew, then stroked its way home again. Her tongue darted all around his, teasing and testing, tasting and tantalizing. He sucked, drawing her tongue into his mouth, stroking the underside of it with his tongue, drawing her tongue across the sharpness of his teeth by way of contrast. Their mouths fit together perfectly, and it made him think of more carnal pairings. Yup. She would fit him in bed, too.

She was eager and athletic, but still all woman. Just the way he liked his partners in love. She went for the buttons on his shirt again, and this time he let her undo them and push the soft flannel aside.

"Oh my," she sighed as her palms slid across his chest. Her fingers slipped through the dark hair there, and his pectoral muscles jumped spasmodically. Wow, that felt good. He'd had no idea how much he missed this skin-to-skin human contact. No wonder his shrink told him a while back that he seriously needed to get laid. And here he thought the guy had been referring to how surly a patient he was. *Sorry, Doc.*

Anna moved restlessly beneath him and one of her legs came up to wrap around his thighs, her foot tucking up under his butt cheek in the most suggestive fashion. Her entire body undulated against his, seeking. Wanting. As if she hadn't experienced pleasure like this in a *very* long time.

He'd meant what he said before, though. He wasn't

going to take advantage of her being upset to get her in the sack. As horny and uncomfortable as he was, he was a better man than this. Or at least he ought to be a better man than this.

Cursing at himself, he pushed away from her, sitting upright on the edge of the couch while her body spooned around his, kitten-like.

"What's wrong?" she asked in a small, hurt voice. "Did I do something wrong?"

"What?" He stared down at her. "No! Hell no!"

"Then why did you stop?"

"Because I'm trying not to be a giant jerk. I refuse to take advantage of you."

"Oh." She sounded disappointed. *Preach, sister.* His woody was complaining in the most strident of terms about this whole be-a-gentleman thing being total crap.

He stared down at her, supremely frustrated. She was eager and willing. And he wanted her so bad his body was cramping with desire.

But dammit, he genuinely liked her.

He was *not* going to be a colossal asshole and have cheap sex with her. This was supposed to be a new chapter in his life. All the shrinks said so. Although, to be honest, he was really looking for an ending he could be okay with.

The thought made him go perfectly still. Had he really been that lost in despair?

All the more reason why he shouldn't just tumble into the sack with this woman. She had baggage of her own, obviously. He didn't need to add to it.

Reggie shifted on his bed, and Brett smiled fondly at the dog. He couldn't seriously consider checking out with Reggie to look after. If not him, who would feed the dog and take him out for the painfully slow walks Reg loved so much? He wasn't like other dogs. Couldn't romp and jump and run, but his mind was still willing. He wanted to wrestle and play. It took a special kind of gentle to make Reggie feel like a real dog without hurting him. Until Reggie crossed the rainbow bridge, he was stuck here on Earth, too. Hell would have to wait.

Nope. No one else would take care of the mangy mutt properly. Not after the silly, heroic dog jumped in front of Brett to protect him and nearly lost his life— but saved Brett's.

From the same IED that did kill his men.

Had it not been for that one bark of warning Reggie'd managed to get out before the bomb blew, that instant of jumping in front of Brett and pushing him back by leaning on his thighs—

—They said close counted only in horseshoes and hand grenades. Turned out they were right. He'd moved back just far enough to make the difference. He'd lived. His guys had not. The simple, brutal luck of the draw in war.

Speaking of Reggie, the dog must've sensed Brett thinking about him, for he slowly climbed to his feet and stepped off his soft dog bed. Brett watched fondly as the dog limped over to him and nudged his hand. Saved by the dog.

Aloud, Brett said, "I gotta take Reggie out. I'll be back in a few."

He didn't look back at Anna as he shrugged into his heavy sheepskin coat and ducked outside. Twilight lay upon the land, all the colors leeched away by encroaching night. The entire valley was a study in shadows and contrasts. Grays and blacks, devoid of vibrancy. He'd always hated this time of day. And now it was a perfect metaphor for his life.

Reggie moved over to his favorite spot to take a dump and did so in a leisurely fashion. Brett grinned fondly at the old guy. Even taking a squat made Reggie smile over his shoulder at Brett.

Reggie trotted over to him with his stilted gait and leaned against his leg. The two of them watched the last of the light fade. The clouds were low and pregnant tonight, heavy with moisture.

There would be snow, and plenty of it before morning. The cold was deep and still, but the air was damp against his face. Soon now, the snow would start. Brett felt it in his bones. He'd been away from home so long he'd forgotten how a rancher felt the rhythms of the land and the seasons and the weather like this.

Hell, he'd run away from all of this as fast as he could when he'd turned eighteen.

The cabin door opened behind him and a band of golden light spilled out onto the ground.

"You done, Reggie?" he asked aloud for Anna's benefit behind him.

A big wag of a bushy tail and a toothy smile were his answer.

"All right, then. I've got a lamb bone in the freezer for you."

The dog heard the word *bone* and made a Reggie-speed beeline for the house. The dog pushed past Anna before she could get out of his way, and Brett followed more slowly.

"Wanna give Reggie a treat and become his favorite person in the whole world?" he asked Anna.

"Sure."

"In the freezer door. There's a bag of bones."

While Anna fetched a bone, he knelt in front of the stove and loaded it up with split wood from the big pile beside the hearth. This cabin was ugly, but it was tight and cozy. If the stove got ahead of the storm now, the place would stay reasonably warm through the night.

Reggie had just settled in his bed for a nice, long gnaw when the windows rattled suddenly. Anna looked up in alarm.

"The gust front is here," Brett commented.

"There's a storm coming?" Anna asked quickly. "I should get down the mountain and back to my place!"

Brett moved over to the front window to peer out. "Too late. Storm's here."

Anna made a sound of dismay.

"I promise I won't hurt you."

She stared at him quizzically. "Why would you say something like that?"

"Well, uh, today. My outburst. And after I took down that guy in the diner…" He paused, drew a deep breath and barged onward, "I thought you might be afraid of me."

"Should I be afraid of you?" She asked the question calmly enough. She didn't sound scared of him. He wasn't sure if that made her brave or stupid.

"There's nothing to be afraid of." *Liar.* "I have control of myself." *Maybe.* "I do have some unfortunate reflexes left over from living in combat zones for the past decade. But I'm told those reflexes will dull over time and maybe even fade away." *And that was the biggest lie of all.* He'd been more on edge since he'd gotten home than he'd ever been overseas. His temper had a hair trigger, and he couldn't seem to rein it in.

"I'd hardly call your reflexes unfortunate if they kept you alive," she replied.

He blinked, startled. "That's what I told the shrinks!"

She shrugged. "See? You're acting perfectly reasonably. There's not a thing to be afraid of with you. As long as I don't try to kill you and trigger any self-defense reflexes in you, we'll be fine."

It sounded so easy when she put it like that. Almost doable, even. Was it possible that he could truly find his way back to a normal life?

Chapter 8

Anna studied Brett as the flickering glow from the stove lit his face in harsh planes and angles. He did, indeed, look dangerous. Honed by violence. But she knew crazy, and he was not it. In pain? Yes. Crazy? No.

He seemed afraid of himself, which she couldn't understand. Of course, he'd taken down the punk in the diner. The kid was armed and threatening her. Any sane man with an ounce of training and courage would have done the same. As for Jimbo this afternoon, Brett had *not* read the situation incorrectly. She'd been scared silly, and it was entirely possible that Jimbo would have dragged her outside and choked her to death had Brett not intervened.

She strolled over to the cabin's front window to peer out. In the warm light passing out through the glass into the cold night, great flakes of snow the size of silver dollars were falling so thick and fast she could barely make out Brett's truck only a dozen yards from the window. "You weren't kidding when you said the storm's here," she exclaimed. "I may be stuck here overnight."

He gave her a "well, duh" look, and then grinned as if he was pleased by this development.

Huh. He'd struck her as a hard-core loner, maybe even a bit antisocial the first time she'd come up here to return his necklace. But the man currently at the kitchen counter emptying a pouch of frozen vegetables and pasta into a skillet was open and relaxed. Maybe that kiss had been as therapeutic for him as it had been for her.

Brett was the first man she'd kissed since Eddie. Not that she had voluntarily kissed Eddie for a long time before his death. He was mean when he was drunk, and the last few years he was drunk pretty much all the time.

She'd forgotten how fantastic it could be to kiss a man without fear and to be kissed back with respect. Something inside her had broken free of wherever it had been hiding, and it felt good. Really good. Maybe she wasn't as damaged as she thought she was. Given that she hadn't been the least bit attracted to a man since Eddie died, she'd figured that her interest in men had been permanently burned out of her. But maybe not.

She was eager to see how much further her renewed interest in men extended. Of course, she couldn't possibly ask Brett to indulge in such an exploration. *Hey, Brett. I wanna find out how close to having sex I can go without freaking out. I want you to seduce me, and then be prepared to stop on a dime when I say so.* Right. Like any man would agree to that.

Eddie would have killed her—for real—if she'd ever tried a stunt like that on him.

Brett turned around just then and caught her blatantly staring at him. "What?" he muttered.

"Do you have any idea how sexy it is to see a man in a kitchen cooking for me?"

He glanced over his shoulder at the tiny kitchenette in the corner. "It's not much of a kitchen."

"Doesn't have to be with a man like you in it—" She broke off, appalled. "I'm sorry. That was rude of me to say."

"I don't think so. Thank you, in fact."

She risked meeting his gaze. Brett wasn't messing with her. He truly didn't seem offended. Eddie had flown into rages at the idea of being relegated to kitchen duty. He was a Man, and Men didn't do menial housework.

She might have set aside the idea of seducing Brett, but that didn't stop her mind from working on ways to get him to kiss her again. They ate side by side on the couch in front of the wood-burning stove, which was pouring out heat like crazy.

He took her plate from her, carried it to the sink and washed it while she watched on in shock. Now *that* was the sexiest thing she'd ever seen. Brett opened the refrigerator, poked his head inside and emerged with a can of beer.

Oh, God. Her mind went blank as the old terror rushed over her. Her eyes darted to the front door, and she calculated how long it would take her to run down the mountain to the main house. Did she have enough clothing not to freeze to death along the way? Would she get lost in the dark and the snow? Freezing to death was preferable to dying by violence—

"Are you okay?" Brett asked in concern. "What's wrong?"

Dammit. He had to go and be all observant again. "Um, everything's great. Fine. Just fine."

He plopped down on the other end of the sofa, studying her over the can of beer. He said evenly, "We've already had this discussion. I can sniff a lie at twenty paces. What gives?"

"Eddie used to drink sometimes."

"How'd that go?" he asked. His voice was laced with enough skepticism that she could almost believe he'd known the real Eddie. The born-again bastard who hid behind the pretty face, winning smile and charming way with the ladies.

She opened her mouth to say that it had been fine, but something in Brett's eyes stopped her. He was going to weigh her words. Measure them for truth. This was a test to see if she could and would be honest with him. As the moment stretched out, it began to feel more important. As if this was some sort of turning point in their relationship for him.

She closed her mouth. And considered his question seriously. Marrying Eddie had been the biggest mistake of her life. She had ruined her future and ultimately destroyed her own soul.

Taking a deep breath, she opened her mouth and let truth come out. The first real truth she'd told anyone, ever, about her life with Eddie Billingham. "Being married to Eddie was hell on Earth."

"I can imagine. He was a gigantic asshole in high school."

"How did you see that when nobody else did?" she exclaimed.

"I wasn't a girl whose panties he was trying to get into. I played football with him. And he was as dirty a player as I ever saw. Cheated all the time. Lied to the coach and to referees. I can think of at least three guys from opposing teams who had promising football careers ahead of them whom Eddie targeted. Destroyed knees on two of them. Gave the third guy a concussion so bad he was never allowed to play football again."

"Yeah, well, he ruined me, too."

Brett surged partially off the couch at that, and then sank back carefully. He set the beer down on the floor and turned his full attention to her. "What did he do to you, Anna?"

She shook her head. She really didn't want to talk about any of this. All of it was stuffed into a drawer somewhere in the back of her mind, closed tight and locked away with every mental padlock she could summon. "I shouldn't have said anything." She added lightly, "My mama taught me it's not Christian to speak ill of the dead, you know."

"Bullshit."

She stared at Brett. At length, she mumbled, "What?"

"That's a stinking pile of steaming crap, Anna. People who were bad in life are still bad in death. Dying doesn't suddenly make you a good guy."

He delivered the words with such bitterness that she blurted, "Who are *you* talking about right now?"

It was his turn to stop, blink, and consider her question at length. She waited him out, giving him time and space to come up with an answer. Finally, he muttered, "Myself."

"What?" she squawked. "You're not a bad person!"

"You don't know me."

"Yes, Brett, I do. You saved me from that robber, and you saved me again today from Jimbo Billingham. Without thinking, you just acted heroically. It's your core nature to be a good guy. You didn't have to put yourself out for me. You weren't in any danger. But you leaped into the fray and put yourself in harm's way to protect me."

"Don't kid yourself. I wasn't in any danger from the kid and his knife, or from Jimbo. I'm a highly trained Special Forces commando with years and years of combat experience. Neither of those assholes stood a chance against me." He paused, then added, "Had I still been on active duty, I would be in a world of trouble for not finding a nonviolent way to diffuse both situations. The military doesn't want guys like me running around acting like Rambo."

She could see that. Still. He needed to take credit for saving her. Twice. She tried, "So where were the other people in the diner, or in your parents' living room? None of them stepped forward to even complain, let alone intervene. Face it, Brett. You're a hero at heart, whether you like it or not."

"Aw hell, honey. I'm a lot of things, but a hero is not one of them."

She knew that feeling well enough. Everyone who wasn't friends with Eddie thought she was the poor, grieving widow of the town's golden boy. It was all *such* a lie. After all, Jimbo had not been wrong earlier. She *had* killed his brother.

She stared into the fire, visible through the tempered-glass front of the stove, for a long time, letting the sluggish dance of flames and the steady glow of the embers mesmerize her. She lost herself in the silence and the warmth, and the primal allure of the fire. If only she could disappear entirely. The world would be a better place. She didn't deserve to live in a world that included heroes like Brett who'd left the best part of themselves on foreign battlefields so others could be free.

A log popped loudly, startling the hell out of her and knocking her out of her reverie. Reggie woke up, stood carefully, turned around a couple of times and lay down on his other side.

"What happened to Reggie?" she asked idly. "Do you know how he got hurt?"

"Yeah. I know."

She glanced over at Brett. He had finished his beer apparently, for he started slowly twisting the can in his hands, turning it into an aluminum rope.

"Well? What happened to him?" she prompted him.

"IED."

"I E what?" she echoed.

"Improvised Explosive Device."

"There was a bomb here on the ranch?" She was aghast at the notion.

"No. In Afghanistan."

She looked from Brett to the dog and back to Brett. "I don't understand."

"Reggie was a military working dog. Ran with my platoon in Afghanistan. We were out on patrol, and he found an IED the hard way."

"Ohmigosh! That poor, poor dog!"

Brett's face contorted into a mask of pain so deep it was hard for her to look at it. She was torn between going to Reggie to comfort him and going to the man to console him. She settled for murmuring, "It must have been hard to see him hurt."

Brett shook his head. The man looked wired so tight that he couldn't even form words. That did it. She slid across the couch to him and laid her palms on his cheeks. "It's okay, Brett. You're here. Alive. Safe. And so is Reggie. You both made it."

Brett stunned her by pitching forward and burying his face against her neck. If she wasn't mistaken, that was a sob that shook his chest in a racking shudder. Good grief. How traumatic had seeing Reggie hurt been? She wrapped her arms around Brett's head, her fingers sliding through his silky, short hair, pulling him closer. He shifted a little so his ear pressed against her chest over her heart. She caught herself rocking slightly, as if she were comforting an upset child.

How much suffering must it have taken to break a man this tough? Fear coursed through her that she wasn't strong enough to bear whatever agonies he must have endured. But she could hold him. She could offer silent comfort. Her heartbeat. She only prayed it was enough.

His arms slid around her waist, and he hung on for dear life. Pain radiated from him in waves so overpowering she wasn't sure she could breathe under the weight of it. How in the world was he surviving with all this agony and grief locked inside him? No wonder he'd come up here to this cabin to get away from the world.

Not that it was good for him, of course. In dealing with the weight of her own grief and guilt, she'd discovered that running away from it and distracting herself with projects and people had been easier than actually trying to face it. But running also hadn't cured what ailed her.

She glanced over at Reggie, sprawled on his side, sleeping peacefully in front of the fire, his black coat gleaming softly. He wasn't hanging onto the trauma of nearly being blown up. The dog was thoroughly enjoying this moment, content to be warm and dry and indoors on a stormy night. Reggie wasn't hung up about the past, and undoubtedly wasn't fretting about the future.

"The problem with us humans is we overthink everything," she murmured.

Brett snorted against her chest. "That's the understatement of the century."

She stroked her hand through his hair, trying to convey with her touch that she sympathized with his pain and wanted to comfort him.

He groaned very faintly, under his breath, and she didn't think he'd intended for her to hear that sound of heart-wrenching grief.

"You're not alone, Brett. I'm right here with you."

"It's not safe to be with me," he ground out. He started to push away from her, but she tightened her grip on him, unwilling to let him run away from this moment. She sensed that he needed this possibly even more than she did.

"I trust you, Brett. You won't hurt me."

Another sound escaped him, this time laced with self-loathing.

"You're not a bad man. I *know* it. Deep down in my heart."

"You're wrong, Anna. Very, very wrong."

"Name me one terrible thing you've done. Something really despicable."

"How about attacking Jimbo? I damn near strangled him to death."

"You're forgetting that he was attempting to strangle me. He told me he was going to kill me. You did, in fact, save my life."

"He said that?" Brett asked quickly.

She winced mentally because the next obvious question to ask would be why he'd wanted to kill her. She blatantly diverted Brett, saying, "You saw how scared I was and rushed to the rescue without a second thought."

"It would be more accurate to say that I saw how scared you were and something snapped inside my head. That I dropped into a violent fugue state and blindly attacked a man who, fortunately in this case, deserved the violence I unleashed on him. But what about the next time? What if I mistake a situation, read it wrong, and hurt or kill an innocent person? I'm a ticking time bomb, Anna. No matter what you say, you're not going to convince me I'm a good person."

"Regardless. Rescuing me from Jimbo was really sweet of you."

He lifted his head from her chest, pulled back enough to stare down at her. "Are you freaking serious? You actually think I'm *sweet*?"

He started to chuckle, and she replied defensively, "Yes, I do. I can't remember the last time someone came roaring to my defense like that."

Speaking of things snapping inside his head, she saw in his eyes the moment when something else clicked in his noggin. His smile faded and he asked cautiously,

"What else—who else—have you needed defending from?"

And it was her turn to shut down. "Nothing. Nobody. It was just an expression—"

His eyebrows came together in a frown, and she broke off, realizing she'd blurted the same old, tired lie she always told when asked about her marriage to Eddie.

"Fine. It wasn't nothing," she huffed. "But I don't want to talk about it."

He stared at her for a moment and then nodded, as if accepting that she was trying to tell him the truth. "We make a hell of a pair, don't we?" he muttered.

"If you're referring to our mutual unspoken contest of who's more messed up than the other one, I suppose we do."

He grinned at her. "I've got you dead to rights on that score, kid."

The smile drained away from her face, leaving her feeling decades older than her twenty-seven years. She highly doubted that he would win the contest. He was a soldier, paid and ordered to kill enemy combatants. She had no such excuse.

"Don't you go and cry on me again," he said in alarm. "I suck at tears."

"I thought you did pretty good before," she managed to say lightly.

"Aw, Anna. Come here." He gathered her into a hug, and this time it was her ear plastered to his heart. It thumped slow and steady and strong, like the man in whom it lived. Why couldn't he see himself the way she saw him?

She slipped her arms around his waist, which was narrow and hard, completely devoid of any flab. The man didn't know the meaning of *body fat*, apparently. Her palms measured the long ridges of muscle down each side of his spine. They might as well have been carved from stone they were so hard. She slid her hands up, following the line of his back, and as he shifted position and pulled her a little closer, bulges of muscle moved as well, giving way to the hard edge of his shoulder blade.

Nope. No body fat at all. It was enough to make a girl feel a wee bit inadequate. But she'd never been the kind of girl to do hard-core workouts. She'd always been active—a hiker, camper, and outdoorsy kid growing up—but hours in a gym with weights and cardio and sweat? Not so much.

The heartbeat beneath her ear changed, thudding harder and faster. All of a sudden, her palms felt electrified by the heat of his skin, and her simple exploration shifted, morphed into something with definite sexual undertones.

She might as well be groping a tiger. Brett's size and power and lethal training were all right there, in her hands. This was no boy holding her. This wasn't even a regular man. This was a warrior. A soldier.

Caution roared through her. *Danger! Danger!*

And yet, she was drawn to it. Drawn to Brett. God, was she some sort of junkie for dangerous men? In hindsight, Eddie had given her all kinds of warning signs of trouble to come, even before they'd run away from Sunny Creek at the ripe old age of eighteen and eloped.

He'd gotten mean when drunk, even in high school. He'd always apologized profusely and showered her with attention, particularly in front of the other girls in school, which had played right into her desperate need for approval and acceptance. He'd dragged her into the "cool" crowd whether the other kids had wanted her there or not. She'd been so needy and insecure that she'd overlooked the fists through walls, the ugly way he'd looked at her when she talked to other boys, how he occasionally manhandled her, and the time he'd torn her beloved teddy bear to shreds.

Her own parents had divorced when she was little, and she'd never seen what a healthy relationship looked like. She should have known better, but she'd had no measuring stick—

"Where'd you go off to on me, Anna?" Brett murmured.

Oh! Her attention jerked back to the man whose bare back she was feeling up. She realized with a start that she was digging her nails into his bare flesh and loosened her grip instantly. "I'm so sorry!"

"It's okay. I'm pretty tough. What were you thinking about that turned you into a cat with its claws out?"

She laughed a little. "I was thinking about high school."

He groaned. "What a shit show that was."

She lifted her head to stare up at him. "You were the most popular kid in your class. Quarterback of the football team. Homecoming king, for crying out loud. What did you have to complain about?"

He snorted. "My old man was determined to make a Marine out of me, like he'd been. My little sisters had boys sniffing all over them and none of my brothers would help me keep the losers away from them. The girl I thought I was going to marry cheated on me with my best friend, and truth be told, I was horny pretty much every waking minute. Teenage hormones were hell."

She nodded. "No kidding. I followed mine to Hollywood and paid the price big-time."

"Fill in the blanks for me. You dated Eddie in high school. After graduation the two of you moved to Hollywood and got married. Yes?"

She nodded.

"Then he sucked at acting and couldn't get any jobs. What did you do?"

"I went to night school and got an accounting degree. I got a job as a bookkeeper for a small movie production company that made porn films."

"Holy cow. There've got to be some stories there. But let's get back to that later."

"I didn't see the films getting made. I sat in a crappy office and crunched numbers. Although I can tell you how much any kind of sex toy you can think of costs purchased in bulk from a wholesale supplier."

He grinned down at her. "Now there's a hell of a life skill."

She released his back with one hand to swat him on the upper arm.

He caught her hand with his own, twining his fingers between hers. "Your hands are so small and soft. Mine are all scarred and calloused."

"I like your hands. They've seen hard work. And they toughened and survived."

"You've got to quit romanticizing me in your mind, Anna."

"Well, I'm sorry," she declared. "I happen to find you romantic. Deal with it."

His gaze caught hers, and all of a sudden, they were staring into each other's eyes. The air shimmered with tension in the blink of an eye, and she couldn't seem to look away. When she finally did manage to tear her gaze away from his blue-as-the-ocean gaze, darned if she didn't catch herself staring at his lips.

The lower one was slightly fuller than the top one, and a faint shadow of mustache outlined the bow of his upper lip. His tongue slid across his lips slowly, unconsciously, and now his mouth glistened slightly, its fullness and warmth as tempting as sin.

"You gotta stop looking at me like that," he muttered.

"Like how?" she murmured back. Good grief, her heart was going a mile a minute, and she couldn't seem to catch a breath.

"Like you want to eat me alive."

Like she—

Huh. She kind of did want to eat him all up. Well, that was new. The last time she'd panted after a boy had been Eddie back when she was sixteen or so, and he'd been the prettiest thing she'd ever seen.

Brett wasn't boyishly pretty like Eddie had been. But he was ruggedly handsome in a more mature way. His skin was tanned and roughened by years outdoors, there were wrinkles at the corners of his eyes that had more to do with sun and laughter than age, and his facial features were harder, more chiseled than Eddie's had been. But it was their eyes that differed the most. Eddie's had gone dead, or maybe always had been flat and dead, and she'd been too young and naive to notice it. But Brett's eyes? Ah, Brett's eyes were so *alive*. Intelligence and awareness filled his blue gaze, along with humor, sadness and, right now, heavy-lidded passion.

He leaned forward one millimeter at a time, so slowly she could've run to the kitchen sink and back, no doubt giving her plenty of time to evade him as he closed in on her.

But for once, she didn't want to evade a man. She wanted to kiss Brett again. In fact, he was taking altogether too long to get on with it! She leaned forward quickly and planted her mouth on his before she could talk herself out of doing what felt good for once.

His mouth opened against hers, and his tongue swept into her mouth, simultaneously exploring and claiming his territory. This time there was no tentative smooching. This kiss was carnal and Brett made no apology for it. He leaned back, drawing her up his body, sprawling her atop him in the most blatantly suggestive fashion. And he never broke their kiss, never stopped sucking and tasting and devouring her, branding his territory. Although truth be told, she did her best to return the favor, claiming his mouth for herself, relishing the way his lips opened beneath hers, the way his tongue welcomed and tangled with hers as she tasted his mouth back.

Kissing him was like falling into darkness. Not a scary abyss, but a soft, welcoming night that embraced her like a velvet blanket and welled up within her with feelings she couldn't remember feeling before. Was this what real attraction felt like? Well, no wonder her girlfriends made such a fuss about sex!

His hand pulled up the hem of her shirt and then paused on her waist, an unspoken question. Was it okay for him to proceed? She arched into his deliciously muscular body, offering hers to him.

His hand didn't move, and she mumbled impatiently against his lips, "Touch me, Brett."

His lips curved into a smile beneath hers. His palm

burned like fire on her skin, leaving a trail of devastation in its wake as it traced the waistline of her jeans. His splayed hand spanned much of the width of her back and made her feel small and fragile. But for once, she didn't hate that sensation. With Eddie, he'd used her petite stature against her to bully her. But Brett's hand was sliding carefully up her ribs, cherishing her and treating her as if she might break if he played too rough.

For her part, she unbuttoned his shirt between their bodies, pushing aside the flannel shirt eagerly. Her own tank top had slid up in the front a bit, too, and the heat of his washboard-hard belly against her naked skin was enough to make her gasp into his mouth.

"You feel so good," he muttered against her lips.

"Ha. You have no idea," she mumbled back. She shifted her weight, slipping her leg between his hip and the sofa back, straddling his hips as she tried to climb down his throat. Wanton urges surged through her, and a need to get as close to this man as she possibly could had her pulling up her own shirt to bare even more of her body to his.

His hand hovered over her bra clasp behind her, and she broke off her tongue tonsillectomy long enough to challenge, "Do it. I dare you."

A gust of silent laughter filled her mouth, and he neatly popped open her bra. Now her whole back was bare to his roaming palm, and he rubbed up and down her spine slowly, melting away the last vestiges of tension she was holding in her body. She might as well have been a pat of butter melting in his hand.

She plunged her hands into his hair, resting her full weight on him as she tilted her head to kiss his mouth, his jaw, his temple, his ear. She dipped her tongue into his ear and swirled it around once. Twice. He groaned aloud, and she abruptly became aware that the front of his jeans was filled and hard against her nether regions.

She stilled, absorbing the shocking realization that she'd done this to him. Little old mousy, unlovable her. She'd turned on this hot, mature, confident man. "Thank you," she murmured to him.

"For what?" he asked back, kissing his way across the base of her neck, pausing to lick the pulsing fluttering wildly in the hollow of her throat.

"For finding me a little attractive."

"A little? Don't sell yourself short, Anna."

Gratitude warmed her belly. "Thank you for that, too."

He pulled back to stare down at her sprawled all over him. "That's not the first time you've said something like that. How big a jerk *was* Eddie to you?"

Sadness filled her eyes as she smiled up at him. There were no words for the horror of living with Eddie Billingham.

"Good thing he's dead, or I'd have to kill him myself," Brett growled.

She kissed him for that, too emotional for words.

Brett reversed their positions, putting her on her back with him stretched out beside her, his body plastered down the length of her side. He lazily stroked her hair out of her face and stared down at her in the flickering firelight. "Damn, you're beautiful."

She shook her head, her throat still too tight for speech.

"You're the kind of woman I could make love to for hours and hours and still not be tired of."

She gaped up at him, mouth open. She couldn't help

it. No man had ever said anything like that to her and actually meant it. Even in his most romantic moments, Eddie had been a wham-bam-thank-you-ma'am kind of guy.

"It's your call, Anna."

"What's my call?" She was missing something significant, but for the life of her she didn't know where he was going with that comment.

"If you ever want to make love—" He corrected himself. "When you want to make love with me, you let me know. I'm ready, willing and able. But it's your call. You obviously have some baggage in your past to work out, and I'm not about to add to it. Say the word, and I'm there."

He stilled, his gaze shifting to the fire, his hand resting quietly on her bare stomach.

That was it? He wasn't going to make out with her anymore until she said so? What the heck?

"I, um, don't want you to stop kissing me," she said tentatively.

He glanced down at her sidelong, a sexy come-hither look that invited her to kiss him as much as she wanted to. Oh, he was a tease! She reached up and tugged his hair, pulling him down to her.

He kissed her chastely, forcing her to deepen the kiss and go hunting for his tongue and all the clever things he could do with it. Frustrated, she tugged on the back of his muscular neck, pulling him deeper into the kiss. She wriggled beneath him where he lay half across her, pressing her achy, tender breasts against the wall of his chest. Oh, yeah. That felt better.

He smiled against her lips, not breaking the contact, but not advancing it either.

Finally, she lost all patience and blurted, "Oh, for the love of Mike. Would you please stop being such a gentleman and take me to bed already?"

Chapter 9

Brett's heart actually, no kidding, skipped a beat. She wanted him enough to fight through her fear and heartbreak? The magnitude of the gift did not escape him. In fact it scared the hell out of him. Not that he feared he wouldn't be decent to her or make sex good for her. He just wasn't sure he deserved her trust or caring. "You're sure?" he asked aloud.

"Uh-huh."

"Say it." He wanted there to be no mistakes here, no misunderstandings, no later recriminations. If he made love to her, it truly had to be her call.

"I want you to make love to me, Brett. Is that good enough for you?"

Carefully, slowly, so as not to scare her, he stood up, scooped her into his arms and carried her into the tiny bedroom, filled almost wall to wall with a big, old-fashioned iron bed. He took his time, giving her every opportunity to change her mind, and he watched her face for any sign of stress. So far, so good.

The bed was piled high with pillows and quilts, which he leaned down far enough for Anna to grab and throw back. He laid her on the bed and she gasped.

He froze. "What's wrong?" he asked quickly.

"The sheets are freezing!"

Thank God it was nothing more serious than that. He murmured, "We'll fix that fast enough."

He stretched out beside her and she rolled partially on top of him eagerly. Did he dare believe that she really wanted this? Wanted *him*?

He used his foot to hook the covers and pull them up far enough to reach by hand. He covered both of them and savored the weight of her body on his, pressing him down into the down mattress topper. Her honeyed hair fell in a curtain around both of them, its vanilla scent wafting around him in a cloud of comforting invitation.

His erection was so painfully hard he struggled to ignore it. But he sensed that he absolutely had to take it slow with Anna. Eddie had obviously been as big an asshole in bed as he'd been on a football field.

"Warmer now?" he murmured.

"Yes, thank you. But, um, Brett. Aren't we supposed to take our clothes off to do this?"

"Well, now," he drawled. "It's not always necessary, and it can be hot to sneak off in a corner in a crowded room and hike up a woman's skirt, pull down her panties, unzip my fly and press into her from behind when no one's looking. It's pretty sexy to be in a roomful of people, silently doing the deed, having to make no sounds, and having hot, secret sex while not a soul's the wiser."

"In public?" she gasped, sounding scandalized.

"Sure. If two people are consenting adults and no one else knows what's going on to get offended, why not?"

"But…but…in public? With other people around? That's…"

"Scandalous? Naughty? Hot as hell?" he suggested, smiling up at her.

"All of the above." She sounded a little disgruntled. In need of an education in sexual adventure, was she? Well, he was the man for the job.

"About those clothes," he murmured. He sat up, taking Anna with him so she ended up in his lap, straddling his hips. He quickly divested her of her plaid blouse, tank top and sagging bra. Only a little light came in through the door, but it was enough to see the perfect curve of her breasts. They weren't huge, but they were so damned round and full and pink-tipped that he all but came in his pants right then. It didn't help that it had been way, way too long since he'd had a woman.

Getting off their jeans was awkward, and they ended up laughing, tangled up with each other and the bedsheets. He stared down at her as the laughter faded from his eyes. "Ah, you're good for my soul, Anna."

"I think you're about to be very good for mine, too." From another woman in any other situation, it would have been a cheesy line. But she said it so sincerely, so hesitantly, that he realized she was genuinely nervous about having sex with him.

"I promise I'll make it better than good for you," he whispered.

She smiled at him, running her fingers through his

hair. He loved it when she did that. It was as if she was really seeing *him*. She was totally present with him. A lot of the groupie chicks who hung out at the bars Spec Ops guys frequented were all hung up on the idea of doing soldiers. But they hardly cared which soldier they screwed and barely managed to remember a guy's name. It was all very impersonal and routine.

But this moment was a big deal for Anna. And shockingly, it felt like a big deal to him, too. What was it about her that made this more than mere sex?

More unsure of himself than he'd been in a long time, he lowered himself slowly to kiss her. Words failed him as her sleek, warm body pressed against his, all soft curves and sexy, smooth flesh. Man, it had been a long time since he'd been with a woman. And his body wasn't letting him forget it. He clenched his teeth against the lust pounding through his erection, impatient to get inside her and mindlessly slam into her.

In an act of supreme self-discipline, he eased down her body, kissing his way across the soft swell of her belly, nuzzling the junction between her legs, and kissing his way down to her dainty foot and back up her leg. Nibbling the soft flesh behind her knee made her giggle and tug his hair, pulling him back up to kiss her luscious mouth. He couldn't get enough of her berry-plump lips. It was an effort not to devour her whole, but the last thing in the world he wanted to do was scare her.

"Are you okay?" he asked, murmuring the words against the sweetness of her mouth.

"I'm great. You?" she responded, sounding a little surprised. She wasn't used to practicing rolling consent, obviously.

"Ready for more?"

"If you don't quit asking me stupid questions like that, I'm going to start seriously doubting your mental capacity."

"I'm just trying to respect your wishes and not assume too much."

"Assume this. I want you, and I want you *now.*" Her legs wrapped around his hips, her foot tucking up underneath his butt cheek and urging him into closer proximity with her.

"Slow down, baby," he laughed. "Gotta be safe." He fumbled in his wallet, which thankfully sat on the nightstand, and came up with a condom. He noted to self: if she was going to make a habit of getting snowed in with him, he was going to have to stock up on those the next time he went to town.

He ripped open the packet and quickly rolled the condom down his straining erection. Man. He hadn't been this turned on since... Well, he couldn't remember since when.

He rolled back to Anna and her open, welcoming arms. Who knew such a generous, brave woman lurked under her quiet, withdrawn exterior? What kind of an asshole did Eddie have to be to walk away from a woman like this?

He sank into her embrace, and it felt like coming home. For the first time he'd been stateside, he truly felt like he was back. He kissed her gently, reverently, silently conveying his thanks for that.

But then her clever tongue slipped into his mouth and stroked his tongue sexily. She plunged her tongue in and out of his mouth in blatant imitation of the sex she was clearly telegraphing that she wanted.

"Last chance to say no," he ground out.

"Yes. Yes, yes, yes!"

Grinning, he positioned himself and slowly, carefully, by millimeters, eased into her tight heat. She obviously hadn't had sex in a while or her passage wouldn't be so tight he had to push this hard to enter her. She gripped him with both arms and legs, though, murmuring words of encouragement and making little gasps that were all pleasure.

A lifetime later, he was finally seated all the way to the hilt in her, gasping himself with the incredible sensation of being sheathed in all that heat and throbbing flesh. "You okay?" he managed to ask without panting like a dog on a hot summer day.

"Better than okay. Amazing. Fantastic. Spectacular," she replied.

"Aw, baby, we haven't even gotten to the good part yet."

"Show me?"

He lifted up on his elbows to stare down at her. "Don't tell me Eddie couldn't manage to give you real pleasure."

A sad little smile curved the perfect bow of her mouth.

He stared into her eyes in patent disbelief. "Well, then. We'll have to fix that, won't we?"

Silently vowing to himself not to come until she'd had a full-on, screaming orgasm, he started to move slowly, slowly within her, a gentle slide to accommodate her tightness to his size. Gradually, her muscles relaxed and her internal lubrication announced her readiness for more.

He took each of her hands in his, lacing their fingers together, his forearms resting on top of hers as he set up a steady, unhurried rhythm. In and out, in and out, piston-like, never relenting, but never demanding. He stared down into her big blue eyes, turned on like he'd never been before by the building wonder in them. Pleasure gradually glazed them over until he knew she was lost in something bigger than both of them, in a towering place of pure sensation. And he'd taken her there. A surge of pride passed through him that he could give her this.

Only then did he pick up the speed and intensity, driving into her more forcefully, careful not to hurt her but unleashing the beast within him a little bit more. A sheen of perspiration broke out all over his body, and her palms moved slickly across his back, sliding down to clutch desperately at his ass. "Still okay?" he panted, doing everything in his power to keep himself from exploding like a supernova.

"Yes," she whispered. "Yes. Yes. Yes," she gasped in time with his thrusts.

"More?" She'd reduced him to monosyllabic grunts, but he'd be damned if he didn't check in with her and make sure she was still okay.

"Yes!"

Thank goodness. He wasn't sure how much longer he could hold on to his control, not to mention his sanity. He turned his desire loose then, surging up into her body with abandon, reveling in going so deep he touched her womb. Her hips rose to meet his, matching his abandon, as the two of them frantically sought something just beyond their reach.

He, of course, knew what lay just over the edge, but he wasn't sure she did. Just a little bit more. A little bit further. One more nudge. One last, powerful surge into her, and she shattered, crying out, a long, keening sound of pleasure torn from the depths of her soul. And that was all it took. The sound of her orgasm ripped through him and he yelled hoarsely as the mother of all orgasms exploded through him. His entire being convulsed around where their bodies met. His soul emptied into hers, and his body shuddered violently as he gave her everything he had, everything he was.

They stilled, and she stared up at him, awe written on her face. He knew the feeling. He had no words at all for what they'd just shared.

She said in a small voice, out of breath, "So that's what all the fuss is about."

Startled, he threw back his head and laughed. Eventually, he managed to splutter, "That is, indeed, what all the fuss is about."

"Oh. Oh my. That was very nice."

"Nice?" he echoed. "I must be losing my touch if that was just nice."

She swatted his upper arm. "Behave yourself. You know full well that was amazing."

He pressed down to kiss her gently. "It was. Thank you."

"Um, I think I'm the one who should be thanking you. It has never been like that for me before."

"Well, then we'll have to do it again. There's a whole lot more to show you where that came from."

She smiled up at him then, and it was as if she bestowed a benediction on him. It flowed through him like soothing waters across his parched soul. Maybe he was going to be all right someday, after all. Maybe there was hope for him yet. If a woman like her could look at him like that, maybe there was still some small part of his soul that hadn't been corrupted and destroyed by war.

He rolled onto his back, gathering her in his arms and taking her with him. He pulled the covers up over them both and found himself staring up at the wood planks of the ceiling in the dim glow from the fire. A deep, profound silence filled the cabin and filled his soul. He couldn't remember the last time his mind was quiet like this, really, truly calm.

In combat zones, he had to be on high alert 24/7, always anticipating, always planning, always wary. But here, tonight, with snow falling all around them, and Anna drowsy and content in his arms, he could almost believe that he could let down his guard, and that everything was going to be all right.

He drifted off to sleep, and even as he slipped into unconsciousness, he registered shock at being able to go to sleep without hours of tossing and turning. Who knew the love of a good woman cured so many ills?

Brett was jerked from dreamless slumber some time later by an unholy scream that had him leaping out of bed, taking the knife from under his pillow with him in one lightning-fast roll. He crouched, feral, every nerve jangling, the drive to kill surging through his veins.

Another scream, from within his bed.

His brain was about two steps behind his killer instinct, and he took an aggressive step toward the intruder before he remembered.

Anna.

They'd made love.

It had been incredible.

She'd fallen asleep in his arms.

A third scream, ripped from her throat, sent literal chills down his spine. He threw down the knife and leaped forward, tearing off the blankets and gathering her in his arms.

"Anna, baby. Wake up. What is it? Talk to me!"

Chapter 10

The blood. My God. The blood was everywhere. Covering her until her T-shirt was crimson, drenched with it. A huge puddle of it spread on the floor, sticky and hot against her bare feet. Eddie stared up at her in shock and accusation, his hands grasping the butcher knife she'd buried in his belly. God, the slide of cold steel into his gut had felt so good against her palm. So wrong, but so right—

"Anna. Wake up!"

Someone was shaking her.

She thrashed, horrified, frantic to escape the blood.

"Wake. Up!"

Reluctantly, she opened her eyes, unwilling to face the carnage she had wrought. The human life she had spilled in a gush of scarlet death.

Brett.

What was he doing here—?

Oh.

She'd fallen asleep draped across his chest after the best sex and only orgasm of her entire life.

The recriminations slammed into her then. She didn't deserve to be happy. She'd sacrificed that right when she'd taken Eddie's life. She was supposed to suffer. To isolate herself and punish herself when the law had not done it for her. The police called it an accidental death. Eddie had charged her in a drunken rage while she'd been chopping vegetables for stew. She turned around. He'd impaled himself on the knife with the force of his charge. The police had ruled there wasn't anything she could have done. Accidental death.

But she wondered differently. Could she have moved the knife? Yanked it out of the way? There had been a millisecond of hesitation on her part, and that had made all the difference. It wasn't that she'd consciously decided to kill him. She'd just…frozen. Panicked. And he'd rammed into that blade.

"Anna. Talk to me. Tell me about your dream."

"It was a nightmare. A terrible, bloody, awful nightmare."

He nodded sagely. "Ah, yes. I know those well."

"You do? What do you have nightmares about?"

"Things that would make your toes curl and give you worse dreams than you had tonight," he answered bitterly.

"Nothing could be worse than that."

"Trust me," he retorted.

She shook her head in denial. She'd murdered her husband. Nothing was worse than that. She won, hands down.

They stared into each other's eyes, each unwilling

to share their private horror, each convinced that their own nightmare was worse. God knew, she wasn't about to share hers with him. She couldn't very well insist that he share his with her. Eventually, the terrible tension between them eased as they each carefully tucked away their personal hells into drawers in their minds and closed and locked them tightly shut.

Brett shoved a distracted hand through his hair. "Christ, those screams of yours unnerved me. I'm gonna go get a drink of water. You thirsty?"

"I guess so."

She watched him pull on his jeans, skipping underwear. Leaving the fly undone, he padded barefoot into the other room. *Hubba, hubba.*

She heard the woodstove door open and the thud of him tossing more logs onto the fire. The faucet ran in the kitchen, and then his shadow loomed in the doorway, tall and lean and sexy as hell.

She didn't deserve him. Sleeping with him had been a colossal mistake. She took the glass of water he handed her and drained it in silence. She handed it back to him and he disappeared into the other room, moving with ghostlike silence.

How long she waited for him to return to the bed with her, she didn't know. But he never came back.

Just as well. She didn't have any idea how to explain to him that he'd given her the best night of her life, which made it the second worst night of her life.

She lay in the bed, staring up bleakly at the ceiling until gray lightened the wood planks. The snow must have stopped falling because a little while later brilliant sunshine streamed in through the window. She knew the ground would be covered with a fluffy blanket of blindingly white snow, reflecting the sunshine like a sheet of sparkling diamonds draped over the earth.

The cold was deep this morning, and even the fire in the other room couldn't hold it back. Shivering, she hurried into her clothes and stepped into the main room. It was empty. Both Brett and Reggie were gone. She hurried to the front door and was startled to see his truck was gone, too.

The tracks from his tires were about eight inches deep. With his tracks having broken a path, her car ought to be able to manage that. She stomped into her boots fast and wrapped her coat tightly around her. She had to get out of here before he came back. Before he demanded answers and explanations of what had made her scream in her sleep like that. Before he wanted to make love again, and her resolve to deny herself undeserved pleasure was tested beyond its puny limits.

She opened the door and gasped as the cold bit into her face. She'd forgotten what true winter felt like in her years in California. It cut the flesh away from her bones and sank down into them. She already felt as if she was never going to be warm again. Or maybe that was the ice in her soul freezing her from the inside out.

Her car didn't want to start, but finally caught sluggishly. She revved the engine to keep it from stalling and sat for an endless, terrifying minute to let it warm up a little before she started down the mountain. The road wasn't exactly treacherous, but had she not had Brett's tracks to follow, she would never have been able to stay on the road. She would definitely have ended up stuck in the soft ground beneath the new snow.

The main house came into view, and the road she was on merged with the main driveway, which someone had already plowed this morning. She accelerated on the scraped asphalt and held her breath until she made it to the main road without spotting Brett's truck.

Thank God. A clean escape.

Her cell phone rang, and she jumped about a foot in the air. In severe trepidation, she picked it up to look at the caller ID. *Please don't be Brett. Please don't be Brett...*

Vinny Benson from the junk shop.

Thank God.

She picked up the phone. "Hey, Vinny. Whatchya got for me?"

"I found a really cool dresser that would make a perfect sink cabinet in your bathroom. Just saw a hole out of the top for a sink and take off the back, and it would be awesome. Can you come over today to see it? I already have another customer trying to buy it from me."

"Um, sure. I'm balancing the books at the diner today. It'll take me a few hours, but I can head over after that."

"Great. Call me when you leave so I know when to expect you and can make sure to be here."

"Will do."

Guilt gnawed at her as she made her way back to town. What kind of ingrate had the best sex of her life and then snuck out the morning after as if it had been a shameful thing? She was a horrible person. Brett had shown her vulnerability that she sensed he'd never shown anyone else, and she was spitting in his face by running away from him like this. Maybe she should call him. Apologize.

Crud. She didn't have his phone number.

She could turn around and go back. He would never have to know she'd fled.

But then her resolve hardened. *She. Didn't. Deserve. Him.*

And that was the bottom line.

Brett mentally kicked himself. He should have known she would bolt if he left her alone. Whatever demons haunted her had been riding her hard last night. He'd never heard a woman scream like that, but he would never forget the agony and terror in that awful sound.

Christ. He'd made a complete fool of himself, letting down his guard and revealing what a complete mess he was. No wonder she'd run screaming from him. Literally.

He fed Reggie the breakfast he'd gone to town to get for her and then headed for the cupboard where he kept his liquor. Who the hell cared that it was barely 9:00 a.m.? He needed to drink until he couldn't feel a damned thing.

Except as the level in the whiskey bottle went down, his traitorous feelings *increased*. What was up with that? The liquor was supposed to dull it all into background noise. He might never forgive Anna if she'd managed to ruin his only escape from all the pain.

He fell asleep on the couch and was disgusted when he woke up to realize it was midafternoon, he was stone-cold sober and he was out of both whiskey and beer. Another one of his old man's tactics to force him to get out and mingle with people was that Brett had to do his own grocery shopping. Scowling, nursing a headache and feeling as antisocial as he'd felt in a long damned time, he climbed in his truck and headed for Sunny Creek.

He wasn't looking for her. Really. But she drove the only red hybrid car in town, and when he was stopped at the traffic light and a red hybrid crossed in front of him, headed south out of town, it was impossible to miss. Where was she headed?

Not that it was any of his damned business.

Although it wasn't like he had anywhere else to go. The liquor store would be open for hours, still.

What the hell.

He turned right at the light and followed her toward the south end of town. He dropped back out of habit and training so she wouldn't spot him. The road curved to the east out of Sunny Creek and through McMinn Pass on a nasty little stretch of road that wound up into the McMinn Range and then down the other side of the chain of steep granite upthrusts. That floofy little car of hers was wholly inadequate to be driving the McMinn road at this time of year. Particularly not with how unpredictable the weather had been for the past few weeks.

Irritated with her for taking unnecessary risks, he followed far enough behind that she was just a red dot ahead on the dangerous road. Although maybe her daredevil tendencies shouldn't surprise him. After all, she'd taken him for a test drive, hadn't she? And he was a crap ton more lethal than some car.

Flurries started to fill the air, and he accelerated, halving the distance between himself and Anna so he wouldn't lose sight of her. The road twisted up into the mountains and over the high point of the pass, and then began the treacherous, winding descent down the other side.

Brett was concentrating hard, squinting to keep sight of Anna's taillights, when a big, dirty, dual-wheeled pickup truck roared up behind him, practically drove into his backseat for a second and then whipped around him in a no-passing zone.

He swore at the reckless driver who accelerated past him and roared on down the mountain. The other driver was going awfully fast. A thin layer of snow had accumulated on the road, making it just slick enough that braking would be tricky.

His gut tightened. Intuition whispered a warning at him. That truck was barreling down the mountain toward Anna too fast for safety. He accelerated his own truck, trying to catch up with the other truck. The warning in his gut grew more strident. He caught sight of the truck ahead, and it was overtaking Anna way, *way* too fast. Surely the guy saw her car.

Aw, hell. His gut was shouting at him now. That truck wasn't bearing down on her that fast by mistake. No, no, no, no, no, no, no...

Frantically, he fumbled in his back pocket for his cell phone. He had to warn her! Tell her to pull over and stop. That he was right behind her. Just get out of the way of that—

He saw the moment the truck ahead of him pulled out to pass Anna. No. Not to pass her. To get inside her on the road and bump her toward the steep drop-off to her right.

"Hit your brakes!" he yelled helplessly at Anna, watching in horror as her little car swerved and then righted itself. The truck swerved right again, slamming into her left rear tire hard.

Her car swerved...and started fishtailing violently.

She must have hit her brakes—too late—because the tires locked up and her car went into a skid, sliding sideways toward the edge of the road. She disappeared around a curve, and the truck beside her accelerated with a roar of its engine audible even back here.

Please, God, let the guardrail stop her.

Slowing carefully as he approached the curve, so as not to go off the road himself, he started around the bend.

No sign of the homicidal truck. And then he saw that the guardrail on this stretch of road was missing. A voice inside his skull started screaming, and the sound grew louder and louder as he stopped his truck. He jumped out before the wheels barely stopped turning. He raced over to the edge of the embankment and looked down in horror.

Long skid marks showed where her car had slid much of the way down a steep embankment. The marks stopped about three-quarters of the way down and turned into big splat marks in the rocks. That was where her car had rolled. Heart in his throat, he traced the marks to the bottom of the ravine.

Anna's little red car was upside down, at least two hundred feet below.

His heart stopped. Literally stopped. He couldn't breathe, and a ten-ton weight crushed his chest.

Flashes of his men down. Blown to barely recognizable bits. Blood. Muzzle flashes from the insurgents lying in wait to take out any survivors. Die. They would all die for this...

He slipped and skidded down the steep slope, sitting on his butt as the loose scree carried him downward in a terrifying rush. The scream in his head was replaced by a chant repeating over and over.

Be alive. Be alive. Be alive.

He saw the white curtains of airbags hanging in the windows first. *Please, God, let those have done their jobs. Let her be alive...*

"Anna!" he shouted hoarsely.

He backpedaled hard, digging his heels into the wet, soft dirt, lying out almost flat on his back in an effort to slow his tumultuous descent. Her car had landed at the bottom of a ravine, and the last few yards before he reached her car, the hillside flattened out to a gentle slope. Still, he ended up all but sliding in the back window of her car before he managed to slow his momentum. He looked around fast. No puddles to indicate any leaks from the car, which meant there was probably no imminent danger of fire.

"Anna!" he cried, dropping to his knees to peer inside the car. He ripped away the driver's side air bag from the door frame and spotted her.

She was crumpled in a pile, lying on the roof of the car, her legs still strapped into the seat, inside the partially crumpled car. The steering column poked down to the roof between her belly and her face, and she was curled around it. Lucky it hadn't crushed her.

She had a cut on her forehead and there was plenty of blood on her face from that, but his combat-experienced eyes spotted no major pools of blood to indicate life-threatening bleeding.

Limbs lying at natural angles. Thank God. Breathing shallow and rapid. But that was to be expected. She was white as a sheet. Also to be expected.

He reached across her to release her lap belt, but

the combination of her body weight hanging from the strap and damage to the car made the latch completely inoperable. He reached into his boot for his KA-BAR field knife and commenced sawing at the nylon lap belt. The nylon was tough, but his blade was razor sharp and made quick work of it.

Anna let out a faint grunt as her legs flopped down to the roof.

He ordered loudly, "Talk to me, Anna. Open your eyes!"

She moaned faintly, a sound of protest, and went limp and silent again.

"Wake. Up!" he yelled at her.

Her eyelids fluttered.

"C'mon. I can't move you until you tell me where you hurt. We need to get you to a hospital. You have to wake up and talk to me," he shouted.

"So…loud…" she whispered. "Shh."

Seriously? She was shushing him for shouting? He didn't know whether to laugh or shout some more at her.

"Can you feel your hands and feet?" he tried in a more temperate voice.

"Um." A pause. "Yeah."

Thank God. If her spinal cord was intact, her chances of survival had just gone up tenfold.

"Does anything hurt?" he asked next.

"Everything."

"I got that. Does anything hurt more than everything else? A sharp, stabbing pain anywhere? Some injury that's rising above the background noise of pain?"

"My left arm."

"Where?"

"Wrist."

"Open your eyes. Are you seeing double, or is my face in sharp focus?"

Gradually, she opened her eyes and both lids rose at the same time and in equal amounts. Was it possible she'd managed to avoid serious injury in this terrible crash?

"Only one you. Pretty," she sighed.

Okay, so maybe she'd taken a harder hit on her head than he'd realized. If she was thinking about how he looked at a time like this, she must have at least a concussion.

"Does your head hurt?"

"Neck."

"You must have wrenched it pretty hard. I'm going to wrap my sweatshirt around your neck to immobilize it, okay? Just a precaution." He bloody well *hoped* it was just a precaution. Shrugging out of his sweatshirt, he rolled it from the bottom hem up to the collar, creating a long roll.

"Don't move. Let me do all the work. Your job is just to t relax and not tense anything. Got it?"

"Bossy," she sighed.

"Damn straight I'm the boss," he retorted humorously. "Do what I say, okay? I've got some first aid training and a whole bunch of combat experience, and I need your help to make sure I don't hurt you when I move you."

"'Kay." She sounded like she was getting sleepy. She mustn't slip into shock.

"Stay with me, Anna. Don't go to sleep, okay?" Very carefully, he slipped the fleece tube under her neck, doing his level best not to move her head or neck at all.

"Cold," she murmured.

"As soon as I get you out of there, I'll wrap you up and get you warm. Sound good?" He had to keep getting responses out of her. Keep her engaged with him, if not alert, at least talking.

"Uh-huh."

He used the sleeves to tie the fleece roll around her neck. "How does that feel? Any pain? Numbness in your hands or feet?"

"'S'okay."

He looked around on the ground for something to use as a splint. Nothing. It was all rocks and gravel. He peered in the back of her car and spied several manila folders. Magazine clippings and pictures were scattered all over the back. At a glance, they appeared to be decorating and architecture related.

He had to lie down on his belly to reach into the back, but he snagged three manila folders and stacked them on top of one another. He didn't have anything to tie them on with, so he shrugged out of his T-shirt and used his knife to make a tear at the bottom of it. Cold air hit his skin and he shivered as goose bumps rose on his skin. Anna wasn't wrong. They had to get her out of here before hypothermia complicated her injuries even more. Working fast, he ripped off a long strip of cotton from the bottom of his T-shirt.

He knocked out the remaining bits of glass around the passenger window frame and then, lying on his belly, crawled partway into the tiny space with Anna to reach her injured wrist.

Claustrophobia surged through him, and certainty that the car was closing in on him, crushing him, made breathing nearly impossible. He had to roll on his side to use both hands, which squeezed his shoulder so tightly against the roof of the car that he could barely move. Oh, God.

"You okay?" Anna mumbled.

He glanced at her, all of twelve inches away from him. "Yup. You?"

"You look...pale."

"Yeah, well, you scared the hell out of me. When I saw that truck slam into you..." He closed his eyes for a second, forced down his panic, and finished, "...I died a little inside."

"But I'm alive," she protested weakly.

"And let's keep you that way," he said with false cheer as he wrapped the manila folders around her wrist and tied them tightly in place with the strip of T-shirt fabric. Neck: stabilized. Check. Wrist: splinted. Check.

"Any other injuries you can feel?" he asked her.

Her mint-green eyes were starting to turn a rather dull shade of gray as she mumbled, "Don't...think...so."

Crap. She was trying hard to go into shock on him. "Okay then, Anna. Let's get you out of here. Let me do all the work, okay?"

"'Kay."

"You just stay limp. Got that?"

"Noodle," she sighed.

Cripes. Even on the verge of unconsciousness, she still had a sense of humor. The woman had spunk all right.

"Tell me immediately if you feel any new hurts," he told her. Working on his knees outside the car, he reached for her armpits, hooking his wrists under them. He pulled slowly, easing her through the window as gently as he possibly could.

She groaned, and he stopped instantly. "What hurts?"

"Everything. Keep going."

Apparently, the pain had woken her up a little. That was good, at least. His pulling landed him on his butt with Anna's torso in his lap, her legs the only part of her still left inside the vehicle. He ran his hands down each of her arms, across her collarbones and down her ribs. "Any bones feel broken?" he asked her. "You'd feel a sharp pain when I put pressure on them."

"No." She wriggled a little, burrowing her head into the bend of his thigh and hip.

"Don't you go to sleep on me," he blurted, alarmed. He slid out from under her, ignoring her sound of protest. He lifted her as gently as he could across his back in a fireman's carry, her right arm draped forward over his left shoulder, her legs draped over his right shoulder. Her head hung down beside his left arm. Hanging on to her grimly, he began the long climb back up to his truck.

His lungs burned and his legs screamed in protest long before he got there, but he kept going, one dogged step after the next. No way in hell was he failing Anna today.

Maybe it was the altitude making him light-headed, or maybe he was just a head case, but the Montana mountain kept turning into a hillside in Afghanistan. The gray scree around him became dust and darkness, Anna's body draped over his shoulders became one of his men. Except none of his men had survived the ambush. Only he had walked out. But in his hallucination, he was saving them. They made it out. He *had* been able to help them after all.

Without warning, his truck popped into sight. He'd reached the road. He opened the back door of his crew cab and deposited Anna on the backseat as gently as he could. He spread a wool horse blanket from the storage box in the back of his truck across her. It smelled of hay and horse sweat, but it would keep her warm.

He climbed into the front seat, turned the heat on as high as it would go and headed down the mountain. Hillsdale was only a few miles ahead of him and had an urgent care clinic. It wasn't a full-blown hospital emergency room, but it was the closest medical care to be had.

He called ahead to the clinic on his cell phone to let the staff know he was coming in with Anna, who might be seriously injured, and then he called his cousin, Joe Westlake.

"Sheriff's Office," a male voice answered.

"Joe, thank God it's you. This is Brett Morgan."

"What's going on, Brett?" Joe asked tersely. He was a military veteran himself and must have recognized the tension in Brett's voice.

"Anna Larkin was just run off the road by a heavy-duty pickup truck on the McMinn Pass road. East side of the pass, about a quarter of the way down. Her car slid and rolled a couple hundred feet down an embankment. I've pulled her out of the car and am taking her to the clinic in Hillsdale. She doesn't seem seriously injured at a glance. But I need you to check out her car. See if you can find any evidence of who specifically ran her off the road."

"I'm on it." Joe's breathing accelerated as he obviously left his office at a run and headed for his SUV. "How do you know she was run off the road and didn't just slide off?"

"I saw it."

"What?" An engine started in the background. "Tell me exactly what you saw."

"I was a ways back from her. It was snowing lightly, and I only had her taillights in sight. A big silver truck with a trailer-hauling package—dual rear wheels, cut-out tailgate—blew past me in a no-passing zone. He ran right up on Anna's tail, and when she was taking a left-hand curve, pulled up on her left side and bumped her twice. She lost control and went off the road and down a long embankment."

"Did you get a license plate?"

Brett answered in chagrin, "No. Tailgate was down and I couldn't see it. Not that I would have known to memorize it, anyway."

"Continue," Joe ordered.

"When I got to where she went off the road, I saw there was no guardrail installed. Bastard must have known there wouldn't be anything there to stop her."

"You're talking about attempted murder, Brett."

"That would be why I'm calling you, Mr. Law Enforcement."

"I'll be there as soon as I can and will check it out. Maybe I can get a paint sample from where he hit her. Let me know what the doc says about her."

"Will do." Brett threw down the cell phone on the seat beside him and accelerated as another panic attack threatened to overwhelm him. Mustn't have a flash-back now. He was driving, for God's sake. Clenching the wheel until his hands hurt, he forced himself to stay here in the present. With Anna. She needed him. Flashes of driving a badly damaged Humvee frantically back to base in search of help kept intruding upon the Montana road.

He hung on to reality, but by a thread.

He reached Hillsdale and drove the last few blocks to the urgent care clinic in a cold sweat that had nothing to do with being shirtless. He parked in front and saw a nurse and a doctor waiting in the doorway with a rolling gurney. They transferred Anna to the bed and then the pair whisked her away, abruptly leaving him standing alone in the snow and cold.

And that was when his knees started to shake. He staggered into the waiting room and fell into a chair, shaking from head to foot. He'd done it. He'd held it together long enough to save Anna. But he was wrung out, both physically and emotionally, from the effort. It had to be enough. Anna had to be okay. She *had* to.

"Here's a blanket," a young woman said.

He looked up at the receptionist and took the blanket as she stepped back hastily from him. Just how bad did he look? He glanced over at an aquarium full of brightly colored tropical fish and saw his dim reflection in the glass. He looked like a crazy man, covered in dust, his hair sticking up in all directions and his eyes wild.

Ah. It was his eyes that had scared the receptionist. Funny, but he never seemed to scare Anna. And she'd seen him nearly kill people. Twice. Which begged the question of whether she was brave as hell or just too foolish for words.

He wrapped the blanket around his shoulders and realized his right knee was bouncing up and down in a rapid-fire staccato that he couldn't seem to stop. *She has to be okay. She has to be okay.* The rhythm burned into his brain, a litany that was the only thing anchoring him to sanity.

Time passed, and his hold on reality slipped more

and more until he was clinging to the present, to a facade of calm, by the slimmest of margins. With each minute, his imagination ran away with him, envisioning Anna having terrible internal injuries he hadn't spotted. Had he been too freaked out to do a proper safety check before moving her? He replayed every second on the mountain in his head frantically. What had he missed?

At least a hundred years passed before the doctor came out into the waiting room. He was a tall, athletic man with coffee-colored skin. "Mr. Morgan? I'm Benjamin Cooper."

Brett surged to his feet, the blanket falling to the floor behind him. "Is she all right?"

"Yes. She fractured her wrist and has a grade two concussion. She's asking for you, and I need you to go to her. See if you can calm her down. She's agitated and talking a lot about someone named Eddie."

"Her ex-husband."

"Do you have his number? I'll call him—"

Brett cut the doctor off. "He's dead. I'm with her now."

The doctor shrugged. "Works for me. If you come this way, I'll take you to her."

Brett followed the doctor down the hall to a room full of machines and monitors. Thankfully, Anna wasn't hooked to many of them. Just a blood pressure monitor. She looked pale and small in the hospital bed, and when he paused in the doorway, the prettiest smile he'd ever seen broke across her face. It lit up the whole damned room and felt like a burst of sunshine in his chest.

He rushed to her side, and gently took her uninjured right hand that she held up to him. The smile on his face was so big it hurt, but it wasn't half the size of the smile in his heart. Her left hand lay on top of the blankets in a molded plastic splint held on by wide bands of Velcro. "How are you feeling?" he murmured.

"Like I got run off the road by a truck and rolled down a giant hill. Well, I slid most of the way. The car only rolled at the end."

Which probably explained how she'd lived through that crash.

She couldn't be dying if she was making jokes. Right? He glanced over at Dr. Cooper. "What's the prognosis, Doc?"

"Like I said before, she has fractured her wrist. It's not a serious break, and she should wear that splint twenty-four/seven for the next four weeks. I'll re-x-ray the wrist then to see if she can lose the splint. She can take the splint off to bathe, but she may not do anything at all with that hand while it's out of the cast. That includes washing your hair or yourself, Anna," he added sternly.

She nodded meekly.

"As for her concussion, she may feel dizziness, nausea and loss of balance for the next few days. I want someone with her around the clock. If her speech begins to slur, or she experiences memory loss or disorientation, I want her back here ASAP."

"I don't have anyone to stay with me—"

Brett cut her off. "I'll stay with her."

"But—"

"No *buts*." He shot her a quelling glance. "And no arguments."

She subsided, looking uncertain. Not used to being taken care of, was she? Well, they would have to correct that.

While the nurse helped Anna get dressed, Brett stepped out to the front counter and filled out paperwork. The matter of payment came up, and he charged the cost of today's visit to his credit card. Not only did he receive annual income from the ranch in a substantial trust fund, but he'd drawn combat pay on top of his regular military pay for years without spending hardly a dime of it. There was nowhere to spend US dollars in miles-from-nowhere war zones, as it turned out. And he couldn't think of a better way to blow a few thousand bucks than to ensure Anna's health and well-being.

At length, she was bundled into his truck's front seat, and he pointed the truck toward Sunny Creek. On the assumption that she didn't need to drive right past the scene of her near death again today, he took the long route around the McMinn Range to Sunny Creek. Not to mention, he wasn't sure his nerves could take it. Going the long way turned their half-hour drive into over an hour, but she dozed on and off the whole ride back.

When they got back to her place, he asked her, "Should I call someone to come over to stay with you?"

"No!" Anna exclaimed. She winced in pain and repeated in a whisper, "No."

"That was quite the emphatic answer. You don't have any friends in town?"

"Mostly, I have enemies. Eddie had a lot of friends and a big family."

"Then why did you come back here?" he asked curiously.

"I think I came back to punish myself. Or at least to let Eddie's family punish me."

Whoa. He hadn't expected so baldly honest an answer. Must be the painkillers talking. "Do you miss your mother?"

"No."

That was emphatic. He'd had some epic fights with both of his parents over the years, but they'd always gotten past the arguments and forgiven each other. He couldn't imagine being abandoned by his family. Although, now that he thought about it, he'd made a pretty good-faith effort to push them away since he'd gotten home. He made a mental note to stop by the main house for dinner sometime soon.

He had just tucked her into her bed with a mug of chicken noodle soup he'd found in her kitchen cupboard when his cell phone rang. He glanced at the caller ID— Joe Westlake.

"I have to take this. You drink your soup and try to get some rest," he admonished Anna.

"Sheesh. You're fussier than a wet chicken."

"Have you ever seen a wet chicken?" he retorted. "They look like crazy, homeless aliens."

Her laughter floated down the hall behind him as he stepped into the living room. "What have you got for me, Joe?" he muttered quietly.

"Nothing. By the time I got there, her car was completely engulfed in flames."

"What?" he squawked. "It wasn't on fire when we left. There wasn't even a fuel leak. Believe me, Joe. I'm a Spec Ops type. That was the first thing I looked for when I got there. I swear, that car wasn't smoldering, let alone leaking."

"I believe you. Fire chief says it looks like someone doused the car in gas and lit it up. He's got an arson guy coming out from Butte to take a look at it tomorrow. I've roped it off as a crime scene and one of my deputies will be out there all night to make sure no one tampers with it any further. But the car's a total loss. Any evidence we might have found about who ran her off the road has been destroyed."

Brett swore under his breath.

"I hate to say it, but I think you're right. Someone tried to kill Anna."

Chapter 11

Anna didn't know what to make of a man who not only was proficient in a kitchen, but who was willing to fuss over her. Brett plumped pillows and fetched blankets and kept bringing her food and hot drinks until she thought she was going to burst. It was so sweet of him, though, that she didn't have the heart to tell him she couldn't eat another bite if she tried.

The evening grew late, and she'd barely finished a single yawn before Brett scooped her up in his arms off the living room sofa to carry her back to her bedroom. "Really, Brett. I'm capable of walking by myself."

"Congratulations," he murmured, striding down the hall.

"You can put me down," she tried.

Nope. No dice. He carried her all the way into her bedroom and laid her down in her bed. She was going to have to get up to use the restroom before she slept, but she wasn't about to tell him that. No way did she want him carrying her into the bathroom and trying to babysit her in there!

"I'll be on the couch. If you need anything at all during the night, just call out and I'll be right here."

She looked up at him shyly. "I don't know how to thank you, Brett. I don't deserve any of this—"

"Will you stop with that deserving/not deserving stuff?" he snapped.

Her head hurt too much to argue with him tonight, so she merely frowned up at him. What must it be like to see the best in people? To believe that the world was a decent place and that most people were good-hearted?

In spite of a throbbing headache, she managed to sleep and startled herself by not waking up until morning light streamed through the window. Her wrist was hurting this morning, but her head felt better. She padded into the living room to say good-morning to Brett, except he was gone.

She was disappointed, but by the same token, he didn't exactly strike her as the domestic type. She fried herself a few eggs one-handed and made toast.

She'd finished eating and was rinsing off her plate in the sink when she heard the front door open. She froze, panicked that it was Jimbo or one of Eddie's friends. It would figure that she'd just found a reason to live, and *that* would be when one of Eddie's family offed her.

"Anna?" She recognized Brett's voice and sagged in relief.

A scrabble of claws on hardwood warned her that Reggie had come to visit, and she squatted down, smiling, to welcome the Lab into her house. He trotted into the kitchen with his stiff-legged gait, but smiled and wagged his tail when he caught sight of her. She gave his ears a hearty rub with her good hand and the dog leaned against her affectionately.

Reggie turned around and headed back toward the front door, and she followed behind him, stopping cold when she reached the main room. Brett held a rifle in one hand and a nylon duffel bag in the other. He set the bag down and opened it, laying out three pistols and a half-dozen boxes of ammunition. Alarm roared through her. She hated and feared guns, and didn't like the idea of any of them in her house.

Good grief. "Expecting a war?" she asked cautiously.

"Just taking a few precautions."

She frowned. "Against what?"

"I don't know. That's why I'm prepared for anything."

She'd been in a car accident with some jerk with road rage, and Brett was overreacting. A lot. But he also was recently returned from a war zone, and who knew how that affected his view of the world.

Still, she hated guns. She'd lived in fear of Eddie getting the bright idea to bring one into the house and mixing it with his drinking and drugs. But from the grim look on Brett's face, he wasn't going to be talked out of his weapons.

Instead, she asked a question that had been bugging her since yesterday. "How was it that you found me so soon after I went off the road?"

His face reddened. "I followed you out of Sunny Creek. I was in town and saw your car. I was curious about why you left my place without saying goodbye and I wondered where you were going." He added in a rush, "I shouldn't have followed you. It was weird and stalker-y. I'm sorry."

"I'm glad you were there to help me. I don't know what would have happened to me if you hadn't gotten there so fast."

His expression closed down grimly as if he didn't want to think about that either. After a moment, he mumbled, "It's just that I have trust issues—"

She cut him off gently. "Really. It's okay. I didn't give you any reason to trust me when I left your place the way I did yesterday morning. I shouldn't have left without at least thanking you for the time we spent together. It was amazing, by the way. Likewise, you shouldn't have followed me. But it all worked out for the best. Let's call it even, okay?"

He nodded in agreement.

"Is there any way I can talk you out of having that arsenal in my house?" she tried.

"Not a chance."

"Why?" she challenged.

"Because your safety is important to me."

"In the first place, my safety is my business. And in the second place, no one's trying to kill me. At least not today. As long as Jimbo Billingham and his drunk buddies aren't around, I'm fine."

"You have no way of knowing if someone else is out to harm you," he bit out. A note of desperation entered his voice.

"Who would hurt me? I'm nobody."

He shoved a hand through his hair. "God, I hate it when you put yourself down."

"Just keeping it real, Brett."

"You're putting me down at the same time, you know."

She stared. "How's that?"

"I like you. I find you attractive. Interesting. If you're nobody, what does that say about my taste in women?"

He made a good point. Not that it changed her mind about her relative worth as a human being, of course. She scowled at him, and he scowled back.

If he was determined to babysit her back to health, this was going to be a long weekend. Very long.

He seemed agitated as well and picked up a piece of sandpaper. He attacked hand sanding the carved wood trim on the wainscoting and made short work of sanding the door frames she hadn't gotten to. He spent several hours in silence, staining the wood he'd just sanded, and she let him stew. If he wouldn't respect her wishes in her own home and take his guns and his overprotective attitude outside, she had nothing to say to him.

But when he headed for the kitchen with a crowbar, that was when she protested. "What on earth are you thinking about doing with that crowbar?"

"You plan to redo that god-awful avocado, 1970s nightmare of a kitchen, don't you?" he asked.

"Eventually. When I can afford it."

"Consider it done."

"But I can't afford—"

"I've got nothing better to do, and I'm sick of sitting around the cabin by myself."

"But—"

"Think about it like this. I'm bigger than you, I'm meaner than you, you're the one with the concussion, and I'm the one with the crowbar."

She did stand up with some idea of stopping him, but

before she could get to the kitchen, she heard a mighty rending of wood followed by a crash.

"What on earth?" she exclaimed, bolting for the kitchen.

An entire counter was torn off its cabinets and lying on the floor.

"Stop!" she shouted over the kitchen sink being ripped free of its moorings.

"Out with the old and in with the new!" he shouted back.

She hadn't given him permission to reinvent her entire life, darn it! But that was exactly what he seemed set on doing. Sheesh. Sleep with a man once, and he thought he could just come in and rip up a woman's kitchen.

She didn't even want to think about how she was going to pay for new cabinets, counters, floors…heck, appliances. "You have to let me help," she insisted.

"Nope. You're hurt. Stay over there out of the way."

Helplessly, she watched as he efficiently emptied her drawers and cabinets into plastic storage bins that he'd carried in as part of his suite of tools. He carried the bins into her dining room, and then destroyed the rest of her kitchen. Cabinets came off the walls, linoleum came up off the floor and he started to unhook appliances.

"You can't carry all this stuff out by yourself," she declared.

"You're right. That's why a few hands from Runaway Ranch—" He broke off as the sound of a truck engine became audible in the driveway beside her house. "Speak of the devil. Hank Mathers and a few of the guys just pulled into your driveway with a flatbed truck and gloves to help me haul off this trash."

She watched in amazement as the entire contents of her kitchen disappeared out the back door. In short order, she stood in a bare room, stripped down to the laths and studs. She officially was kitchen-less. "And how am I supposed to eat and cook and wash up now?" she demanded.

"That's what takeout is for. And in the meantime, do you feel up to a field trip?" he asked.

She glared at him. "Are you always this bossy?"

"Bossy's my middle name."

"Has anyone ever told you that you remind them a lot of your mother? On a bad day?"

He just grinned and helped her into a coat. The pain-killers she'd taken upon waking were kicking in and her headache and wrist were mostly dull throbs and not actual distractions.

"You're a bully, Brett Morgan."

"Guilty as charged." He moved toward her purposefully as if to pick her up bodily.

She stopped him with a hand on his chest, glaring as menacingly as she could manage. "I swear, if you pick me up, I won't go with you wherever you're planning to take me."

He grinned at her unrepentantly. "Fine. I'll just kiss you, then."

He handled her like spun glass and his kiss was far too gentle and short for her taste. Worse, he stepped back from her before she could get her arms around him and demand more. The man seriously was an awful tease.

She did let him take her good arm as they went outside to his truck. Yesterday's snowmelt had frozen overnight into a thin layer of ice on the sidewalk. The last thing she needed was to fall and bang her head again or land on her fractured wrist.

She dozed as he drove all the way to Butte and parked beside a kitchen design store. She eyed it warily. "This place looks expensive. I was planning to buy vintage stuff from Vinny Benson. He's keeping an eye out for cabinets that are the size I need. In fact, he called yesterday morning to tell me he might have a dresser I could turn into a bathroom sink cabinet."

"You could wait for months or years for the right kitchen cabinets to show up at his place. Better to order exactly what you want and have a functioning kitchen."

Horror slammed through her. She couldn't afford this? Not by a mile.

She opened her mouth to refuse flatly to go inside, but he cut her off before she could speak. "I don't want to hear a word about the cost. This is my gift to you."

"It's way too much. It's entirely inappropriate, Brett," she retorted.

"I never have gone in for the whole appropriate thing. How about you agree that whenever I drop by for supper in the future, you have to feed me in the kitchen I built for you? Would that make you feel better?"

She scowled at him, appalled. "No!"

His smile faded and he spoke seriously. "Anna, let me do this. Think of it as therapy for me. Trust me. If my old man knew I was getting out of the cabin to work on your place, he'd pay for your whole damned house."

She opened her mouth. Closed it. What was a person supposed to say in response to that? She would find a way to pay him back. Somehow.

Brett refused to let her ask about the price of anything in the kitchen store, from cabinets to appliances.

And when she tried to choose basic models, he casually told the salesman to upgrade them. He had even brought the exact measurements of her kitchen with him. Fortunately, she liked the original layout, so he wouldn't be tearing out her plumbing and wiring to reconfigure the space. That would save some money, at least.

She was in shock by the time Brett handed over a credit card and casually paid for the entire order without ever letting her see the grand total. It had to be thousands of dollars, though.

She tried one last time to stop him. "Brett—"

"My father can afford a thousand of your kitchens. Hush."

He led her out to the truck. If only she weren't starting to droop. And her pain meds were wearing off. She would put up the mother of all fights against this...

...She woke up as the truck turned into her driveway and dusk was falling. Brett made her stay in the truck while he went inside and presumably searched the house. Which was total overkill, but not worth arguing over. And besides, his concern for her sent warmth through her that had nothing to do with the truck's excellent heater.

He came outside to open her door and escort her inside. His mama hadn't missed a trick when it came to training him to be a gentleman. They shared pizza they ate out of the box lid, à la college coed, and she called it an early night.

The same nightmare that always visited her in the wee hours came again, and she woke to Brett leaning over, coaxing her to wake. Her throat was dry, and her entire body shook.

"Geez, Anna. What do you dream about that makes you scream like that?"

She blinked up at him in dismay. He would know if she lied, so she answered, "I dream about Eddie's death."

"How did he die? I've been out of the country for the past few years and didn't catch the local gossip while I was gone."

"He was stabbed."

"God, I'm sorry. He was an asshole, but no one deserves to be murdered."

Brett's words might as well have been knives stabbed right into her heart. As amazing a fantasy as it was to play house with him, the truth hadn't changed. She had no business allowing herself to be happy. She closed her eyes, and rolled away from him, hoping he would take the hint and leave.

He didn't. In fact, she felt the covers rise and he slid in behind her, his big body spooning hers, his arm coming around her gently.

She squeezed her eyes shut, silent tears escaping to run down her face onto the pillow. She was bad. Horrible. A killer, whether intentional or not.

Brett might be a soldier, but he didn't kill in cold blood. He engaged in combat with violent enemies who would kill him if he didn't defend himself. She had long given up on defending herself from Eddie when he'd charged her that night. If only she had moved the knife. If only. If only. The refrain played in her head like a broken record.

She should tell Brett the truth. She owed it to him if he was considering getting involved with her. Being with her came with baggage he deserved to know about.

But she couldn't bring herself to confess her sins to him. For once, she was happy, and it was entirely possible Brett would walk away from her if he found out she'd killed her own husband and then hidden that fact.

Truth was, Brett could never despise her as much as she despised herself.

Chapter 12

Brett held Anna patiently, waiting for nearly an hour until her body finally relaxed in his arms into sleep. He knew she wasn't afraid of him. So what, then, made her so tense after her nightmare? Had it frightened her that much? Had she seen Eddie's murder? As a civilian, she wouldn't be accustomed to what violent death looked like. Unlike him. He carried far too many images and memories of what war did to human bodies. To innocents. To his friends and comrades.

But lying here in the dark with Anna cuddled up against him all warm and soft, the images were a little more distant for a change. A little less personal. He hoped it was progress and not just his being tired after a long day of hard physical labor. Whatever its source, he was grateful for it.

He was on the verge of drifting off to sleep himself

when he heard a noise that didn't belong to the furnace or the creaks of an old house. It wasn't much—something brushing against something else. Maybe branches of a bush rattling against the house or a person. But it was enough. Instantly alert, he eased his arm out from underneath Anna and rolled out of bed, landing silently on bare feet. He took the pistol with him that he'd stuffed under his pillow.

Crouching, he moved out into the hallway, pistol first. His rifle lay on the floor beside the sofa where he'd left it when he'd bolted into the bedroom to comfort Anna. But the noise had come from the back of the house. Outside. Damn. His pistol would have to provide enough firepower to handle the intruder.

He eased into the combat zone of a kitchen, freezing as he heard a shoe scuff on the back stoop. The back doorknob moved slightly. It was locked, but someone was testing the knob. An intruder was trying to gain entry to the house, was he? Bastard was in for a hell of a nasty surprise, then. A commando was waiting just on the other side of the door.

Brett moved forward, planning to slide to the wall to the right of the door. But from behind him, Reggie growled. It wasn't loud, just a low rumble in the dog's chest, but it was enough to spook the wannabe intruder. He heard the slap of running footsteps down the driveway.

Swearing, he sprinted through the house, slowing only enough to scoop up the rifle. He threw open the front door and raced out onto the porch.

Headlights were just disappearing around the corner. He ran out into the front yard to get a better look at the car. The lights belonged to a truck, but he didn't get a good enough look at the vehicle even to tell its color or model. Dammit. Was that the truck from McMinn Pass?

He went back inside and dialed the sheriff's office on his cell phone. A deputy was on duty and took his terse report, promising to send a cruiser to spend the rest of the night in front of Anna's house and to tell Joe about the incident first thing in the morning.

He doubted anyone would be back to bother Anna tonight, but he was glad for the cop car out front. When the cruiser arrived, he had a quiet word with the deputy inside, informing the guy that he was armed inside the house but would be careful not to shoot in the direction of the squad car. He went back inside and sat on the sofa, going through the breathing exercises Spec Ops guys used to calm and focus themselves.

It dawned on him as the last battle readiness finally drained away that his feet were half-frozen. He'd been running around outside barefoot all this time. Taking the rifle with him this time, he went back to Anna's room.

Thank God. She was still asleep. All the excitement outside hadn't disturbed her. He lifted the covers and eased into bed beside her. She stirred, turning in her sleep. Her arms came around him and her feet tangled with his.

"What on Earth?" she exclaimed sleepily. "You're an ice cube!"

"I was outside."

"What for?"

"Just checking on things." No need to terrify her after whoever was snooping around had been chased away. Tomorrow morning would be soon enough to let her know that someone was stalking her.

"I don't deserve you—" she started.

He kissed her to cut off the familiar refrain. Her mouth was soft and warm and lazy beneath his, and he could kiss her like this until the end of time and be a happy man. He leaned over her on one elbow and pushed her hair off her face with his free hand.

Her uninjured hand tugged at his shirt, lifting it up until her palm could smooth over his waist and around to his back. She pulled him down to her, and he was elated to sink into her, kissing her thoroughly, outlining her mouth with his tongue and then dipping inside to all that plump, wet, slippery invitation. Her tongue touched his and it was on. He groaned and deepened the kiss, plunging his free hand into her hair and lifting her to meet him.

His T-shirt bunched up under her fingers, and he stopped kissing her long enough to shrug out of it. She went to work awkwardly on his fly and zipper while he pushed up the oversize T-shirt she'd slept in, being careful of the splint on her wrist.

A sleek, naked hip slid under his hand, the sharp indent of her waist, and then the swelling fullness of her breast filled his palm. His body raged with desire as he wriggled free of his jeans. And then her body was arching up eagerly into his, her bare skin warm and soft. She ran her fingers through his chest hair and then circled a hand around his neck, tugging him down to kiss her again.

It was a miracle that he remembered to pause long enough to don a condom given how badly he wanted to be inside her this very instant.

She was waiting for him with open arms when he

returned, and he rolled over onto his back, taking her with him until she sprawled on top of him.

"I don't want to hurt you, Anna. You do what you want tonight, okay?" Her eyes lit so brightly with possibilities in the dark that he half laughed and half groaned. "Why do I think I'm going to regret saying that?"

"I promise you won't regret it," she replied earnestly.

Using her good hand, she pushed upright, straddling his thighs. Running her fingertips around the base of his erection, she cupped him lower, squeezing just enough to make him groan with pleasure. And then she shifted her weight higher, guiding him to her entrance.

He braced himself, gritting his teeth against the storm of pleasure roaring through him. *Must. Not. Explode.*

She slid onto him, sheathing him by slow degrees in such heat and tightness that he could no longer form words, let alone string them together into thoughts. She rocked her hips experimentally, and a purring noise slipped out of her throat. Pleasure spiked through him almost painfully intense.

She did it again, and this time the groan came from him.

She started to move, rocking her hips back and forth, finding a rhythm that made the room go black behind her gorgeous face as the entire world narrowed down to just her riding him, her head thrown back, her good hand on his stomach to balance herself.

His hips refused to stay still and he surged up into her, meeting her where she moved, pressing up every time she pushed down onto him. Deep. So incredibly deep inside her he went. Deep enough to lose himself completely. Deep enough to forget everything but her and the joy she gave him. Deep enough to heal his soul.

She tensed above him and her tempo increased. He reached up to push gently on her stomach, leaning her back over his thighs and increasing the pressure on her pleasure spot.

She cried out, an undulating sound ripped from deep within her, and her internal muscles clenched him spasmodically as she shuddered in violent release. It was arguably the most beautiful thing he'd ever seen.

He sat up, wrapped his arms around her and rolled her over onto her back without ever leaving her tight, clenching heat. He picked up the rhythm from before, driving deeply into her this time, being careful not to jostle her too much. He reached between them to rub his fingertip across the engorged, pulsing bud of her desire, and she cried out again.

This time he went with her over the edge, his face buried against her neck as he emptied his soul into her. She completely ravaged him, and he was a happy man for it.

He pressed up over her, careful of her splinted wrist. "How's your head? Any pain?"

She smiled up at him. "How could I feel anything but pleasure with you?"

He leaned down to kiss her gently and carefully disengaged their bodies so he wouldn't hurt her. "I'm a selfish bastard for making love to you when you're hurt—"

Soft fingertips pressed against his lips. "You apologize all the time. If I didn't want that, I would have said something and you would have respected my wishes."

He might not like her saying she didn't deserve to be

happy all the time, but she had a point, too. He probably did apologize too much. It was just that if she knew about all the baggage inside his head, she might not want to be with him.

"Why were you outside in the middle of the night?" she asked him.

Crap. He'd been hoping to put off this conversation until tomorrow.

"There was someone at your back door trying to get into the house. Someone's trying to kill you, Anna."

She stared up at him in the dark, stunned. Kill her? "That's ridiculous. It was probably just the wind rattling the doorknob."

"Not unless the wind sprints for a truck parked in front of your house and peels out down the street when I go outside after him."

He wasn't kidding about a stranger having been outside her house! Surely this was some sort of paranoid delusion on his part. *Please* let it be a delusion. Except he wasn't the least bit delusional. Had Jimbo come for her? Or was it someone else she didn't know to fear?

"I was hoping not to have this conversation until tomorrow morning when you'd had a good night's sleep," he responded reluctantly.

"I'm wide awake now and not going back to sleep any time soon."

He sighed and said, "Whoever was driving that truck up in the McMinn Pass intentionally ran you off the road."

She pounced on his declaration. "How can you be sure about that?"

"I was there. Remember? The truck that hit you

passed me to get to you, then waited till that stretch of road with no guardrail and swerved into you until you went over the edge of the road. I saw the whole thing."

"It could have been an accident. The road was slick, and maybe the driver lost control of his or her truck."

He rolled his eyes obviously enough that she saw it in the dark. "I assure you. The truck was entirely under control when it rammed you." He hesitated for a moment, then continued grimly, "After I pulled you out of your car and took you to the clinic, I called Joe Westlake. Before he could get to your car to check it out, someone came back, doused your car in something flammable like gasoline, and lit it on fire. Why would anyone do that unless he was trying to hide evidence?"

"My car burned up?" she exclaimed in dismay. All of a sudden the hypothetical idea of Eddie's family taking revenge on her was entirely tangible. Someone had killed her car and erased the evidence just like they would do to her if they ever caught her alone.

Whoever ran her off the road could have been the same person who'd just tried to get into her house.

To finish her off.

A sharp desire to live speared into her gut. Huh. Was that because she hadn't actually faced death before the kid in the diner pulled a knife on her, or was it because she'd met Brett, and her will to live had come surging back?

The practical considerations of getting to and from work when the weather got bad or grocery shopping, or even how she would afford a new car, paled in comparison with the realization that she had a would-be killer stalking her. For real.

"And you're sure the car didn't start on fire by itself?" she asked.

"It took me a while to get you out of your car, and nothing was sparking or providing an ignition source for any spilled fuel when I was there." He continued, "Your car was torched."

"You said my car wasn't visible from the side of the road, right?" she asked.

"Correct. Only you, me and whoever was driving that truck knew your car was down there."

She gulped. "And why destroy my car unless the truck driver had something to hide? Like his paint on my car, maybe?"

"That would be my guess," Brett replied.

The tightness in her belly only increased as the truth sank into her mind. She was a target. For death.

Brett said grimly, "As for your would-be visitor a little while ago, why would anyone try to get into your house in the middle of the night unless he meant you harm?"

She felt sick to her stomach, hot and cold all over. "What am I supposed to do now?"

"Let me and the sheriff do what we do best. We'll figure this out."

Jimbo Billingham had said specifically that he planned to kill her. She had just never seen him as the kind of guy with any follow-through. He was a lot like Eddie—basically lazy and not inclined to exert himself to do much of anything in life.

As if he'd picked the thought out of her brain, Brett asked, "Did Jimbo specifically say he was going to kill you when he assaulted you at my parents' house?"

She winced at the memory of Jimbo's damning

words and answered reluctantly, "He said I got away with murdering his brother, and he was going to see to it I get the justice I deserve. Then he put his arm around my throat and…" Her voice faltered, but she pushed onward miserably. "…And he asked me how it felt to be killed. He asked me if…" She squeezed her eyes shut briefly and then forced herself to finish. "He asked if I was as scared as Eddie when he died."

"What the hell?" Brett exclaimed.

She wanted to curl up and disappear. Just fade away until nothing of her remained. Consciously, she'd thought coming home to Sunny Creek would be anonymous. Quiet. God knew, it was the smallest, most isolated corner of nowhere that she could think of.

But deep in her heart, maybe punishment was what she'd been hoping for when she came back to Eddie's hometown. How sick was that?

Had it not been for Brett's abrupt appearance in her life, she might just have let her wannabe murderer succeed. But now? Now, she looked at Brett's rugged profile in the dark and couldn't imagine just giving up.

Truth be told, she'd desperately wanted to go back in time to before she'd made the disastrous decision to run away with Eddie. Reset her life. Maybe that was why she'd really come back here—in hopes of getting a do-over at life.

And here she was, getting her do-over, finding a great guy who seemed to like her too, and Eddie was still managing to ruin her life. Although, in his defense, she was the one who'd stuck a knife in his gut and severed a major artery. This was her mess.

Her mess.

She looked up at Brett earnestly. "I really appreciate your offer to help me. Honestly, I do. But this is my problem, and I don't expect you to get involved in it. You have issues of your own to sort out, and the last thing you need is to take on all of my baggage."

"You're not equipped to handle it. I am."

"That doesn't mean you're obligated to handle my problems!" she exclaimed. "In fact, I'd prefer it if you didn't!"

As soon as the words left her mouth, she knew them to be a lie. She loved the fact that he was willing to help her. She loved feeling safe for a change, and goodness knew, she loved feeling like somebody decent and kind cared for her. But he didn't get the fact that she truly, genuinely deserved none of it.

He seemed determined to forgive her for any past sins, but he didn't know the truth. He didn't understand that she was beyond redemption. Her sin was unforgivable. She might have been able to move that knife, but she hadn't even tried. She'd been so terrified when Eddie rushed her that she'd frozen. She'd just stood there and watched that blade slide into his belly.

Truthfully, she hadn't even remembered that she had a knife in her hand. The look in his eyes that night— he was finally going to kill her. The moment had come when he'd snapped completely. She'd known for a while that it was coming, that he was working himself up into enough of a rage to kill her. It took several months, but the escalating violence, the increasingly enraged drunkenness, the verbal threats—they'd created a pattern that was crystal clear to her.

Oh, it was bad enough that she'd stabbed Eddie. But the thing she'd never admitted to anyone, not even to herself until this very minute, was that she'd given up. She'd wanted to die. She'd wanted him to kill her.

And that was the thing she simply couldn't forgive herself for.

Chapter 13

Anna went back to work at the diner on Monday morning. Her wrist hurt and she still had a lingering headache that no painkiller would touch, but she couldn't afford to miss any more work. She was going to have to get a car soon, and that would wipe out the rest of her savings. It would have to be a junker, but the weather was going to get too bad soon for her to walk to and from work and the grocery store.

All work on her house would have to come to a stop for the foreseeable future. The new kitchen was due to be installed in about a week. Until then, she would live on canned tuna fish and leftovers from the diner. Patricia and Petunia didn't mind if the waitresses grabbed a salad or a piece of pie now and then.

How she was going to dig out of her financial hole was overshadowed, however, by the loss of Brett. He'd climbed out of her bed silently, dressed without uttering a word and left her house after she'd lied to him about not wanting his help. At her insistence, he'd taken his guns with him.

When she left for work, she thought she might have glimpsed his truck down the street, but she couldn't be sure without staring at it, and she wasn't willing to chance his taking it as an invitation to come talk with her.

A few days later, Hank Mathers stopped by to pick up the various power tools Brett had left at her place. The ranch foreman had been kind to her, inquiring after her health. But he'd also made a point of mentioning that Brett was in a bad way.

Great. Something else to lay at the altar of her failures. She'd hurt a man who was already vulnerable. A good man. A wounded hero.

How much lower could she go?

She trudged through her days, going through the motions of living. But she wasn't really engaged with anyone or anything around her. Even the arrival of the beautiful new kitchen only made her cry. She had to find a way to pay back the Morgans for it, and she had no idea how she would manage that. She was barely covering her bills now, and she still had a car to buy and the rest of her house to fix up.

It was near the end of her shift on Friday when she looked up and saw possibly the one person she dreaded seeing more than Jimbo Billingham walk into the diner. Mona Billingham—Eddie and Jimbo's mother.

They hadn't spoken since Eddie's death. Anna had arranged a small memorial service for Eddie in Los Angeles that had been attended most notably by his mourning drug dealer. Mona hadn't come to it, which was probably just as well. Instead, the woman had held a big funeral for Eddie in Sunny Creek—and Anna had not been invited. Which was also probably just as well.

When Anna arrived in Sunny Creek a few weeks after the funeral, people were *still* talking about the drunken wake that the police had to be called in to break up.

Anna hadn't seen Eddie's mother since her last, disastrous visit to Los Angeles about a year ago. Mona had screamed at Anna for ruining her beautiful baby boy. There'd been no telling the woman that drugs, alcohol, age, and dissipation were responsible for destroying his looks. Nope, it had all been Anna's fault, and Mona—drunk herself on the last night of her visit—had declared that Anna deserved to die for what she'd done to Eddie.

Maybe Mona was right. Maybe another woman would have been better for him. Maybe another woman would have propped up his ego and fed his fantasies of stardom. But Anna had been too realistic, too practical, to play along with his delusions.

Come to think of it, right after Mona's visit had been when Eddie started talking about killing her.

Shaking herself out of the awful memories, she lurched forward to greet Mona. Her feet dragged, and an urge to turn and run as fast as she could in the other direction nearly overcame her. "Would you like a booth today, Mona? Or would you rather sit at the counter?"

Eddie's mother looked her up and down disdainfully. "You look like crap."

"Thank you. You're looking well," she said pleasantly. No way was she getting into a confrontation with

Eddie's mother in front of a dozen customers, all of whom would gossip like crazy. Anna didn't even have to glance over her shoulder to know every single person in the diner was watching this exchange with avid interest. "How about a nice booth over here?"

Mona slid into the vinyl banquette and demanded a cup of coffee while Anna handed her a menu. She recalled that her ex-mother-in-law liked her coffee more like ice cream than actual coffee, and Anna loaded up the cup with sugar and milk.

"What can I get for you today?" Anna asked, order pad held at the ready. As if the puny notebook would protect her from Mona's barbs. Not.

"My son back would be nice."

Great. It was going to be like that, huh? She gritted her teeth and said politely, "The special today is deep-dish potpie. It's a mix of chicken and vegetables in a cream sauce, topped by Petunia's homemade puff pastry. It's delicious. Can I bring you one of those?"

"Fine," Mona spat.

Anna escaped gratefully, heading for the order window. Petunia said from the kitchen, "Are you all right, sweetie? I can come out and deal with her if you'd rather not speak to her."

"No, that's all right. I can handle her. And we both live in this town. It was inevitable that we would see each other eventually."

"If you're sure," Petunia responded doubtfully. Then, "Mona's waving for you."

This time, Anna armed herself with a coffeepot. It wasn't as if she could actually pour the scalding liquid on the woman's lap, but the idea of being able to do it comforted her. Lord, she was more of a sadist than she'd ever realized. Either that, or the entire Billingham clan had a special gift for getting under her skin.

"Can I refill your coffee?" Anna asked Mona. When the woman didn't respond immediately, she started to turn away, grateful to escape.

"Don't you run away from me, girlie. I have things to say to you."

"I'm working, ma'am. And I have other customers to take care of." She let a little steel enter her voice as she added, "This is neither the time nor place for a personal conversation."

Mona leaned over toward her, and that was when Anna smelled alcohol on the woman's breath. Uh-oh. As she recalled, Mona was nearly as nasty a drunk as her son.

She hastily refilled Mona's coffee cup and retreated, ignoring the woman's demands that she stand and listen to what Mona had to say. Nope. Not happening in this lifetime.

The potpie came up on the counter, and Anna mentally girded herself to deliver it. She carried the hot dish over to Mona and set it down on the table. "Be careful. It's hot." She looked the woman dead in the eye. "It will burn you if you're not careful."

"Are you threatening me? You? Threatening *me*?" Mona threw her head back and cackled loudly, and heads turned in her direction.

Well, hell. So much for not being today's hot topic of gossip. She tried so damned hard not to draw attention to herself and to live quietly, but these Billinghams were determined not to let her do that. She supposed she could see their point of view. If someone had killed a loved one of hers, she would be out for blood, too. No doubt about it. Coming back to Sunny Creek had been a colossal mistake.

But in the meantime, she had to deal with her ex-husband's vicious and inebriated mother—and all the wagging tongues just dying to wag in the other booths.

Maybe she just wasn't getting enough sleep, or maybe she was tired of being the brunt of all the nasty gossip in this town. But something reckless broke loose in her chest, and she went with the impulse for once and told the unvarnished truth.

"You're drunk, Mona. Why don't you go home and sleep it off. If you want to talk with me, come back later, when you're sober. And then I'll tell you just what kind of monster your precious Eddie turned out to be."

She turned on her heel and pulled up short as every face in the diner gaped at her. Tough. They could all just get over the whole cult of Eddie Billingham. It was high time people in this town knew what a terrible man he'd really been.

"Don't you walk away from me!" Mona screeched.

Anna felt the woman coming and managed to get turned around before Mona's arms closed around her. She threw her splint up and Mona's hand slammed into it. Daggers of pain shot up Anna's arm to her elbow, but the impact made Mona pull back sharply, shaking her own hand.

Anna spoke with icy calm, enunciating each word with precision. "Eddie used to hit me, too. I guess I see now where he learned to do that. He was a mean drunk, too. And by the way, he was drunk pretty much all the time. He used to go to auditions so plastered he couldn't say his lines, let alone remember them."

"How. Dare. You!" Mona howled.

"Oh, I'll dare a lot more," Anna retorted, advancing menacingly. "I've had it with you Billinghams. Eddie made my life a living hell for ten years, and I'm not about to let you and Jimbo do the same thing here."

She tore off her apron, threw it down on the floor at Mona's feet and made a beeline for the backroom where dishes got washed. She stormed through the double doors, and as they swung shut behind her, she sagged against the wall, bravado spent.

Dumb, dumb, dumb! She *knew better* than to antagonize Eddie, and his mother was apparently just like him. She'd all but dared the woman to come after her now. If Mona exercised half the control over Jimbo that she had over Eddie, Jimbo would be knocking down her door, shotgun in hand, before supper tonight.

An urge to run away, to hide under a rock and never come out, washed over her. What the hell had she been thinking? She'd just picked a fight with a deranged drunk, and likely with her deranged, drunken—and armed—son.

Petunia came into the back room and Anna looked up at her miserably. "I'm so sorry, Petunia. You don't have to say it. I'll punch out my time card and pick up my last paycheck on Friday."

"I'm not firing you! I just came back to see if you're all right. It's high time someone called out Mona Billingham. She's a bully and a bitch, and I couldn't be more delighted that you finally gave her a dose of her own medicine."

That was it. Anna broke down in tears and ended up crying on her boss's shoulder until all her mascara was on the older woman's blouse.

Eventually, she collected herself enough to mumble, "I'm so sorry I made a scene. The other customers—"

Petunia cut her off. "The other customers are fine. They'll be thrilled to have had front-row seats at the comeuppance of Mona Billingham."

"But the diner—"

Petunia interrupted again. "The diner will be fine. If anything, that little show you two just put on will be good for business. Folks will flock to the diner to hear all the dirt. Do you want to take the rest of the day off, or do you feel good enough to go back out there? Your tips are going to be fantastic today. Mark my words."

Petunia turned out to be right. The diner had a heavy turnout for supper, and Anna's tips ran at least double their normal amounts. People went out of their way to smile at her, too, although no one brought up her ugly confrontation with Mona even once.

It was kind of wonderful how supportive everyone was. Until she had to go home and face her empty house, and the long night to come, alone. That was when she missed Brett the most.

He'd installed insulation in her attic as part of his home improvement kick last week, and the place was toasty warm now, partially thanks to him. She ate a sandwich that Petunia sent home from the diner for her and went to bed early. Sleep was her only relief from the loneliness and wistful thoughts of Brett.

Tonight, regret for her rash words to Mona kept her up, tossing and turning for hours after she turned off the lights. Brett might have a monster case of survivor's guilt, but she was suffering from straight-up guilt. Plain and simple. On nights like this, she wished the police had charged her with some crime. At least she would feel like she'd paid an appropriate price for freezing on that fateful night that destroyed what was left of her life.

She jolted awake to a loud crash a little after 2:00 a.m., sitting bolt upright before she was sure what had even woken her. Terrified, she crept out of her bed and peeked out into the hallway. All was quiet now. She listened fearfully at the bedroom door for a long time and heard nothing.

A little braver as the silence stretched out, she tiptoed into the living room. A cold breeze stopped her in her tracks as her eyes adjusted to the light from the streetlamps.

One of her front windows was broken. A brick lay on the floor of her living room along with a bunch of shattered shards of glass. Shocked, she retreated to her bedroom to put on shoes and fetch her cell phone. She called the police and finished dressing while she waited for them to arrive.

She moved around the mess, which she hadn't touched at the request of the police, and opened the front door. Joe Westlake stood there in his sheriff's uniform and a thick, fleece-lined jacket.

"Anna? Are you all right?"

"I'm fine. My window's not, however." She stayed by the door as the sheriff moved around her living room looking for clues and taking pictures. Finally, he picked up the brick itself.

"Huh. No note. Usually brick throwers like to deliver a threat along with the brick." He looked up at her keenly. "Which means whoever tossed this at you likely thinks you know why it got thrown at you. Any idea who might hold a grudge against you?"

"I can think of two people. Jimbo and Mona Bill-ingham."

"Have either of them threatened you in any way?"

"Both of them. Jimbo tried to strangle me at a barbe-cue a couple of weeks back at Runaway Ranch. There were a bunch of witnesses. And Mona and I had some words earlier today at Pittypat's." She confessed, "I might have lost my temper a little bit at the end. I told her Eddie was awful and a drunk and used to hit me."

Although sympathy shone in his eyes, Joe said evenly enough, "I never liked that guy."

"How is it you and Brett saw him for what he was, but all of us girls thought he walked on water?"

"We played sports with him. He showed his true colors then." She rolled her eyes and he added, "Don't beat yourself up over it. Lots of abusers are charm-ing bastards on the surface. It's how they attract their victims."

He turned over the brick and examined it with inter-est. "Is it just me or does this look old?"

She looked at the pale, rose color of the brick and its chipped and worn edges. "You're right, it does. Some of the buildings on Main Street are about that color, and they were built before 1900, weren't they?"

He nodded. "I'll have one of my guys take a look down in the old part of town for any buildings that have had work done and might have left old bricks lying around."

"In that case, anyone could have picked it up."

Joe frowned. "We've had several cases of vandalism in this neighborhood recently. Rumor has it a developer is trying to buy up the houses in this area so they can be knocked down and a commercial business park built. Has anyone approached you to buy you out?"

"No. This is the first I've heard of it. I'll have to ask the neighbors if anyone has approached them."

"Let me know what they say," Joe responded.

"In the meantime, do you have a piece of plywood around here that I can use to board up that window for you?"

She gaped, surprised at how thoughtful an offer that was. She wasn't accustomed to law enforcement officials being anything other than pitying and/or condescending toward her. "As a matter of fact, I do. The sheets I used to cover the window frames until I get these windows are still in the garage. There's a box of screws on the top shelf on the right side of the garage that I used to secure them."

"Stay inside. It's cold out and you're not dressed for it. I'll be back in a minute."

She noted that he took a stroll around her front yard with a flashlight before he headed down her driveway toward the shed. Since he didn't stop to take any pictures, she assumed he didn't find any tracks.

With what little help she could provide one-handed, Joe boarded over the window.

As they stood back to survey their handiwork, she asked him, "Did your arson specialist find out anything about how my car burned up?"

"Someone doused it in an accelerant, probably gasoline, but the final tests aren't back yet to confirm that. The arsonist lit it on fire with a plastic cigarette lighter that was found at the scene."

"Did you find any evidence that someone ran me off the road?"

He shrugged. "I have a reliable eyewitness account. That's all the evidence I need. As for the identity of your attacker, I'm afraid I've got nothing. Dozens of people in this area own pickup trucks similar to the one Brett described. Have you by any chance remembered anything more about the driver?"

She answered regretfully, "I barely got a look at him or her. I was paying attention to the road. The person was wearing a baseball cap. That's about all I noticed."

"I'll have cruisers check on your house several times a night until we catch whoever's harassing you. Let me assure you, I take this very seriously. You have a right to feel safe in your own home and in Sunny Creek."

She deeply appreciated his concern, but she also knew full well she'd brought all of this grief down upon her own head. She showed him to the door and he departed, leaving her alone once more. She cleaned up the glass and, at long last, crawled back into bed.

Morning came with heavy gray skies and a promise of snow. She greeted the new day bleary-eyed from lack of sleep and no closer to knowing what she should do. Stay or go. Make a stand here in Sunny Creek or cut her losses and run. Again.

Thoughtfully, Anna walked to the diner to begin her shift.

As luck would have it, a woman Anna knew to be the county clerk came in for lunch, and Anna took advantage of being her waitress to ask, "Is it true that a developer has been trying to buy up properties over in the old lumber mill district?"

The woman shrugged. "I can tell you that as properties go into foreclosure, they're being snapped up fast at the auctions."

Auctions? That sounded alarming.

"Why, just next week the Rogers property will go on the block. Such a sweet old couple."

Anna stared, stunned. The Rogers were retired teachers whose backyard butted up against her back fence. "I spoke with Mrs. Rogers just a few days ago. She gave no indication at all of a problem, and I would think she'd be devastated at the idea of losing their house."

"We've been sending the homeowner letters for upward of two years, trying to get the back taxes paid," the clerk responded.

"Mr. Rogers is deep into senile dementia. Are you sure he's even been opening the letters?"

"Oh, dear. I didn't know. He taught me history many years ago. I think I'll just stop by to speak with them after work today."

Anna moved away, satisfied to have used the town gossip network for good. If she couldn't beat it, she might as well join it.

Just when she thought her life couldn't possibly get any worse, she was reminded that somebody else had bigger problems than she. Poor Mrs. Rogers.

After her shift, Anna walked home, but bypassed her house to stop in at a neighbor's house. He was an artist who, like her, had recently moved to the neighborhood, lured by a cheap house he could renovate. The fellow was distressed to hear about the Rogerses' plight and offered to pitch in a few hundred dollars to help them out.

Too bad she'd alienated Brett already. His family had more money than it knew what to do with. Paying a few back taxes on a modest home would be nothing to them.

But maybe she could get all the neighbors to pitch in a little. It wasn't often that a person got to pick one's neighbors, and even more rare to have a chance to pick neighbors like the Rogerses. Maybe everyone on this block could have a neighborhood yard sale and raise more money. Energized, she canvassed all the neighbors around her and found that few could afford to pitch in cash. But most were willing to pitch in time or old stuff for a sale.

She could do this. She wanted to help out, to make something good of her return to Sunny Creek. Maybe through service to others she could find a little relief from the crushing burden of her guilt. Brett had turned to building her a new kitchen to keep his hands and mind busy. Maybe she should take a lesson from him and find a project of her own. Except the project she craved was him. She dreamed of him at night, worried about his isolation, and wondered a hundred times a day how he was feeling.

It had started to snow by the time she got home, and she shook flakes out of her hair as she stepped inside her house. Her cell phone rang, and she dug it out of her jeans. "Hey, Vinny. What's up?"

"I heard you had a broken window last night. I thought I'd call and let you know I have a piece of glass that will match the glass in those old windows I sold you."

"Wow. That's so thoughtful of you!"

"I can drive it over to Sunny Creek if you want."

"Oh, gosh. That's too much for me to ask of you." Even though she was without a car at the moment, she was determined not to become a charity case. In Los Angeles, she'd been forced into living a trashy life that often embarrassed her and occasionally humiliated her. She'd sworn to herself that life after Eddie would be different.

To Vinny, she said, "I'll come over as soon as I can to pick it up."

"Tonight?"

She rolled her eyes. The guy wasn't the least bit subtle about wanting to date her and was so awkward about it that he was almost—but not quite—cute. "Maybe. It'll depend on how soon I replace my car." She got off the phone fast before he could insist on bringing over the replacement windowpane.

She'd no sooner hung up her coat than somebody pounded on her front door as if they were trying to break through it. Alarmed, she moved over to peer through the peephole. What was Brett doing here?

Her heart leaped in her chest, as if it hadn't beat for days and was jump-starting now, at the sight of him. Blood rushed through her body and nerves came alive. Even her mind shed the sluggish depression of the past few days and she felt awake. Energized.

She opened the door and he blew past her, barging into her living room and demanding, "Why didn't you call me and let me know someone threw a brick into your house?"

"Because it was only a window. It was an act of vandalism, not a death threat."

His blue eyes narrowed in frustration. "Someone is willing to damage your property. Who's to say they're not willing to damage you? Whoever threw that brick is acting out on rage."

Well, when he put it like that, he did give her pause to think. "I won't be run out of my own house, Brett."

"Not in the long term, no. But in the short term, you need to stay somewhere safe so Joe can figure this out without having to spend half his time and energy protecting you from more attacks."

She hadn't thought of it like that. The sheriff's department wasn't exactly brimming with spare guys sitting around waiting to take care of her. Brett was right. She didn't like it, but he was. "I suppose I could call someone. Ask to stay with them for a day or two. Maybe one of the other girls from the diner, or maybe the Rogerses."

"You're coming back to my place." Brett's voice was flat. Firm.

"I can't!"

"Wanna bet?" He strode past her and into her bedroom. "Do you have a suitcase or am I just carrying out an armload of your stuff and throwing it in my truck?"

"Brett!"

He opened the top drawer in her chest of drawers and froze for an instant as he obviously realized it was her lingerie drawer. Then he lurched into motion, grabbing a handful of lace panties and bras and turning around to face her. Red and pink and lavender and black lace spilled from his fingers in a dazzlingly embarrassing display.

"Oh, for crying out loud. Give that stuff to me," she demanded, snatching her underwear and stuffing it in a small suitcase she pulled out from under the bed.

While she pulled out jeans, shirts and socks for a few days, Brett marched into her bathroom and came back with shampoo, conditioner, hairbrush, toothbrush, toothpaste and a random handful of makeup. She took a quick inventory and ducked back into the bathroom to get mascara and moisturizer.

Her cell phone rang again, and she frowned at it. Why was Vinny calling her back? "Hey, Vinny," she said a little less patiently than before.

"Come over to Hillsdale tonight. I've got some steaks we can grill out behind the store, and I've got a cabinet that might work in your kitchen."

"Oh. About that. I went ahead and ordered new cabinets. Brett Morgan convinced me that I might wait forever and not find cabinets the right dimensions for my kitchen."

The silence on the other end of the line was palpably furious. Finally, Vinny muttered, "He did, did he?"

With scant patience, she said, "Look, Vinny, Brett is here now and I'm about to leave with him. I have to go." She disconnected the call without any further ado.

Brett picked up the suitcase she carried out into the living room and herded her to his truck before she came up with any more protests. He'd been at her house a grand total of no more than two minutes.

"Has anyone told you that you do a decent imitation of a tornado?" she asked as they pulled away from her house and into the night.

"I don't like to waste time. If something needs to get done, I do it."

"For the record, it's a little bit exhausting. And by the way, I can't just go hang out with you on your mountain. I have work tomorrow."

"I'll send someone from the ranch down to fill in for you."

"You can't just take over my life like this, Brett."

"I'm not taking it over. I'm saving it. That's different."

"I'm not in mortal danger. Not really. Jimbo and Mona are taking out their anger and grief on me right now, but they'll get over it."

"Until they do, you're with me."

She'd see about that. While a large part of her was grateful that he still gave a damn about her after she'd been a jerk to him, the rest of her was determined to take care of herself and not depend on anyone else.

For the first time in her life, she was strong enough to stand on her own two feet. Which, now that she thought about it, she no doubt owed entirely to Brett. She appreciated it immensely, but she couldn't lean on him forever either. She had to take care of herself.

Chapter 14

Brett didn't stop breathing hard until he'd pulled onto the ranch driveway. The ranch represented safety to him. Of course, it also represented a dozen full-time ranch hands who were all handy with a shotgun and not about to let one of their own get hurt. For that matter, Miranda was nearly as fine a shot as her ex-Marine husband.

The moon was shining tonight, bathing the white-tipped mountains in silvery light that made them look enchanted. The long valley stretched away in front of him, rising up toward the distant peaks that marked the western boundary of the ranch, and he let out a long sigh of relief. He knew this land, and his link to it sank into his bones. It was a part of him as much as he was part of it.

No matter that he'd fled this place as a teen and never come home until now. It hadn't ever left him.

As the ranch and its inhabitants hunkered down into the slower, frozen rhythm of winter, he felt himself starting to slow down and breathe again, too. The woman beside him was a big part of that. She saw him. Really saw him. And she didn't see a head case or a broken soul when she looked at him. She saw the man he was now—or maybe she saw the man he'd once been, a long time ago.

Either way, he felt a deep tie forming to her, as well. Like the mountains around them, she was solid. Dependable. With a quiet magic about her that called to him.

He parked at his cabin and grabbed Anna's suitcase out of the backseat. Reggie greeted him briefly at the door but then went over to Anna right away for an ear scratch. "Traitor," Brett accused him.

Reggie smiled back and leaned against Anna.

Yeah, he liked her, too.

She asked curiously, "How much more snow can fall up here before you get snowed in? Even your truck has to have its limits."

He shrugged. "It's not uncommon to have ten feet of snow on the ground up here by the end of January. But there's a snowmobile in the lean-to behind this cabin. I tuned it up earlier this week. It's good to go."

"You are Mr. Preparedness, aren't you?"

He shrugged modestly. "This is wild country. You have to take the weather seriously up here."

"It amazes me how different Sunny Creek is from here, and yet we're only a dozen miles away."

"Yes, but there's a four-thousand-foot altitude change between there and here."

She laughed. "I know. I feel it when I try to move fast."

"You'll get used to it in a week or two. If you get a persistent headache, let me know. You might have a little altitude sickness. I can take you down to the main house. It's about two thousand feet lower than this cabin."

"I wouldn't dream of imposing on your parents."

"Have you seen the size of that place? They would hardly notice you were there. I got lost in it for the whole first week I was home."

He moved over to the kitchen counter and pulled out the makings of tea. "Would you like something hot to drink?"

"You're drinking tea now?" She sounded surprised.

"I figured I needed a break from booze if I was going to be handling weapons again."

"Well that's responsible of you."

He glanced up at her and pulled a wry face. "When I'm not wallowing in depression and guilt, I'm a reasonably responsible guy."

He took two mugs of steeping tea and carried them over to the sofa. He handed one to Anna.

She murmured, "You never did tell me about how you ended up leaving the military and coming home."

His entire body tensed. "Don't try to be my shrink," he warned her carefully.

"I'm not. I'm just curious. I assume it had to do with the same attack that ended Reggie's career?"

"Yeah," he answered shortly.

"I thought it's supposed to be good to talk about these things," she commented.

"I don't know. How keen are you to tell me all the

gory details of Eddie's death?" he snapped. "I looked it up on the internet. I know you held the knife he impaled himself on. But why don't you tell me the stuff the newspapers didn't cover. How it smelled. What it was like to feel a blade slide into human muscle. How it made you feel. Go ahead. Let's see how eager you are to talk about all of that."

She shut down as if he'd flipped a switch in her brain. Her face froze, and the expression in her eyes became guarded.

"I'm sorry. I'm an asshole. I shouldn't have poked at that. I know it's a sore subject for you."

She smiled at him sadly. "If only it were just that."

Yeah. He knew the feeling.

They sipped their tea in silence, each lost in their own memories. He only hoped hers weren't as horrible as his.

At length, she finished her tea and carried her mug over to the sink. "I think I'm going to call it a night."

"I'll sleep on the couch. You take the bed," he responded.

She frowned. "You're too long for that sofa. You should take the bed. I'll sleep on the couch."

He snorted. "My mama would tan my hide if she thought I relegated any guest of mine to a lumpy old sofa."

"Well,, I'm not letting you sleep on it, either." She huffed. "We're adults, for crying out loud. We can share the same bed without falling all over one another."

Speak for herself. His hands literally itched to touch her. He nodded tersely, mentally girding himself for a very long night to come. "You use the bathroom first." He added in an attempt at levity, "Then you can crawl into the cold bed first and warm it up for me." He owed her some laughter after dredging up bad memories of Eddie's death.

She smiled halfheartedly, more in appreciation of his effort than actual humor.

At least she didn't seem determined to put up any more fight over the sleeping arrangement.

She disappeared into the bathroom, and in deference to her modesty, he pulled on running shorts and a T-shirt to act as makeshift pajamas. Which was kind of ridiculous, given that she'd had her hands and mouth all over him before. Still, he was doing his damnedest to be a gentleman, here.

He turned out the bathroom light and slipped into the bed. His side was ice cold. "Brrr!" he complained.

She commented from her side of the bed. "Mmm. I'm nice and toasty."

"Don't tempt me, woman." He rolled over half on top of her, and she squealed as his cold body hit hers. "Better," he declared.

The humor faded from his eyes as he stared down at her in the moonlight. "I'm sorry I took that potshot at you about your ex. I know that's a painful subject for you."

"Thanks. I'm sorry I poked at your past. I suppose it's all classified anyway and you couldn't talk about it even if you wanted to."

It would be easy to lie to her, to agree that he wasn't allowed to talk about the incident. But the truth was, it just hurt. And the frustration of not remembering got to him sometimes. "It's not classified," he admitted. "But here's the thing. I was in command of a group of guys and we went out on a patrol. Something bad happened, and four of them died."

She stared up at him with sympathy brimming in her eyes. "And you feel responsible," she breathed.

He shook his head. "It's worse than that. I don't remember what happened. I don't know if I'm responsible or not."

She reached up to lay a soft palm on his cheek. "And not knowing is killing you."

He hadn't ever thought of it in such simple terms. "Something like that."

"Will you ever recover your memory, or is it gone for good?" she asked.

He rolled on his back and threw his arm over his eyes. "The doctors don't know. They sent me here, home, to the ranch, to see if the relaxing, familiar setting would help me remember."

"But it hasn't?"

"Not yet. I have a lot of nightmares, but that's about it."

"Maybe those are pieces of it coming back," she said hopefully.

"Nope. They're just violent and involve people I love dying horribly."

"I'm so sorry, Brett. Is there anything I can do to help?"

He laughed shortly. "The first time I didn't have nightmares after I came home was the night we made love." He was *not* going to ask her for sex so he could escape his private hell. God knew, she had a hell of her own to deal with.

He felt her weight shift and uncovered his eyes to see

her leaning over him, propped up on her good elbow. "I've missed you," she said softly.

"Not half as much as I've missed you," he replied soberly.

"Show me?"

He did not need a second invitation. It was a minor miracle that she'd found her way back to him and he wasn't about to blow it this time.

Anna woke up slowly, aware at first of being warm and safe. Then she registered a muscular arm across her stomach. Brett. She smiled lazily, contented and sated after a long night of lovemaking in the cool moonlight streaming in his bedroom window. The dawn was soft and gray, but snow-bright light came in the room—it must have snowed more after they fell asleep. Frost rimmed the windowpanes, announcing that it had gotten colder, as well.

In no hurry to get up, she turned under Brett's arm and snuggled close to his big body. Who knew it could be this nice to sleep with a man? She had always huddled at the far edge of the bed, as far away from Eddie as possible. He hated being disturbed and accused her of putting the bags under his eyes any time she woke him up.

Brett's lips moved lazily against her temple and he murmured, "Good morning."

"How did you sleep?" she murmured.

"Fantastic. Nightmare free."

She smiled against his chest. "I'm sorry I woke you—"

"I'm glad you did. I would hate to miss a minute of

feeling you in my arms like this." One dark blue eye peeled open. "But it's still early. Go back to sleep, love."

Love.

She froze, stunned. Did he realize what he'd just called her? Surely it was just an endearment. Like calling her *darling* or *baby*. It didn't mean anything. It wasn't a pronouncement of the big L.

He snored gently, and she let out a careful relieved breath. Nope. It hadn't meant anything. Thank goodness. She didn't know how she felt about the idea of anyone ever loving her, let alone loving her now, before she'd paid back her debt to society somehow.

Gradually, the tension drained from her and she managed to doze again. The next time she woke up, teeth were nibbling lightly on her ear, and she giggled at the sensation.

"I suppose now I've slept far too late and it's high time I get up," she declared.

"Baby, you can stay in my bed all day long if you'll let me do naughty things to you while you're here."

After last night's marathon, she couldn't believe he was still up for more sex. She'd known Eddie didn't take care of his health over the years, but she'd had no idea how much it had impacted his stamina. "Do you ever get tired?" she asked Brett playfully.

He grinned. "Now and then. It takes about a fifty-mile hike with a full combat pack to get my attention. I'm actually out of shape right now. I started working out again this week, though. Give me a few months, and I'll be back in battle trim."

"Wow. I can't wait to see how long you can go in bed then," she teased.

"I'll be happy to demonstrate." He kissed her on

the tip of her nose. "But right now, I'm starving. How about you?"

"Famished. Can I help cook?"

"Absolutely."

They laughed and generally got in each other's way until they managed to plate up cheese grits, sausage and a big bowl of cut fruit. They sat down beside each other on the sofa to eat.

They had just finished cleaning up when the sound of a loud motor approaching sent Brett over to one side of a front window to peer out cautiously. Anna tensed immediately. What threat did he sense? "Who's out there?" she asked in alarm.

He glanced over at her, surprise written on his face. "It's just my father."

"Oh. The way you rushed over there and hid in the shadows made me worry."

He blinked, looking surprised. "Sorry. It's just habit. I was a soldier for a long time."

When he was the gentle, funny, demanding lover in her arms, she forgot about the warrior he also was. She supposed he would always be a soldier at heart. There would always be some part of him that responded to threats in this way and that reacted instinctively to protect his loved ones. And that was okay. She could live with that side of him. She trusted that part of him never to hurt her.

Which was a weird sensation. She couldn't remember the last time she'd trusted any man. And to trust one with hair-trigger reflexes honed to violence was the last thing she would have expected. But there it was. She trusted Brett Morgan.

She asked him, "Do you want me to make myself scarce in the bedroom?"

Brett threw her a startled look. "Of course not. We're both consenting adults, not teenagers sneaking around. Besides, my father will be thrilled to see you."

"Why?"

But there was no time for Brett to answer her question before John Morgan blew into the cabin on a gust of frigid wind. "I need your help, son—" He broke off and stared at her in open shock where she hovered in the doorway to the bedroom. A big smile broke across his face.

"Hi, Mr. Morgan," she said shyly.

"Well, hello there, Anna. What a pleasure to see you!" John boomed. Huh. Brett hadn't been wrong about the man's enthusiasm at finding her here.

Morgan turned his attention back to his son. "I'm missing almost a hundred head of breeder cows. The new bull looks to have busted through the fence last night and led them out to the north range. Cloud ceiling is too low to take up the helicopter, so we're going to have to find them and bring them in over land."

Brett swore under his breath. "Lemme put on a few more layers of clothes and I'll drive down to the house."

"You'll need to take the snowmobile. There's three feet of snow on the ground outside."

Anna gasped. Three feet? She rushed over to the window, and sure enough, the snow was almost up to the level of the porch, and Brett's truck was buried past the tires. Winter was officially here. With a vengeance. "Can I help look for the cows?" she asked the older Morgan. "I know how to drive a snowmobile."

"We're all hands on deck right now. We could use the help if you're willing."

She nodded and headed for the bedroom after Brett to put on more clothes. They headed outside, and John bundled Reggie onto his snowmobile, riding in front of him, inside the circle of his arms. Meanwhile, she climbed on the snowmobile Brett pulled out of a shed behind the cabin, plastering her front to Brett's back and hanging on tight. Her thighs cupped his, and the engine vibrated through her body provocatively. It was hard to believe that she could get so turned on after all the sex last night, but there was no mistaking the languid desire pulsing through her lower belly. She couldn't get enough of this man.

Even through thick layers of both their coats, he was hard and strong and reassuring in her arms. What had she been thinking to send him away before? Although she still wasn't sure exactly what he saw in her, she wasn't about to fight against it any longer. She'd fallen, hook, line and sinker, for Brett Morgan.

When they got back to the main compound, he pointed the snowmobile toward the main barn, where a cluster of a dozen people stood around snowmobiles. Apparently, a batch of them had just come back from searching one part of the ranch, and a new batch was about to head out while the first ones warmed up and got a bite to eat.

A snowmobile was assigned to Anna, and as soon as it was fueled up, she followed the others onto the vast acreage. Even caught in the grip of winter, the ranch was breathtakingly beautiful. Stands of tall, fluffy pines drooped under blankets of snow, interspersed with the white skeletons of aspen trees. A wide creek ran swift and cold over a bed of gravel, its banks heavy with snow. And above it all the violet and black mountains loomed in breathtaking majesty. A sense of coming home enveloped her as she followed the trail broken by the other snowmobiles deep into the ranch's splendor.

They reached the end of the trail, and John Morgan stopped to let everyone catch up with him. He gave terse instructions on who should fan out in which direction. She was given the task of heading east until she hit the fence line that paralleled the main road and then following it north.

Brett paused beside her long enough to warn her to be cautious of gullies along the drainage points leaving the property, and then he was off, roaring away in another direction.

She turned her machine toward the road, walkie-talkie tucked inside her coat to keep the batteries warm and operational. It was slow going breaking a trail through the deep snow, and more than once, she got showered in snow that got into the neck of her coat and stuck to her mittens. Thank goodness someone had given her a pair of thick wool felt mittens to go over her own knit mittens. Otherwise, she would already have frostbite.

Occasional vehicles came along the road just on the other side of the wire fence, and the drivers usually waved at her and smiled. She must look like a snowman riding a snowmobile. Every time she hit a deep spot in the snow, the treads threw up a rooster tail of snow that showered down on her. Snow stuck to her hat and shoulders and covered the snowmobile in white. It would be fun if the lives of a bunch of valuable and vulnerable cattle weren't at risk.

She'd been riding along the fence for nearly an hour when she heard a gunshot ring out from somewhere nearby. She was passing through a copse of trees in a low area that came out to the road, exactly the kind of place the cows might have congregated to seek shelter from last night's storm. She stopped and looked around. Was that gunshot a signal of some kind that they'd forgotten to tell her about? She pulled out her walkie-talkie to ask, when another shot rang out. Something flew past her face and she ducked instinctively. That had been a chunk of wood. What the heck?

A third gunshot rang out, and she swore she felt the bullet pass by her before it hit a tree and sent another barrage of splinters flying.

Holy crap. Someone was shooting at her!

Panic exploded in her chest.

Ducking low over her snowmobile, she gunned it, hanging on grimly as it jumped forward. She slid back on the seat and had to haul herself back into position using the handlebars as it bumped over uneven ground. Clinging to the machine grimly, she shot away from the road, which was her best guess as to where the bullets were coming from, based on which sides of the trees had been hit.

She wound through the trees and crashed through brush until the road disappeared from view. She kept going several more minutes for good measure, sticking to the woods for cover.

When she finally came to a stop, heart pounding a hole in her chest and her lungs aching from the freezing-cold air, she looked around at trees and more trees stretching in every direction. Where was she?

It was really going to suck if the city slicker got lost

looking for the lost cows and had to pull ranch hands away from the search for the missing cattle to rescue her. The sun was no help—it was completely hidden behind thick cloud cover.

As best she could tell, the ground was rising slightly in front of her. If she was lucky, that was west. She turned ninety degrees to the left, put the rise on her right, and moved out, praying she was headed south and back in the general direction of the main house.

She drove for what felt like forever. Surely she hadn't come this far along the road. Had she overshot the main house? Was she even going in the right direction? She broke out into broad meadows sprawling in between stands of forest. Although they were beautiful, they did nothing to tell her where she was. She checked her cell phone for a signal but got nothing. No surprise way out here in the mountains.

More than once she pulled out the walkie-talkie to call for help, but unwillingness to be a burden made her shove it back inside her coat each time. She would figure this out herself, darn it. She could take care of herself!

She rode for perhaps another twenty increasingly panicked minutes. She was getting low on fuel, and the daylight was starting to fade. If she didn't find the house soon, it was going to get dark, and then she'd be stuck out here for the night. The temperature was dropping, too.

She was about one minute from stopping for good and calling for help when the trees opened up in front of her. And there, across the valley, lay the glorious sight of the stone-and-log mansion and cluster of neat barns behind it. Tears squeezed out of her eyes and froze on her cheeks as she gunned the snowmobile across the valley.

A beautiful young woman with black hair and black eyes met her at the barn. "I'm Willa Mathers. Hank's daughter. You must be Anna. You look half-frozen."

"I am," Anna replied. Now that her panic was draining away, she noticed the deep chill pervading her body. "Was somebody shooting a gun out by the main road a couple of hours ago? Was it a signal?"

Willa frowned. "We use the walkie-talkies to communicate. John doesn't let anyone shoot or hunt on the ranch. The weanling horses look too much like deer, and Miranda would kill anyone who shot one of her horses."

"Oh. Then I think someone shot at me when I was out by the road."

Willa stared hard at her for a few seconds, and then pulled out a walkie-talkie and spoke quickly into it. Then she spoke very calmly to Anna. "Why don't you go on into the house and get warm? I'll put your snowmobile away for you. Brett will be here shortly."

"Did you call him?" Anna asked accusingly.

"I did." Willa looked at her compassionately. "If something happened to you, I'd hate to think what would happen to him. We're just starting to get him back—thanks to you."

Anna blinked, shocked. Thanks to her? "He's the one saving me—" she started.

Willa waved off her words. "I've known Brett my whole life, and I've never seen him like he was when he came home a few months ago. He was getting worse, not better, until you came along. The whole family's grateful to you."

"I swear. I haven't done anything special."

Willa shrugged. "I'd love to sit down with you sometime and talk with you about what you did to get through to him. I'm writing my PhD dissertation on getting through to military patients with intractable psychological issues."

Anna blinked. "Sounds rough."

"It is. Hence my research in the field. Go on inside. I can hear your teeth chattering from here."

Anna trudged up to the main house, and with every step, felt colder. By the time she reached the back door, her hands and feet were screaming with a thousand needles stabbed in them.

She stepped inside and Miranda exclaimed, "Good Lord, child. You look frozen! Take off all those wet clothes and go sit by the fireplace. I'll bring you some hot spiced cider. When you're warmed up, there's a big pot of chili on the stove and plenty of food laid out."

Anna stripped out of her sodden clothing and made her way to the giant hearth. Beneath a steady fire, a huge pile of coals poured out heat, and the stones she sat on soaked heat into her body. The hot mug Miranda brought her warmed her hands until her fingers started to itch ferociously. She knew better than to scratch her reddened flesh, and by the time she'd finished sipping the hot, cinnamon-laced cider, her hands felt better.

She made her way to the kitchen and was stunned by the volume of food there. It was enough to feed a small army. She ladled up a bowl of the thick, meaty chili that was spicy enough to warm her belly from the inside out. Anna was just mopping up the last of it with a hunk of corn bread when Brett burst into the house. He, too, was covered in snow and his cheeks were red.

He took one look at her and strode over to her,

wrapping her up in a bear hug, snowy coat and all. She squealed as snow melted through her shirt and ran down her collar onto her neck. "I just got dry!" she exclaimed.

"Thank God, you're all right," he rasped. "Who shot at you?"

"I have no idea. As best I can tell, the shots came from the road. Could have been anyone driving by who saw me moving in the trees. They must have mistaken me for a deer."

"You were a human wearing a red coat on a snowmobile," he retorted.

"Yes, but I was covered in snow and down in a hollow. I'm sure it was nothing."

"But what if it wasn't?" he replied. The poor man sounded ravaged. "I'm not letting you out of my sight again until we get this thing with you sorted out."

"There's nothing to sort." Although, as much as she wanted to believe that, she wasn't 100 percent sure any more that it was true. It wasn't deer hunting season, and everyone in these parts knew where the Runaway Ranch property lines were. It made no sense to shoot across a fence onto obviously private property.

Brett finally stepped back from her, and she shook off snow and water while he shed his outer layers of clothing. Anna became aware of Miranda standing at the kitchen sink, washing dishes while blatantly eavesdropping. She had no experience with big nosy families, but she supposed this was what one was like.

Over the next few minutes, several more ranch hands came inside to warm up and get a bite to eat. Darkness was falling fast outside. All at once, every walkie-talkie in the house flared to life.

"Found 'em!" someone called. "They're foundering

in deep snow and going to need help to get out of the ravine on the east side of Fly Creek by the north bend."

Everyone but Anna groaned. She looked at Brett questioningly. "They're way out at the north end of the valley. It's going to take hours to bring them in. We'll have to use snowmobiles to break a trail through the snow and then herd them down it. This is going to take a while."

"Can I help?"

He kissed her briefly. "Stay here and help my mother cook more food. We're going to need it when we get back later. And don't leave the house until I get back. Promise me."

She nodded and he kissed her again, hard and fast. But he still packed a world of care into it. With a last crooked grin for her, he hurried out the back door with the others.

Anna turned and found Miranda approaching her. The older woman wrapped her in a brief, hard hug that shocked Anna. Then she loosed Anna and said briskly, "How are you at peeling potatoes?"

Anna laughed. "Pretty good."

"Then roll up your sleeves and let's get to work."

Brett paused outside the main house to have a word with Hank Mathers. He took the older man aside and said low, "Someone shot at Anna earlier. We need to leave a man or two here at the house to keep an eye on her. And they need to be armed."

Hank nodded grimly. "Don't you worry, son. We take care of our own around here." He thumped Brett affectionately on the shoulder.

Brett got the impression that Hank was talking about

him, too. For the first time since he'd gotten home, family and friends' concern didn't feel like a burden. But when it came to Anna's safety, he had no pride.

Bringing the herd of cattle home was cold, grueling work that took hours to complete. But at long last, the herd was locked inside a barn, heads counted, and miraculously, no cows appeared to have been lost.

Brett and the others trudged up to the main house, exhausted but pleased. It felt a lot like returning to base after a tough military mission successfully concluded. The same satisfaction coursed through him. Which stunned him. After he'd been involuntarily retired from the military, he didn't think he would ever find anything to replace the feeling of a job well done in combat.

He took off his coat and went into the great room, where he spied Anna curled in a ball at one end of a big sofa, her cheek resting on her hands, fast asleep. Smiling, he scooped her up in his arms. She opened her eyes sleepily. "Are they okay?"

"The cattle? All under roof and none the worse for wear. They're cozy in a barn and eating some hay."

"Mmm. Good." She snuggled into his arms, and his heart melted a little. At least she appeared to trust him without reservation when she was nearly unconscious. That was a start. He carried her upstairs to his old bedroom, which he hadn't set foot in since he left to join the Army a decade ago.

Lord, it was exactly the way he'd left it. Newspaper clippings about his football team's district win were still tacked to a corkboard. A trophy from a basketball tournament still stood on the dresser, and his varsity jacket still hung on a hook behind the door. Talk about walking into a time warp.

He tucked Anna into his double bed and crawled in beside her, fully clothed. It completely weirded him out to be lying in this bed with a woman. He half expected one of his parents to barge in here and ground him till the end of time for sneaking a girl into the house. But it would have felt weirder still to go to sleep without Anna safe in his arms where he could protect her.

He dreamed of being under fire, with bullets flying and explosions detonating while he searched frantically for his downed comrades, all the while praying desperately that they were still alive. One by one, he found their broken remains, absorbing the blow of each death with increasing agony. The last body he found was Anna's. Her lifeless eyes stared up at him pleadingly, her arms frozen in an attitude of reaching for help. Reaching for him.

He jolted awake, breathing so hard he was lightheaded.

"What's wrong?" Anna asked from beside him.

"Bad dream."

"They seem more real than reality, don't they? I wake up convinced for a minute that they really happened."

He squeezed his eyes closed. "I dreamed you died."

"And you panicked? That's so sweet."

He stared at her. "It's *sweet* that I dreamed you died horribly?"

"No. It's sweet that dreaming of my death bothered you."

Her arms came around him, tugging him closer to her. He laid his ear on her left collarbone, letting the very much alive beat of her heart thump all the way through him, cutting past the terror and brutal images of his dream.

She was warm and soft and here with him now. All that other stuff was gone. Best left in the past. Only she was worth keeping and saving from the carnage he'd just imagined. "I *will* keep you safe," he murmured against her satin skin.

"I know you will," she murmured into his hair. "Sleep now. I'm here."

And to his disbelief, he did drift off to sleep, listening to her heartbeat and relishing her arms around him, protecting him from his nightmares. He still had a lot of crap to work out, and goodness knew, so did she. But for tonight, for this moment, they were both okay. And it was perfect.

Chapter 15

Anna woke up to dim light showing through dark blue curtains—where was she? Oh. Right. Brett's bedroom in the main house. Her bra dug into her rib, and she reached for it to straighten it.

Brett stirred beside her, and she smiled at him. Last night had been intimate in an emotional way that was almost more intense than sex. What did it mean that he was dreaming of her? Did he return at least some of her feelings?

Carefully, she slipped out from under the covers and tiptoed out of the room. She headed downstairs and was not surprised today to see a dozen men eating pancakes that John Morgan was cooking on a big griddle in the kitchen. She was just about to join the men and grab a plate of flapjacks when the back door opened. Joe Westlake stepped inside and traded friendly greetings with everyone. He spotted her, and said quietly, "Can I speak with you for a moment outside?"

Alarmed, she nodded and followed him onto the long, covered back porch, where they were alone.

"I've got some news for you, Anna, and you're not going to like it."

She girded herself for she knew not what.

"Yesterday, Mona Billingham filed a civil lawsuit against you for the wrongful death of her son."

Anna stared at him. Words refused to form in her head, and she was only aware of the heat draining from her face, leaving her frozen.

"I have a summons to serve on you to appear in a preliminary hearing in two weeks' time." He pulled a folded document out of his inner coat pocket. "This is a piece of paper with a lot of legal terms on it that boil down to this—you have to show up for the hearing, and you'd be smart to bring a lawyer with you."

"I can't afford a lawyer!"

"There's a legal aid clinic in Butte, and you can ask for a court-appointed representative. Trust me, Anna. You need a lawyer."

"Can I catch a ride back to town with you?" she asked.

"Sure. But don't you want to tell Brett about this first?"

"No! He has enough problems to deal with. He doesn't need my messes piling on his existing stressors."

Joe frowned. "He's pretty strong—"

"He's dealing with some pretty terrible fallout from his last mission."

Joe pressed his lips together in a thin line of disapproval, but thankfully, he didn't argue with her.

She followed him back to the cruiser and paused beside it. "Am I supposed to ride in the back since I've been sued?"

Joe laughed. "Hell, no. Sit beside me in front. Just don't touch any of the equipment."

She slid into the front seat, eyeing askance the laptop computer mounted at an angle facing the driver, and various radios and cubbyholes with sinister-looking gear in them.

Joe glanced over at her as the car cruised back toward town. "Miranda and John say you're doing good things for Brett."

She shrugged. "I think he's doing more good for me than I am for him."

"He seems happier since he met you. I just wanted to say thanks on behalf of the family."

"Uh, thanks." She wanted to crawl under the seat and hide in shame. Finally, she'd been accused of Eddie's murder. It might be only a civil case, but the truth would come out now, and everyone would know her secrets.

Joe commented, "The lawyer Mona hired is a creep. He's a known ambulance chaser and all around slimy guy. I can recommend a couple of excellent defense lawyers who would love to take him down a few pegs on your behalf."

"That's kind of you, but I really can't afford a lawyer. As you know, my car was just totaled, and I'm in the middle of renovating my house. Plus, I'm trying to help a neighbor not lose her house. I can't take on any more financial burdens, I'm afraid."

"You can't represent yourself, Anna! Mona's lawyer may be a jerk, but he's not incompetent. Without a good lawyer, you're going to face a very large financial penalty."

"How much is Mona suing me for?"

"Ten million dollars."

Anna laughed, partly in disbelief, and partly in genuine humor at the absurdity of that number. "That's the craziest thing I've ever heard."

"Apparently, she blames you for costing her potential income from Eddie's future earnings as an actor."

"She is aware he was a complete failure and never got a single decent job as an actor in Hollywood, right? Not to mention he snorted or shot up or drank away every penny he could lay his hands on. I had to hide my paycheck in a secret bank account so I could even pay the bills every month."

Joe pulled a face. "I was never a member of the Eddie Billingham fan club. But you're still going to have to go through the process of a trial and provide proof of everything you've just told me."

"How am I supposed to prove he was a drunk and an addict? He's dead!"

"I can request reports from the police in California. Please tell me you called them at least a few times."

She rolled her eyes. "I was on a first-name basis with half the police force where we lived."

"Perfect. I'll ask for copies of all those records. When you hire a lawyer, let me know and I'll forward copies to him or her."

She just shook her head. She really couldn't afford to pay a lawyer a dime.

Joe dropped her off at her house, and she slogged through the heavy snow to her front porch. She spent the next hour shoveling snow off her sidewalk and porch.

The one advantage of not having a car was she didn't have to bother shoveling her driveway.

She was just stowing her snow shovel in the ramshackle garage behind her house when a truck pulled into the driveway, but not Brett's truck.

Jimbo Billingham rolled down the window to shout out at her, "I guess you're not so high and mighty now, are you? We're going to make you pay for killing Eddie!"

She leaned on the shovel, winded from the hard workout, and just stared at him. "I've got nothing, Jimbo. You can't squeeze tears from a rock, and you can't squeeze money out of me that I don't have. I don't know what you and your mother hope to accomplish with this lawsuit of yours."

"Yeah, well, now you're dating Brett Morgan. He'll pay up to keep you out of jail."

So *that* was why they were suing her now? They thought they could squeeze the Morgans by way of her? Oh, no way. The Morgans had been nothing but wonderful and welcoming to her.

She advanced toward him, gripping the shovel tightly. "Let me tell you something, Jimbo Billingham. If you want to air the truth out in court, I'm all for it. I'll be happy to testify to all the times Eddie hit me and stole money and got high. Let's really air out the truth. Let's talk about the whores you and Eddie hired when you came to Los Angeles to visit, and let's talk about your mother's drunken stupors on my living room sofa with her son. Yes, indeed. Let's air it *all* out!"

She realized with disgust that she was nearly shouting. She snorted and turned away from Jimbo. He simply wasn't worth the oxygen to even talk to.

"Don't you turn your back on me," Jimbo snarled.

She turned back to face him. "Or else what, Jimbo? You'll hit me like Eddie did? Or date-rape me like you did that girl when you were in the eleventh grade? Or maybe you'll try to run me off the road and kill me, huh?"

He glared at her, eyes narrow. "You're a crazy bitch."

She brandished her shovel at him. "You'd better believe it, Jimbo. And I've had it with you and your mother. Get off my property and don't come back."

He slammed his truck into reverse and spun his tires, throwing up a huge rooster tail of snow in her direction. She dodged it, frustrated at herself for losing her temper with him. One thing she knew from long years of dealing with his brother: losing her temper at a Billingham never led to anything good.

She looked up, and her next-door neighbor, the artist, was standing on his front porch. "You okay?" he called over to her.

She sent him a weak attempt at a smile. "Yes, I'm fine. That was just my ex-brother-in-law. He's not a very nice guy."

"Ya think?" The artist grinned. "Holler if you need anything, okay? Like Emma Rogers says, neighbors stick together."

She was almost reduced to tears by his kindness. Since Brett had arranged for her to take a few days off work already, now was the perfect time to deal with getting herself a car. She went inside to clean up and then headed out, walking to the used car lot about ten blocks away from her house, checkbook in her pocket.

The salesman was kind to her and suggested a car that would almost wipe out her savings but was sturdy, in good shape and capable of handling both mountains and snow. She was sure he was making her a good deal on the vehicle, but she couldn't justify spending all that money when the Rogerses were about to lose their home. She chose the ugliest car on the lot, a junker that looked in grave danger of falling to pieces at the first hard jolt. But, it left her with right at two thousand dollars in her savings. The car salesman reluctantly sold her the car and threw in a full tank of gas.

Her first stop in Fugly, as she immediately dubbed the car, was the county courthouse. She headed for the desk of the county clerk, who'd told her about the Rogerses' home going into foreclosure.

"Hello, Anna," the woman said warmly. "If you're here to deal with a lawsuit, that's upstairs in the District Attorney's office."

The Sunny Creek gossip network was obviously in full swing. "Actually, I'm here to ask if I can pay some of the Rogerses' back taxes. I don't have all the money yet, but if I paid a couple years' worth of their taxes, would that stop their house from being auctioned off?"

"I'm afraid not. The whole amount will have to be cleared."

"Still. I have two thousand dollars, and I'd like to apply that to their taxes."

"You'll lose all of your money if the rest of the taxes aren't paid by the end of next week. I can't let you do that—"

"I insist." If Billie and Mona were going to wipe her out and take all of her worldly possessions from her anyway, she would just as soon have her last money go toward helping a friend in need than to them. "The neighbors are throwing a big yard sale this coming weekend. Hopefully, we'll raise the rest of the money."

The clerk was unhappy at taking her check but did accept it.

There. Now she was officially broke. She didn't have anything left to lose.

Except, of course, the man she'd given her heart to. But as soon as Brett heard her tell the whole truth about what had happened the night Eddie died, he would turn his back on her, too. And then she would truly hit rock bottom.

Honestly, she wished the bottom would get here fast. The waiting was almost worse than having nothing, than being nothing. After all those soul-sucking years with Eddie, she was good at being nothing. It was familiar to her. This whole business of being happy, of making a home for herself, of carving out some peace— that had been the anomaly in her life.

She left the courthouse and headed over to the diner to see if she could pick up some extra shifts. If she was going to eat this week, she needed the work.

When she stepped into the diner, a noticeable hush fell over the customers. Oh, great. Mona and Jimbo had obviously been bragging about their lawsuit here, too. Well, goodie. If she was going to be a pariah to the people she cared about in this town, she might as well be a pariah to everyone.

Embracing her role as outcast, Jezebel and whatever else Jimbo and Mona had called her, she tied on an apron and went to work, painting on a pleasant, wooden mask of politeness. She deflected the sly comments, refused to rise to the subtle pokes and digs, and ignored the outright insults hurled at her over the next few hours. Apparently, Mona's friends had found out Anna was working today and flocked to Pittypat's for the sole purpose of tormenting her.

She was exhausted when she got off her shift, but decided to drive over to Hillsdale to see if Vinny would give her the new windowpane on credit. She started up the McMinn Pass road and came to the spot where she'd been forced off the road. A temporary guardrail had been installed, and she held her breath all the way around the curve until she was past the spot where she'd miraculously avoided death. Of course, the miracle had been Brett's immediate arrival and his medical training. He'd gotten her out of the car, warmed up, and to a doctor before she could freeze to death or go into shock.

As she wound down the east side of the McMinn Range toward Hillsdale, she was able to relax a little and let her thoughts wander. Earlier, it had crossed her mind that she was falling for Brett, and now she circled back to that moment.

She poked and prodded at the idea and could only conclude that she was, indeed, well on the way to falling in love with him. He was all of the things Eddie had not been. Sure, he had nightmares and emotional baggage left over from his military career. But most soldiers did, right? He was a good man and his kind heart and courage would prevail. He would overcome his memories and flashbacks. And now that he was reconnecting with his family, they would get him the rest of way from where he was to well-adjusted. Heck, Willa Mathers was a lot more qualified to counsel Brett than she was.

Well, didn't that just figure? She found a man she could imagine actually spending her life with…just in time to lose him to her screwed-up past. That was pretty much par for the course in how her life had gone.

She pulled into the parking lot of Vinny's junk shop—smiling a little at Brett's insistence on calling it that—and took a deep breath. She couldn't, she *wouldn't*, sleep with Vinny to get that piece of glass. But she had no doubt he was going to make her grovel for it.

"Well, lookee here!" Vinny exclaimed. "It's my favorite girl. Come to run away with me, have you?"

She tried to smile at him, but feared her expression was no more than a hollow parody. "I was wondering if you still have that piece of glass you told me about and what it will cost me. I'm a little short on cash at the moment."

Her tips this afternoon had been awful. Mona's friends had seemed to take pleasure in tipping her just enough to insult her. She would have preferred they not tip her at all rather than leave her the handfuls of pennies that they had. In total, she'd made under twenty dollars in tips.

"I'm sure we can come to some arrangement," Vinny purred. "The glass is back this way."

Oh, God. As she'd feared. His dirty mind had immediately gone to that place. She'd worked around the porn industry for long enough to know a sleazy come-on when she heard one.

She held her ground at the front counter. "I have a little money. What will the glass cost?"

"Come in the back. Let me show it to you."

"Vinny, I'm in a hurry. I need to get back over the pass before it gets dark. Will you give me a price or not?"

"No need to get huffy with me, Missy."

Her molars ground together inside her mouth. Eddie used to call her Missy, and she hated it.

"It's old glass. Thick. Solid. Same vintage as the other windows I sold you."

"A price, Vinny."

"Forty bucks."

"For a piece of old glass that's of no use to anyone else?" she exclaimed. "That's highway robbery."

He shrugged. "Take it or leave it. It's not my window that got a brick through it."

Something clicked inside her head. How did he know that a brick had broken out her window? In fact, now that she thought about it, he'd called her within a matter of hours after the brick incident and had known her window was broken. Warnings flashed inside her head, and she smiled carefully at him. "You're right, of course. I'm sorry I was short with you. It has been a long day, and I had a hard shift at work. You've taken such great care of me and my little house. I don't know what I would have done without your help and advice."

He puffed out his chest and looked somewhat mollified.

"I left my purse in my car. Let me go get it, and then we'll go in the back and have a look at the glass together."

She moved away from the counter quickly, but tried hard not to look like she was fleeing. Which she totally was. Thankfully, Vinny had to go all the way around the far end of the L-shaped counter if he planned to follow her, and she made it out to the parking lot. She did run then, making for her car fast. She jumped inside and pulled out of the parking lot, holding her breath.

She'd been on the road about two minutes when her

cell phone rang. She picked it up from where it sat in a cup holder and looked at the caller ID. *Vinny Benson*. Nope. Not answering it. She tossed the phone on the passenger seat and headed for home, scared out of her mind that she'd just been alone with a man who might actually be stalking her.

She pulled into her driveway, garaged her car and made her way to the house. Leaving the lights off, she sat in the dark of her living room, completely drained by the day's events. If Brett were here, he would tell her to fight back. But she was just so tired of running from it all. She wanted everything to come out once and for all and to be done with her past for better or worse. Was that too much to ask?

Brett scowled at the interior of his cabin, irritated to be here alone, yet again. Anna was consistent in one thing, at least. She was a flight risk. When the going got bad, she could be counted on to run away.

What he didn't know was what had scared her off this time. His mother said something about Joe West-lake stopping by early this morning, but he had yet to get in touch with his cousin to find out what the bastard said to Anna that sent her haring off back to town.

A knock on his cabin door had him jumping to his feet. He threw it open hopefully— "Willa. What brings you up here?"

"Do you have a minute to talk?"

"Yeah, Sure." She was like a kid sister to him. Her father was a single parent and had worked long hours on the ranch while she was growing up. Miranda had just swept her into the family over the years. He did not need her to psychoanalyze him tonight, however.

She took off her coat and perched on the end of his sofa, noting the empty beer can on the floor at his end of the couch. He wasn't going to apologize for drinking to deal with his frustration at Anna.

"I came to talk with you about Anna."

Oh. 'kay. He hadn't seen that one coming. "What about her?"

"Are you aware that she's demonstrating classic symptoms of an abused spouse?"

"How so?" He'd certainly had his suspicions based on things she had let slip, but it was still a shock to have them confirmed.

"She apologizes for everything all the time, even things she's not responsible for. She's withdrawn in social situations with other people. She has zilch for self-esteem. She flinches when people move unexpectedly around her. I could go on, but you get the idea."

"I could be accused of all those things," he replied defensively.

"And you're diagnosable, too. Except your behaviors are clearly a result of combat stress and post-traumatic stress."

He scowled. God, he hated being psychoanalyzed. "Why are you pointing this stuff out to me? Are you trying to tell me I shouldn't be in a relationship with her?" The notion actually started a slow burn of anger in the pit of his stomach.

"Not at all. I just wanted to make sure you were aware that you'll need to cut her some slack. She will take longer to trust you than other women will, and she may never be as confident as you'd like her to be. Once she does trust you, she'll be loyal to the death to you. It will be vital that you not betray her trust. That you're there for her when she needs you."

"I get all that. But tell me this, oh, almost shrink, almost sister of mine. What am I supposed to do when she runs away from me?"

"Let her go. But make sure to follow after her before too long. She needs to know you'll be there for her no matter what she does that she can't stop herself from doing. Her running is a form of self-defense, in the same way your drinking is."

He huffed. "I'm doing a hell of a lot better than I was a few weeks ago."

"I'm aware of that. I've been checking in with the liquor store to monitor your intake of alcohol, and it has gone down significantly."

He stood up, glaring down at her. "Invasion of privacy much?"

She looked up at him unapologetically. "We love you, Brett. We're not abandoning you any more than you're going to abandon the woman you love."

"That I—" He broke off. That he loved? He wasn't in love with Anna... Was he?

Willa snorted. "You didn't seriously think you could hide it from your mother or me, did you?"

"Leave me alone. And while you're at it, keep your nose out of my business. If I still needed a shrink, I'd be in a military hospital somewhere."

"The way I heard it, your shrinks sent you here to shake loose some suppressed memory," she snapped.

He had to give her credit for doing her homework. "Since when did you grow such a spine, kid?"

"Since I started dealing with stubborn-jerk soldiers like you."

He said affectionately, "Get out, Willa, and leave me to my sulking."

"Go after her, Brett. She's worth fighting for."

"I've had too much to drink to get behind the wheel tonight. But I'll drive into town tomorrow and see her."

"Promise?"

He stood up and Willa stood with him. He gave her a warm hug and gently shoved her toward the door. She left, her laughter drifting back to him.

He fell onto the couch, staring in disbelief at Reggie, who thumped his tail on the floor without picking up his head. Aloud, Brett grumbled, "Love? Really? How the hell did *that* happen?"

Chapter 16

Anna had another rough day at the diner. Mona's pals seemed to revel in coming in to make her life miserable. The good news was that Anna was simply too wiped out emotionally to care. She went through the motions of taking orders, serving food, and pouring drinks without feeling much of anything. Petunia even came out of the kitchen at one point to ask Anna if she was all right or wanted to leave early.

She plodded home, choosing to walk because it was a sunny day and her car, Fugly, had only a certain number of miles left in its old bones. The sun set behind the distant mountains in spectacular shades of orange and red, mauve and violet. She turned onto her sidewalk and frowned. Why were the lights on in her house?

She stopped, peering cautiously through the one remaining front window. Vinny hadn't broken into her house had he? Or maybe Jimbo? She took a step backward, fumbling in her purse for her cell phone to call the police.

Her front door opened, and a tall male figure loomed, silhouetted by light spilling out onto her lawn. But she knew those shoulders. Recognized those narrow hips and muscular legs in tight jeans.

"Brett? What on Earth are you doing here?"

"Making you supper. It's almost ready. Hungry?"

He had no idea. She'd been eating here and there at the diner, attempting to avoid spending any money on food that she didn't have to. Paying her bills and keeping the electricity turned on was going to be more important for a while than mere food.

She climbed the front steps and smelled something cheesy and tomatoey. She swayed, dizzy with hunger as Brett took her coat from her shoulders and hung it on the coat tree. There was a table in her dining room! And it was set with china, silver, tall white candles, and white roses in a short vase between them.

"Where did that come from? I don't have a dining room set!"

"You do now. I couldn't very well serve you a romantic dinner on the floor, now, could I?"

She spied a beautiful antique walnut hutch on the far wall, and ran her hand over the smoothly finished antique table and delicate lines of the matching chairs. She didn't even want to know what it had cost. "Brett—"

He pressed his fingertips to her lips. "Don't say it. I like to do nice things for you, and I have more money than I know what to do with. You're only allowed to say, 'Thank you. I accept.'"

She sighed, near tears over his kindness. "Thank you. I accept."

"Sit down while I pour the wine. The salad is ready, and by the time we're done with that, the lasagna will be out of the oven."

"Good grief. I had no idea you can cook."

"I can follow a recipe, and my mother is the best cook I've ever met. It's her lasagna recipe."

"Thank you, Miranda, wherever you are tonight," Anna declared, lifting her wineglass.

"A toast," Brett murmured. "To better times."

Ha. Nothing but misery awaited her for the foreseeable future. Smiling wistfully, she let him clink his glass against hers. She sipped the wine, which was crisp and rich in flavor with bold undertones she couldn't name. She was no expert at wine, but even she could tell this stuff was high quality.

The wine was so smooth that she finished a full glass of it before she barely realized she had. Brett refilled her glass and then left to bring in the dish of lasagna. It turned out to be as delicious as advertised, and she finished another glass of wine.

Determined not to get drunk and maudlin, she waved off a refill but did take seconds of the lasagna. Brett told her lighthearted stories of his days in basic training, and the dinner conversation involved a lot of laughter.

She pushed back her plate, stuffed. Brett did the same, smiling at her around the candles. "Why did you do all this, Brett? I keep being a total jerk and taking off every time you're nice to me."

He stood up and came over to her, holding his hand out to her. Perplexed, she laid her hand in his larger one. He led her into the living room, where he turned off all the lights but a single lamp and set his cell phone on a small stereo speaker. Sexy jazz music began to play.

"Is this a seduction?" she asked, a smile playing at the corners of her mouth.

"This is me telling you that I'm not going anywhere. I get that this…thing…between us scares the hell out of you. It scares me too, sometimes. But then I think about how you make me feel, and I know it'll be okay."

"You're going to have to push my jaw shut for me," she muttered. "I'm too speechless to do it myself."

He leaned down and kissed her, a light, fleeting kiss that had her looping her arms around his shoulders. He swayed to the music, turning her around the room in a not quite dizzying glide. He paused, kissed her again, and then was swaying and turning again.

"What are you doing to me?" she whispered.

"Trying to convince you that maybe I'm worth sticking around for."

She buried her face in his neck and inhaled the woodsy scent of his aftershave with relish. "You're not the problem," she mumbled. "I am."

With a single finger under her chin, he raised her face and kissed her lightly. "There's no need to hide from me. I think you're perfect just the way you are."

"But I'm not!"

"Hush, Anna. Tonight, there's no outside world. There's just the two of us. Just this room and the darkness, and the music, and whatever we create between us."

God, that sounded so nice. One last night with him before he found out about the lawsuit and before she told him the whole truth—because God knew, she wasn't going to make him hear it from her sitting on the witness stand. One last night where he thought she was worthy of him. One last moment of happiness before she stepped into the cold and silence and loneliness of her future. One last goodbye.

She wrapped her arms around his neck and leaned into him, loving the feel of his strong, hard body against hers. She felt his stomach muscles contract through the thin cotton of his dress shirt, and she saw the vein pounding in his neck under his jaw. It was such a turn-on to realize that she made his heart beat faster. That she caused that hard bulge behind his zipper.

His fingers were at the buttons of her blouse, and the fabric fell away from her collarbones, but instantly, his mouth replaced the cloth, sipping at the hollow there, kissing across her neck to her other shoulder. Another few buttons opened, and his kisses followed the swell of her breast downward into the valley between her breasts.

"You smell like vanilla," he murmured. "I could smell you all night long."

"You can if you'd like but I can think of better ways to spend the night," she responded.

He chuckled against her flesh. "So can I, thank you very much."

She pulled his shirt free of his belt and began to work on the buttons as her own shirt fell wide open. His hands cupped her breasts, and he stared down reverently at her chest. No man had ever looked at her like that before Brett. She carefully memorized the look in his eyes, tucking it away for the long years ahead.

She pushed his shirt open and leaned forward to kiss his chest. At her touch, his pectoral muscles jumped under his skin, and she memorized that along with the clean, masculine scent of him. A scent she would never, ever forget.

His hand slid around behind her ribs, and her bra fell loose around her. He pushed the lace aside and his mouth closed on the tip of her breast hungrily. His tongue swirled around the sensitive bud and she cried out, arching into him, offering herself up to him. Tonight, she would hold back nothing. If he wanted all of her, she was his for the taking.

And take her he did. After he finished stripping her naked, he swept his arm behind her knees and picked her up in his arms. He carried her over to her bed, which, surprise, surprise, was conveniently turned down already. He'd thought of everything, hadn't he?

"You planned this out, didn't you?" she accused as he stripped off his pants and socks and leaned down over her.

"Every detail of it," he replied matter-of-factly.

Oh, my. "Well, then, what comes next?"

"I thought I might kiss you from head to toe and see if I can find all your ticklish spots. It's important to know all of those so I can avoid them—or use them to my advantage."

"You're such a soldier," she teased. "Looking for the enemy's weaknesses."

"Ah, but you're not the enemy. And the idea is for both of us to win this war."

She smiled up at him, but the smile faded from her face as she got a good look at the expression in his eyes. He was focused. Intent. But he was also laying his heart out to her tonight. It was all there in his eyes. And it humbled her to see him so invested in making her happy. She didn't deserve him—

No. She wasn't going to have such thoughts tonight. This was their own private world where nothing else mattered or intruded. Just the two of them and the love they made between them.

He did, indeed, discover all her ticklish spots and found a few she didn't know she had. Who knew the inside of her ear was so ticklish, or the spot between her toes?

"Turnabout's fair play, Mister," she declared a little while later. "Where are you ticklish?"

He grinned at her as she knelt over him, her hair spilling over her shoulders. "I believe that's for me to know and you to find out."

"Challenge accepted, Brett Morgan."

Within three minutes, she had him laughing helplessly and guarding his ribs from her with his elbows plastered to his sides. She pushed up on his chest with her hands. "It's a good thing the bad guys never figured out how ticklish you are. They could have skipped all the guns and violence and just snuck into your tent and tickled you into submission."

He smiled up at her. "I don't let anyone know that my ribs are my personal kryptonite. I trust you'll keep that little fact to yourself? I'd hate to have men working for me know my greatest weakness."

"My lips are sealed," she declared.

"I sincerely hope not," he murmured, sitting up and wrapping her in his arms. I have plans for those lips that don't involve them being closed."

She ran her fingers through his thick, silky hair. "Show me?"

"Gladly."

He rolled her onto her back and sank into her body.

It felt like coming home. This was where she belonged. Joined to him in every possible way, moving to the easy rhythm of the music drifting around them. Smiling up at him as wonder filled his eyes, and then feeling the same wonder fill her gaze.

They fit perfectly. Physically, emotionally, even psychologically. They both had their burdens to bear, but they were perfectly suited to help one another. As the music from the living room built to a crescendo around them, so did their love. The pulsing bass rhythm became their flesh straining together. The soaring notes of the melody became her soul, breaking free and flying up, up, into infinity as he brought her such pleasure that it could not be contained. His entire body shuddered in her arms and she was right there with him, emptied and filled all at once, lifted out of herself but joined with him. In short, it was perfect.

And at the moment of climax when she cried out in exquisite pleasure, she heard him groan, "I love you, Anna."

And it all came crashing down around her head.

Brett felt the exact moment when she ran away from him. Oh, her body still encased his throbbing erection, and her breasts still cushioned his heaving chest. But she left him, going to that place of private pain where she let nobody in.

He pushed her damp hair back off her face and stared down at her. "Look at me, Anna," he said gently, but firmly.

She blinked and focused on him, coming back momentarily from her private hell. He spoke quickly before he lost her again. "I'm not going anywhere. I know you have big issues to work out. That you struggle to trust anyone. But no matter what, I'm not leaving you."

"I'll bet I can make you change your mind," she said faintly.

"I'll bet you can't. There's nothing you can say to scare me off."

"How about this? I killed Eddie."

"I know. You were holding a knife and he impaled himself on it."

"I saw him coming. I had time to move the knife, but I didn't. I froze. It's my fault he's dead."

"Lots of people freeze in panic situations. The fact that you did doesn't make you a murderer. It makes you normal. Eddie charged you and scared you to death."

She shook her head a little. "Then how about this? I wanted Eddie to kill me."

That made him pull back far enough to get a good look down at her. "Why?"

"Because I let him do all those terrible things to me. I could have left, but I didn't. I stayed year after year. At first, I was too stubborn to admit to anyone else what a terrible mistake I'd made. But then, after a while, it became…normal."

"Normal how?" he asked carefully. Anna had a wild look in her eyes, and he sensed that at long last he was getting to the heart of the matter with her.

"Hitting me was how he showed me love. I…liked it…when he hit me, because it meant he saw me. It meant he felt something for me. His being angry at me was better than being invisible. Don't you see? I disappeared. He was the only person who saw me anymore."

Her voice became hoarse and she sounded like she was struggling to form words. "I…loved him…for that.

He messed me up so bad that I wanted him to hit me and push me around."

Brett frowned, struggling to comprehend what she was saying.

She continued all in a rush. "I'm *broken*, Brett. I want to be treated terribly. I'm afraid that I actually crave suffering. I'm not worthy of anything else."

"Then why do you enjoy sex with me so much?" he asked logically. "I'm the only person you've ever experienced orgasms with, right?"

She nodded miserably.

"I don't hurt you. I treat you with tenderness and respect. And you like that."

She frowned a little as if she was having trouble puzzling through his logic.

"I've seen women who enjoy pain. Hell, I've seen some guys who like it." He shrugged. "It's not my kink, but if they like it, more power to them. Thing is, you're not one of those people. You get turned on by romance and making out. You like it when I kiss you all over and touch you and make you wet with my fingers."

He demonstrated, and in a matter of seconds had her writhing on the tips of his fingers. He whispered, "Feel how responsive you are to me, Anna. This is what you crave."

He plunged two fingers into her slippery heat while he rubbed his thumb around and around her clitoris. He was merciless, driving her until she cried out sharply, arching up off the bed, keening in pleasure.

"You've been telling yourself you're broken for so long that you've convinced yourself it's the truth. But Anna, I know your body. I know your heart. And you're just fine. Eddie was broken. And God knows, his family is broken. But you are *whole*. You're healthy. You're the sane one. He was the head case."

Anna stared up at him long and hard. He wasn't sure if he got through to her, but he was certain he'd given her a lot to think about. Which wasn't necessarily a good thing. Picking up the rhythm of a new song coming in from the living room, he made love to her again, as slow and lazy and sexy as the saxophone wailing out the blues.

Many hours, and many songs later, he finally watched Anna fall asleep in his arms. He'd given it his best shot. He'd shot every weapon in his arsenal in an effort to convince her of his feelings for her and that she was a lovable person. The rest was up to her.

Chapter 17

Anna had never been so happy and so sad at the same time in her life. Brett had given her the one perfect night she'd always dreamed of experiencing in her life. But now that it was almost over, harsh reality was about to come back with a vengeance, and she had to gird herself mentally and emotionally to face the music.

She was tired, but not sleepy, and enjoyed just lying beside Brett in the dark, listening to his quiet breathing. She wanted to soak up every last morsel of this night and preserve it carefully for the times that came next. Her life was, in effect, over, but this had been a lovely way to end it.

The bedside clock read a little after 4:00 a.m. when Brett's breathing changed. It sped up, becoming light and fast. She rolled over on her side to look at him, and in the shadow of the alarm clock saw his features contorted in anguish. Oh, dear. He was having a nightmare.

Should she wake him up? Let him sleep through it?

His breathing shifted again. He drew in a long, slow breath from the bottom of his belly to the top of his throat, held his breath for several seconds, and then released his breath slowly. She counted the seconds in worry until he drew his next long, deep breath. What was he doing? He was still definitely asleep. His eyeballs were fluttering rapidly underneath his eyelids. He was perfectly still for perhaps a minute, but then he began to thrash. The more he moved, the more tangled in the bed sheets he became, and the more agitated he became. That was it. She was waking him up. He was going to hurt himself or accidentally hurt her.

"Brett," she said quietly. "It's just a dream. Wake up."

He thrashed some more.

"Brett," she said more strongly.

Still no reaction from him.

Concerned, she raised herself up over him and actually threw her arm and a leg across him to hold him down and protect herself as she moved in to force him out of his nightmare.

His eyes shot open, but she wasn't sure he was awake yet. He was staring at something invisible with a look of horror painted on his face.

"Tell me what you see," she tried. "Describe it to me."

"They'll be dead, all of them, if I can't find the bodies. Bastards will find them first and slit their throats. Have to get to them. Ribs hurt so damn bad. Can't breathe. Gotta move."

"Who are you looking for, Brett?"

"My guys!" he replied urgently. "Where the hell are they? So dark out here. Lost my NVGs."

She frowned. NVGs? Night vision goggles, maybe? She stared down at Brett, who was now twitching beneath her as if he was acting out something he was seeing in his mind's eye. Should she try to shake him out of this or just go with his dream? If only she knew what to do!

Her gut said to go with it, so she murmured, "What are you doing right now?"

"Climbing back up the hill. Better vantage point to spot my guys—" He swore explosively, making her jump.

"What happened?" she tried.

"One of my guys. Roll him over—" A pause, and then Brett groaned in such pain that she could hardly stand to hear the sound. Surely the soldier in his dream was dead.

"Anna," he mumbled. "Can't lose you. Don't die. Come back to me."

"I'm right here, Brett. I'm fine."

If he heard her, he in no way acknowledged her. He started twitching again. *He must be moving in his nightmare again.*

"Thank God," he muttered.

"What?"

"Two of my guys—"

"No!" he moaned. "Anna. The blood. Don't bleed out on me, baby. I can't lose you—"

"Brett! I'm not dead! I'm in bed with you! Feel my body. I'm alive."

He shook his head and looked off into a horror only he could see, somewhere over her right shoulder. It dawned on her that perhaps this wasn't just a nightmare. Maybe this was some sort of flashback. Crud. She really didn't know what to do to help him now.

"Keep talking to me, Brett. What's going on?"

"Everywhere I look, she's dead. How can Anna be dead over there and up on that hill, and down the road? I keep losing her…" His voice trailed off, and she was stunned to spy a tear escaping his eye.

Had she really been hurting him that badly every time she fled him? She'd had no idea he felt so strongly about her or that he needed her so much.

Pain knifed through her so hot and sharp she nearly doubled over from it. If she'd had any idea at all he was forming such strong feelings for her, she would have left him, left Sunny Creek long ago. He in no way deserved the pain that was bound to come from caring deeply about her. God, what had she done? She was okay with destroying herself, but she couldn't bear the thought of destroying him.

She had to cut her losses—his losses—now and spare him as much pain as she humanly could. She'd already done too much damage if he was having hallucinations of her dying on some mountain in a faraway war zone.

She smoothed her hand over his brow and shushed him like she would a child, and he gradually quieted, dropping back into sleep.

She leaned down and kissed him with all the love in her heart. She kissed his furrowed brow, and his tense jaw, and then she kissed him one last time on the mouth, a benediction and a blessing, a thank-you for everything that they'd shared and a heartfelt apology for everything to come.

And then she did the only thing she could if she loved him. She slipped out of bed, dressed silently and left.

* * *

Brett woke up slowly, surprised at how late he'd slept this morning. It was after 10:00 a.m. Huh. He never slept past seven or so. Stretching out the kinks, he was surprised to register that he almost felt like he had a hangover, except he hadn't gotten drunk last night. He frowned in recollection. He'd had only a few glasses of wine. The rest of it came back. Dinner with Anna. An evening of romance and lovemaking for the ages. He'd given her everything he had in his soul to share with her—his desire, his passion and, yes, his love. He'd bared his soul to her.

She'd seemed to understand what he'd done, to appreciate it, even. But she'd also been afraid. He just had to trust that she would come around and ultimately take him at face value. She had to believe that he loved her and trust him enough to accept that he knew what he was doing in choosing her. At some point, she had to come to terms with being lovable and deserving of his affection.

He rolled over to gather her into his arms—

And there was only empty space where she'd been last night.

He sighed. Great. He supposed he should have expected her to pull another runner. He'd laid a lot on her; it had to be hard for her to absorb it all. He got up and was surprised to see that she had already cleaned up the last dishes from last night and tidied the kitchen. The white roses were now on the kitchen table.

He hunted around but found no note from her. Not going to give him any clues as to what was going on in her head, was she? He took a deep breath. He'd taken the leap of faith. Now it was up to her to do the same.

Except when Anna's quitting time from work came and went and there was no sign of her, he began to worry. He climbed in his truck and drove over to Pittypat's and was met at the door by one of the owners.

"Hey, Patricia, I'm looking for Anna Larkin. When did she leave work today? Did she say anything about needing to go somewhere or do an errand?"

"She didn't come in to work today. I figured she must have had something she had to do for the lawsuit."

His brows slammed together. "What lawsuit?"

"Mona Billingham sued her for the wrongful death of her son."

He snorted in disgust. "That's absurd. Eddie was an animal and abused her for years."

Patricia lowered her voice and leaned in close to murmur, "You and I both know that, but Mona's got all her friends coming in here and harassing Anna. I would throw them all out on their ears, but Anna won't let me. She keeps saying it's no more than she deserves. That girl. Sometimes I just want to shake some sense into her."

He knew the feeling. "If she stops by, tell her to call me, will you?"

"Of course."

He headed over to the courthouse to find out what he could about this lawsuit and to see if Anna had been there today. No one had seen Anna, although a couple of people privately complained under their breath to him about the unpleasant lawyer Mona had hired.

Why hadn't Anna mentioned any of this to him? Of course, he knew the answer. She was determined not to depend on anyone else, or heaven forbid, cause anyone else any trouble. He left the courthouse and heard his name called from behind.

He turned around to see his cousin striding toward him. "Hey, Joe."

"What brings you to my neck of the woods, Brett?"

"I'm looking for Anna. She didn't show up at work today, and she didn't call to say she wasn't coming in."

"That doesn't sound like her. She's a responsible sort. Nice lady. Kindhearted to a fault. You heard about what she did for her neighbors, didn't you?"

"No. What?"

"You didn't hear this from me, but it's all the talk among the courthouse staff. She paid off two thousand dollars' worth of tax debt for the couple that lives behind her. Apparently, the old man has dementia and hasn't been paying the taxes, and the house is going to be foreclosed on. The way I hear it, Anna emptied her savings account to do it."

Brett frowned. "When did she do this?"

"Couple of days ago. Right after she totaled her car."

She paid part of the Rogerses' taxes rather than buy herself a decent car? That sounded like her. "Are the Rogers in the clear now?" he asked.

"Not the way I hear it. An auction is going ahead to sell their house out from under them. Damned shame. They're good people."

He spun around on his heel and headed right back into the courthouse, walking along beside his cousin. He headed for the tax office, checkbook in hand.

A gray-haired woman looked up from the high counter as he walked in. "Can I help you?"

"I'm here to pay off the rest of the Rogerses' taxes."

"Oh, dear. I'm afraid it's too late for that. The foreclosure auction for their house has started."

"Where is it?" he demanded.

"It's right here. We're accepting bids for the house."

"What's the highest bid you've got?"

"I can't tell you that—"

"I'm going to double it, whatever it is. Give me the damned number so I can write a check!"

"I should think that anything in the range about twenty thousand dollars would get you the house."

Scowling ferociously at the notion of that sweet couple's entire life being worth only twenty grand, he slashed a pen across a check angrily. "There's a bid for forty thousand dollars. If anyone outbids that, my phone number is on the check. You call me, and I'll top it. Got that?"

The woman nodded, her eyes wide.

Irritated as hell, he stomped out of the tax office.

Joe was just coming down the wide staircase from whatever business had brought him here, and said, "We meet again."

"You haven't seen Anna around town today by any chance, have you?"

"Nope. Why?"

"I'm worried about her. My gut's telling me something's not right."

Joe looked at him keenly. "I'm inclined to listen to your gut. It was honed in war. When's the last time you saw her?"

"Last night late. When I woke up this morning she was gone."

"So it's like that between you, huh? Guess I won't be asking her out, then."

Possessiveness growled in his gut, but was appeased a little when Joe grinned at him and said, "You two make a good couple. I'm happy for you."

When it got dark and there was still no sign of Anna, Brett was anything but happy. Her car was still in her garage, so she hadn't fled Montana, at least. But where was she?

When 10:00 p.m. came and passed, Brett broke. He called Joe's cell phone.

"What's up, Brett?" Joe asked sleepily.

"She's still not home. Something's terribly wrong."

Abruptly, Joe was alert. "Meet me down at the station."

Brett bolted out the front door of Anna's house and ran for his truck. His gut was shouting at him, the same way it had the night as his squad had walked into that damned ambush. Flashes of going out on patrol into the black night came and went in his mind's eye. They'd geared up like always. But someone had gotten a hold of a contraband bottle of whiskey the night before. Unused to drinking any alcohol, his guys all had headaches that day. His gut had rumbled that this wasn't a good night to take them out. But orders were orders, and they would learn not to drink on the damned job—

He broke every speed limit on his way to the police station and burst into the brightly lit office.

Joe was there, waiting for him. "Normally, we can't file a missing persons report for a couple of days. But I'm willing to make an exception in this case."

"Thanks," Brett replied. "Can we ping her phone?"

"We can try. Coverage isn't great up in the mountains, though."

Sure enough, when Joe searched for her phone signal, he only got a message back that the number was unavailable. Brett cursed at the computer screen.

"Has she got any enemies? People out to harm her?" Joe asked.

"Yeah. The Billinghams."

"I'm willing to go pay them a visit if you'd like."

"I'd like."

In five minutes, Joe's police SUV parked in front of the Billingham house. It was a 1960s-vintage brick ranch with a fair bit of trash and old cars parked behind it. There were lights on in the windows. Joe ordered, "Stay in the car, Brett. Let me handle this."

Cursing and fidgeting, he complied, but he didn't like it. The front door of the Billingham home opened and Joe had a conversation with whoever stood beyond the opening. At length, Joe came back to the vehicle.

"Well?" Brett demanded.

"Jimbo says he doesn't know anything about Anna's whereabouts."

"Is he lying?"

"Unknown. He was evasive with me when I asked if Mona was home so I could talk with her. He claimed she's out of town."

Brett shook his head. "Apparently, she and some of her friends have been going into Pittypat's daily to harass Anna. I find it hard to believe that she would leave town when she's having so much fun getting revenge."

"Hmm. Maybe I'll park one of my guys down the street and wait to see if Mona comes home. I'd like to have a chat with her, too. Gauge her reactions."

Stymied, Brett was tempted to punch something. "There has to be something we can do. I can feel it. She's in trouble, Joe."

* * *

Anna's head felt like it had been split in two. She reached for it—or she tried to reach for it—but her hands wouldn't move. Her wrists hurt, too—her left one in the cast aching, the right one stinging like it had been burned. She felt stiff and sore all over. She tried to move, to stretch. But her feet wouldn't move either.

She opened her eyes and got the shock of her life. She was tied to a chair, which explained why she couldn't move. But more shocking were the rough stone walls arching up overhead. An oil lantern cast dim light on the damp granite walls. How on earth had she ended up in what looked like a cave? She had no recollection of getting here...

She cast back in her mind for the last thing she did remember...

...Dancing with Brett. And making love with him. She winced as memory came back to her of kissing him goodbye one last time and slipping out of bed. She'd cleaned up the kitchen from their romantic dinner and read the mail she hadn't opened last night.

A letter came with a court date in two weeks' time for some sort of legal hearing. She had to enter a plea, apparently. She might as well plead guilty to whatever they were charging her with. It would save everyone a lot of time and trouble. She remembered thinking that it was time to put her affairs in order.

Anna frowned, trying to remember what came next. But frowning made her head throb so bad she had to pause and wait for the jackhammers in her skull to subside before she tried again to piece together what had happened.

She had put on her coat...

Had headed outside… Where had she been going?

Oh. Right. She was going to go to the diner to warn Petunia and Patricia that when her trial happened, they were going to have to hire a new waitress/bookkeeper. The two women were very particular about who worked for them, and it might take the pair some weeks to get just the person they both wanted.

Did she ever reach the diner?

As hard as she tried, she couldn't remember talking to the twin owners of Pittypat's. Walking out the front door of her little house was the last thing she could recall, and no matter how she tried, nothing between that moment and now was coming back to her.

She looked around the cave as best she could from her chair. A tunnel opened up behind her, presumably leading outside. No light came in from the opening, though. She was alone in the cave. Which was a mixed blessing, she supposed. No one was here to kill her, but no one was here to feed her or untie her, either. She must have been knocked out, or maybe drugged. Goodness knew, her brain was fuzzy enough for her to have been drugged.

She probably ought to feel some sort of panic, but at the moment, matter-of-fact detachment was about all she could summon. Was she in shock, perhaps? Or maybe still under the influence of drugs.

She tested the ropes holding her. Someone had trussed her up tightly. From what she could see of the knots tying her wrists down to the chair arms and tying her ankles to the chair legs, someone had done a thorough job. She tried to wriggle within the bonds, to stretch her aching muscles and relieve a little of the discomfort, but there was only so much she could do tied to a chair.

Over the next half hour or so, her mind gradually cleared, and with clarity came terror. Who had done this to her? Why? What did they want with her? Was this the work of some random psychopath, or was this a specific attack aimed at her?

And the all-important question occurred to her: Was she going to die?

Ironically, death was what she'd wanted for a long time. And now she might just get her wish. She probably ought to be grateful to her kidnapper for hastening the inevitable and saving her the trouble of having to find a way to destroy what remained of her life that didn't involve actually committing suicide.

She tried to settle into a state of calm acceptance of whatever was going to come. Her entire life had been pointing at this moment. And now the end was here.

But without warning, Brett's face flashed in her mind's eye. His impassioned plea for her to value her own life rolled through her mind. Was he right? Should she trust his judgment and accept that a man like him wouldn't fall for her if she didn't have something of value to offer? Over and over, his speech rolled through her mind.

At first, she discounted it as the talk of a man in bed with a woman. Of course he was going to say nice things to get her to have sex with him. But as the last of whatever she'd been drugged with cleared from her mind, logical thought also returned. Brett didn't have to butter her up to get her to sleep with him.

Okay, so maybe he'd actually believed what he said. She replayed his exhortation to trust him and to value herself over a few more times. Was there some truth to what he said? Should she believe him?

One thing about being tied to a chair. It gave a girl plenty of time to think about her life. To pass the time and keep her from freaking out in the oppressive silence, she replayed the events from when she'd been an insecure, lonely teen and Eddie Billingham first noticed her.

In retrospect and with the wisdom of age, she could see now how he'd targeted her as a naive and vulnerable victim. He needed complete control, and she'd been too unsure and shy to fight him on anything. They'd been a match made in hell. She'd enabled his aggression and control issues, and he'd enabled her weakness and inability to stand up for herself.

She walked back through the memories of their years in Hollywood, trying to honestly tally up her mistakes and Eddie's. Maybe it took knowing Brett to get her there, but she was finally able to take a hard, honest look at her disastrous marriage.

At the end of the day, Eddie's list of failures was miles longer than hers. She hadn't been perfect, but if she were to be brutally honest, she'd been a much better wife than Eddie deserved for a lot longer than he'd deserved to have her.

Huh.

She wasn't quite sure what to do with that realization. Instead, she forced herself to move on to examining the night that Eddie died. Most of the time she did everything in her power not to think about it. But now, with death looming near, she opened that drawer in her mind and let the memories flow.

He'd been passed out drunk on the couch when she'd

come home. It had been their anniversary, and she was going to cook him a nice dinner. A roast was ready to go into the oven, and she was chopping potatoes and carrots and onions to go with it. The onions made her cry, and tears were running down her face when she heard him wake up. He'd shouted at her to bring him a beer, but she was in a hurry to get the roast in the oven before it got too late.

He'd come into the kitchen swearing at her. He'd called her a whore, which only made her tired anymore. He'd called her a slut and a bitch and worse for so long she was numb to the insults. His eyes had been cold and flat, the way they got when he was about to use his fists on her. Except tonight he reached for his belt.

That was new. The ominous slither of leather from around his waist got her attention in a big way and terror shivered through her. And then he'd charged at her, lunging forward to grab her. He'd always been fast, even though he'd gotten paunchy the past few years.

She whipped around to face him and that stupid butcher knife had been in her fist. He'd raised his arm, belt in hand, bellowing about how he was going to kill her this time—

Her mind had gone blank. Certainty that this time he was going to do it broke over her like a bucket of ice water. The shock and relief were so great she couldn't even draw breath.

That had been when he hit the knife. He'd been staring into her eyes and hadn't looked down. Hadn't realized that foot-long blade was sticking out in her hand. He'd run right onto it. The tip plunged into his belly so fast she didn't have any chance to pull it out before it was seated to the hilt in his gut. He'd stopped. Looked down in surprise. And she'd done the same.

Her fist was still wrapped around the handle, and the rest of the knife wasn't visible. The whole thing was buried in the soft flesh of his belly. Blood started to pour out, soaking his T-shirt in an instant and soaking his pants in a few seconds more.

He staggered back. Dropped the belt. He yanked the knife out of his gut, and then the blood really came, gushing through the cut in his T-shirt. He looked up at her and said without emotion, "You fucking bitch." And then he'd fallen to his knees. Pitched over on his side. And died in a spreading pool of his own blood.

It had happened so damned fast. He'd been dead in a matter of seconds.

The coroner said the knife had severed the abdominal aorta. Eddie's heart had pumped most of the blood in his body out of the cut in a matter of a few heartbeats. The coroner also said that even if a skilled surgeon had been standing over Eddie the exact second he was stabbed, he still couldn't have been saved. That was how fast he'd bled to death.

Sitting in that chair facing death had a way of stripping everything down to the essential truths. For perhaps the first time ever, she was totally, brutally honest with herself. Guilt aside, and suicidal urges aside, could she have moved that knife in time to stop Eddie from impaling himself on it? The thing was, she'd been looking at that belt coming at her, and she'd been scared to death. She really had frozen in panic.

Yes, there had probably been a millisecond to yank the knife aside. But she'd been in no condition to do it. She'd been paralyzed with terror.

Huh. Maybe the police had been right when they'd absolved her of blame for his death.

For the first time since that horrible night, she was willing to entertain the idea that maybe Eddie had been responsible for his own death. Maybe it was staring down her own death that finally led her to see that, or maybe it was Brett's influence that brought her to the moment. But either way, she was glad she got there before she died.

Although if she wasn't directly responsible for Eddie's death, maybe she didn't deserve to die after all.

The idea broke over her like a tidal wave, stopping in its tracks every other thought passing through her head. Utter stillness of mind, body, and soul came over her. Was Brett right? Did she really deserve to live?

She waited, listening to her soul. At length, a tiny, hesitant voice in the back of her head whispered that maybe, just maybe, she wasn't a bad person.

That tiny voice's message slammed into her with the force of a religious revelation. It rocked her to her core.

And that was when fear exploded in her gut. Finally, at long last, she didn't want to die. Yet, here she was, alone, tied up, at the mercy of an unknown attacker. She had to get out of here!

"I can't just sit around doing nothing, Joe!" Brett exploded. "There has to be something we can do. Someone we can interview."

"You tell me who. Name me anyone else who has some beef with her, and I'm all over pulling them in and interrogating them."

"Vinny Benson."

"The guy with the junk shop in Hillsdale?" Joe blurted, surprised.

"He has the hots for her. She said he's been coming on to her. Calls her all the time."

"When's the last time you know that he spoke to her?" Joe asked.

"Anna said he called her the morning after her front window got broken. Said he had a matching piece of glass for her. Offered to bring it to her in Sunny Creek." He snapped his fingers in recollection. "Oh, and he called her again to invite her to dinner that evening. I was with her when the call came in. She seemed a little creeped out."

Joe frowned. "How the hell did he know her window got broken only a few hours after it got busted?"

Brett and Joe traded grim looks, and as one, headed for Joe's SUV.

They were on their way out the door when one of the deputies called out, waving a handful of papers he snatched out of a printer, "Hey, I just got Anna Larkin's call log from the phone company."

Joe snagged the papers on the way past, but kept going with Brett right on his heels. They climbed in the SUV and Joe shoved the phone records at Brett. "Look through these while I drive."

Brett started with the last calls first. "Here's a phone call from Hillsdale the day Anna disappeared. She didn't' answer it. And..." He swore. "There are about six calls from Benson the day before that, all in the evening. She didn't answer any of them."

"Maybe he was stalking her," Joe commented. "The frequent, unanswered calls fit the pattern."

"Drive faster, buddy," Brett ground out.

* * *

Anna rocked back and forth until her chair tipped over backward. Unlike the movies, the damned chair didn't break, and she managed to hit the back of her head, hard, on the stone floor. As if her head didn't already hurt enough, now it throbbed so badly that her vision was a little fuzzy.

She managed to roll onto her right side, but the ropes dug into her flesh even worse now. And she had to pee. This was going to get very unpleasant very soon if someone didn't come untie her.

Her mouth was parched, her lips cracking from dehydration. Her stomach growled with hunger, too. But none of that mattered. If she didn't find a way out of here, she was dead.

Brett would never forgive her if she died on him. He said he wanted a future with her. And if he would have her, she wanted a future with him, too.

Think, Anna. There has to be something you can do.

She looked around the cave for something, anything to help her. There was only rock and more rock. And that lantern hanging on a high hook. Steel tracks crossed the floor like a mini-railroad used to pass through here. This must be an old mine. This area was historically known for sapphire deposits.

Where there were mines, there were tools. And there were shards of chiseled rock. She squinted, trying to focus her eyes on the ground in the corners. Over there. Some scree was piled up beside the wall. How to get to it, though?

She experimented, and with great effort was able to roll onto her knees and face. It was terribly uncomfortable and she scraped her face all to heck but was able to inchworm her way across the cave, literally a few inches at a time.

It was laborious in the extreme and now her face was killing her along with her head. But she was determined to get out of here. The man she loved was waiting for her.

I'm coming, Brett. Just hang in there. Have faith in me. I didn't run away this time.

Joe parked the SUV in front of the junk shop and Brett said warningly, "Don't tell me to sit in the car. Anna has been missing for twenty-four hours and I'm not sitting anywhere."

Joe rolled his eyes. "Then promise me you'll let me do the talking. This is a legal matter, and if you mess it up a criminal could walk free."

Brett nodded tersely and climbed out. They stepped inside the junk shop and a voice yelled from the back of the store, "Be with you in a sec."

"That's Vinny," Brett murmured.

Joe nodded, then moved quickly and quietly past the front counter toward the storeroom in the back. Brett recognized his cousin's intent to take a look around the nonpublic portion of the store and fell in behind Joe, rolling silently from heel to toe with each step, moving fast and catlike.

Every sense on high alert, he moved into the jungle of antiques and assorted junk stacked high in the storeroom. He was alert for any unexpected movements, and his hands itched to hold a weapon to be ready to take out any threats.

He cast his awareness outward. Was Anna here somewhere? Tied up maybe? Unable to let him know she was nearby? He didn't know if he would instinctively sense her or not, but he tried anyway. He was a desperate man.

If she was here, he didn't feel her presence.

Joe hand signaled him to fan out and work his way down the right side of the room. Joe would take the middle. Brett nodded and moved into the far aisle between piles of junk. Staying low, he moved fast, peering between stacks of crap, clearing every possible nook and cranny where a human being could be stashed.

"Hey! You're not allowed back here!" That was Vinny, ahead and to the left.

"Mr. Benson, I'm Sheriff Westlake."

"I know who you are. What can I do for you today?"

Joe spoke casually, much more so than Brett would have been able to manage, "I'm trying to find Anna Larkin. I need to speak with her about a legal matter. I hear you two are friends, and I was wondering if you by any chance know how I can get a hold of her."

His search of the right side of the storeroom complete, Brett sprinted silently back to the front of the big space. Crouching, he peeked out from behind a bulky rolltop desk and saw that Joe blocked Vinny's line of sight back this way. Perfect. Brett darted across the open space, and this time worked his way up the far left aisle in search of Anna.

"Have you called her cell phone? I've got her number if you need it."

"That would be helpful. Thanks, man," Joe said pleasantly.

Brett half listened as Vinny rattled off the number he already knew by heart, the rest of his attention on his search. Dammit. He reached the end of the left half of the storeroom without spotting anyplace Vinny could be hiding her.

"When's the last time you saw Anna?" Joe asked.

Vinny hemmed and hawed for a shade too long and then said, "Oh. Yeah. I remember now. She came in a few days ago looking for a piece of glass for a broken window. I told her I'd be on the lookout for it. Antique glass, you know. Hard to find. Has to be matched carefully." He added in a bragging tone, "In fact, I just found her the right piece of it yesterday. It's right over here."

He was lying. He'd called Anna and told her three days ago that he had the glass.

"How well do you know Anna?" Joe asked a little less casually.

"Why?" Vinny retorted, sounding a bit defensive.

"Would you say you're close friends?"

"Why do you care how close we are?" Vinny was sounding a lot defensive now.

Joe leaned on the guy even harder. "How close does she think you two are?"

"She thinks we're plenty close!" Vinny was definitely ticked off.

"That's not the way I hear it. I hear she thinks you're creepy. A stalker, even."

"Get out of my store and don't come back unless you have a search warrant!" Vinny shouted.

Joe's voice was silky smooth. "Where are you going, Vinny? That's a big bag of gear you've got there. Mind if I take a look at it?"

"Yes, I damned well mind! Get out of here. You're not even supposed to be in the back room anyway. I'll call your boss!"

Joe snorted gratifyingly. "I am the boss. I'm the

county sheriff. But feel free to call the governor of Montana if you don't like how I'm doing my job."

Brett heard Joe start to move and took the cue, darting back to the front of the storeroom and slipping out into the showroom. He moved silently out the front door and raced over to Joe's SUV, easing inside just as Joe was escorted off the premises by one very red-faced Vinny.

Joe climbed into the SUV thoughtfully. "He got awfully mad as soon as I asked him about his relationship with Anna."

"He's lying," Brett declared hotly.

"Caught that, did you? Why do you suppose he did that?"

"Why don't you march back in there, put him in a headlock and ask him?"

"Patience, Brett. We're going to head on down the street a little ways, park the car, and see what develops."

"What did you see?" Brett demanded. He sensed that Joe wasn't telling him everything.

"Our friend Vinny was packing a bag. Looked like the kind of stuff someone might take on a camping trip. Food, jugs of water. Lantern fuel. Blankets. Rope. Lots of rope, in fact."

"And?"

Joe stared at him. "Wow. You really are off your game, aren't you?"

He answered raggedly, "I love her, man."

Joe shot him a sympathetic look. "Think about it, Brett. If you were holding a prisoner in some isolated location, what kind of supplies would you need?"

He lurched in his seat. "Son of a—"

"Slow down, there. You can't barge in and confront

him. He'll refuse to tell you a thing. If he thinks we're on to him, ole Vinny may not show up to feed Annie or give her water. We have to let him go and hope he leads us to her."

"What if the bastard's just going out camping, and we waste a bunch of time following him?"

"First thing tomorrow morning, I can officially declare Anna missing and call up every reserve deputy in the county. I'll have dozens of men and women out looking for her by noon tomorrow. But in the meantime, I smell a rat with this guy."

"What about Mona Billingham?" Brett asked.

"My guy saw her roll in about two thirty last night. He probably should have arrested her for driving drunk based on his description of how she wove down the street in her car and staggered into her house, but I told him to back off for the same reason we're backing off Vinny. I can't spook whoever's got her. I've got two deputies staking out the Billingham house. If either Jimbo or Mona leaves, one of my guys will follow them."

At least Joe wasn't disputing the fact that Anna had fallen victim to foul play. Brett was grateful for that, at least.

"Here we go," Joe said tightly.

Brett looked up and saw a silver pickup truck pull out of the parking lot beside Vinny's store. "That looks a lot like the truck that forced Anna off the road."

"Funny that," Joe commented. "Take these binoculars and keep an eye on him while I drive."

"Gladly." Brett plastered the field glasses to his eyes. "Take us to her, you son of a bitch."

It took Ann nearly as long to turn around so her hands faced the wall as it did to cross the entire space.

She felt around with her floor-side hand until she found a jagged shard of sharp rock. She fumbled with it and dropped it a few times but eventually managed to pick it up so the sharp edge was facing backward toward her wrists. She started to saw at the tough nylon rope.

Unlike the movies, she didn't make fast progress. Crud. This was going to take a while. Tears of fear and frustration ran down her face, but she kept at it, rubbing the stone doggedly across her ropes.

But at least she wasn't just sitting here waiting to die. She would do whatever it took to get out of here alive. She had to live for Brett, darn it.

Vinny drove into the mountains above Hillsdale, and Joe was forced to drop back a long ways on the deserted roads so Vinny wouldn't spot them. The pavement gave out, and they were able to follow Vinny for a little while just from the plume of dust his truck left behind. But then they hit the snow line and quickly lost sight of him on the narrow, winding road through skinny pine trees.

They came to an intersection and Joe stopped, swearing. "Did you see which way he went?"

Brett swore even more vehemently. "No. The trees blocked him. He could have gone any direction."

"The good news is none of these roads go more than a few miles in any direction. We need to go back to town. Organize a search party."

Panic threatened to overtake Brett. Flashes of vast expanses of barren, foreign mountains distracted him, but he fought like hell to stay present. To keep thinking. For Anna.

"It could take days or weeks to search miles of these

mountains. The bastard will finish playing with her and kill her long before then."

"Let's not think the worst, Brett—"

"He kidnapped her! He's going to take out his sick fantasies on her and then he'll have no choice but to silence her for good."

Joe didn't refute the claim. While Brett appreciated his cousin's honesty with him, his gut clenched so hard he could barely stay upright at the thought of that sick bastard laying hands on her.

Joe turned the SUV around and pointed it back toward Sunny Creek, and Brett gave in to panic. The flashbacks came faster now, more insistent. He couldn't hold them off any longer. Images of that night came roaring back. They'd left base camp not long after full dark to patrol a road through a mountain pass. The local insurgents used it to cross from one valley to the next, and a coalition medical convoy needed to use the pass the following day to get badly needed medical supplies to a forward operating location.

They'd driven to the base of the mountain, but then they'd proceeded on foot. Rico—the dog handler— and Reggie had gone first. Zimmerman, the one who'd found the whiskey, had moved up beside Rico. Brett caught only snatches of the conversation, but Zimm thought his girlfriend was cheating on him and was bitching about it to Rico.

They didn't expect opposition until they neared the summit. Which was why, when Reggie started acting jumpy, no one had paid particular attention. He'd been a little twitchy recently anyway. The veterinarian back at base camp said Reggie was showing signs of battle fatigue and was about due to be retired. But he was beloved by the squad, and they'd all argued to keep him out there a little longer.

Brett sat bolt upright in his seat. "Take me to the ranch right now!"

"What?" Joe bit out.

"Reggie. He's a military working dog. He can track a scent like nobody's business."

Joe nodded and guided the SUV toward the ranch. "Call ahead and tell Uncle John to gather all the men he's got and arm them like it's World War Three."

Brett made the call.

"Dad, it's Brett. We have a lead on where Anna may be. It's possible that Vinny Benson kidnapped her and is hiding her in the McMinn Range. I need you to get all the guys and guns you can, load up Reggie and meet us at the western base of the McMinn road as fast as you can."

Joe added, "Have him bring an article of clothing Anna has worn recently."

Brett nodded and relayed the instruction.

His old man hadn't been a Green Berett for nothing. John replied tersely, "Roger. I'll have the whole damned cavalry there in thirty minutes."

Given that it was a solid twenty-minute drive from the ranch to the road, Brett was impressed. Still, he couldn't resist saying, "Hurry, Dad."

Anna thought she heard a noise and froze, listening hard. She heard blood pounding in her ears, but nothing else. She'd made some progress after she got the hang of using a jagged spot on the rock to pick at the nylon fibers, rather than just sawing at them. She guessed she was halfway through the rope, but she couldn't really see it from her awkward position on the floor.

"Well, well, well. Haven't we been a resourceful prisoner while I was gone?" a familiar voice said from behind her.

Vinny.

"So. You're as sick and twisted as I thought you might be," she said scornfully. No way in hell was she showing this guy fear. She'd learned early from Eddie that predators fed on it.

"You'll change your tune soon enough. When you have to beg me for your life."

She didn't have an answer for that. She supposed she would beg if that was what it took to get back to Brett alive. She frantically tried to palm the shard of rock as Vinny came over and righted her chair.

Must distract him. Keep him from noticing the partially shredded rope.

"Well, lookee at that. You've been trying to free yourself."

Dammit.

"That's okay. I'm going to untie you anyway. I have other plans for you and me tonight." He leaned down and licked her face, his wet tongue running all the way from her jaw to her temple. Oh, God. Disgust rolled through her. She held herself rigid and didn't pull away, but it was hard to stay still.

"I like the taste of your tears. You'll cry for me tonight, won't you?"

A shudder of revulsion passed through her. She took a deep breath, plucked up her courage and said gamely enough, "I'm not going to do anything but pee all over you if you don't let me go to the bathroom."

"Oh. Yeah. Right. Didn't think about that." He untied her wrists and stepped back all the way to the other side of the cave, perhaps twenty feet away. "Untie your feet. You can use that bucket over there."

She bent down to untie her own ankles and heard the snick of shotgun shells being chambered behind her. "Don't go getting any bright ideas, now. I'd hate to have to shoot you before I'm done with you."

Her mind went into a strange survival overdrive. He planned to rape her, did he? Surely, at some point during that process, he would make himself vulnerable to her. He would have to come in close proximity to her to do the deed. That would be when she would make her move.

Until then, she would do her best to lull him into a false sense of security. God knew, she knew all about acting cowed and submissive. If Eddie had taught her nothing else, it was how to act like a mouse.

She ignored her humiliation at having to drop her pants and pee in front of him. It was all part of the game now. A life-and-death game of cat and mouse. Except Vinny didn't realize that she wasn't the mouse at all.

Joe led the convoy of trucks filled with angry ranch hands up to the intersection where they'd lost Anna. Brett jumped out and lifted Reggie down from his father's truck. Even Miranda had come along, a shotgun across her lap and a look in her eye that promised hell to pay for whoever had messed with her family.

Brett had never been Reggie's handler, but he'd seen Rico work the black Lab more times than he could count. Now, he could only pray the dog would recognize commands from a handler he'd never been trained to work with.

He set Reggie down in the middle of the intersection and unclipped the leash from his collar. Brett held out Anna's mittens and hat that Miranda had brought along under Reggie's nose and then looked the dog in the eye. "Search, Reggie. Search."

The dog looked up at him intently for a moment, his brown eyes soft and wise. And then the dog did an odd thing. He took another long sniff at the hat and mittens, as if he was cementing the scent in his mind. And then his nose went to the ground.

Praise the Lord and pass the potatoes. Reggie seemed to know what Brett wanted of him. He held his breath as the dog moved in a slow circle around the intersection. All of a sudden, Reggie took off down one of the side roads, moving with confidence.

Of course, with his crippled hips, he wasn't fast, and Brett and others had no trouble jogging along behind the dog and keeping up with him. Now and then Reggie would crisscross back and forth across the road, and then he would proceed straight ahead again.

Miranda drove along slowly behind the search party in a pickup truck for as long as they kept to the road.

But then Reggie veered off into the trees, and it became a lot harder to keep up with the dog, who followed the trail without any regard for low branches and brush that conspired to slow down and confound the humans behind him.

Brett followed the black tail that stood up like a flag in front of him and blinked hard as memory of Reggie's tail standing up just like that flashed into his mind's eye. The road had narrowed, and a landslide had blocked it partially. They had to climb up and over a tall pile of debris, exposing themselves to anyone above them. Reggie had hesitated, and Rico had muttered something under his breath about the rocks cutting Reggie's feet and picked up the dog.

He blinked hard. *Montana. Anna.* The trees thinned as the dog led them higher up the mountainside. Barren rocks surrounded him, and reality blended with memory until Brett couldn't tell one from the other. Details of the ambush were coming back to him thick and fast now. Stuff he hadn't remembered about that night.

He'd forgotten that Reggie had wriggled to get down, unhappy at being held. Brett remembered signaling Zimmerman to fall back and let Rico and Reggie clear the far side of the landslide, but that Zimm had ignored him. Zimm had spotted something ahead in the darkness and wanted to check it out.

Reggie disappeared over the edge of the rock pile, then Rico and Zimm had dropped out of sight. He raised his hand to call a halt. Signaled for his guys to fan out on their bellies across the summit of the mound of dirt and rock, but they never got there. Zimmerman cried out, and they'd all rushed forward, ignoring his order to take up protected firing positions. Brett went on ahead to check on Rico and Zimm and let his guys cover him from behind. He'd topped the rise—

His mind went blank, and abruptly, he was on a Montana mountain with the woman he loved out here somewhere. Reggie paused, panting, and Brett caught up to the elderly dog.

"You're doing great, buddy." He gave the dog a brief ear scratch, let him catch his breath and then held out Anna's mittens and hat again. "Search, Reggie."

He could swear the dog nodded at him. Reggie did a tight three-sixty, reacquired the scent and pressed on gamely, his limp more pronounced. But that dog didn't have any quit in him. Brett suspected Reggie would drop dead before he stopped tracking Anna.

Please, God, let this work.

Anna schooled her face to pleased surprise as Vinny laid out a picnic on a boulder not far from where he'd tied her up again. At least she was sitting on the ground now and not stuck in that damned chair. Unfortunately, he'd tied her wrists together behind her back, so her shoulders were still screaming at her. She felt the wall at her back and located a little jut in the rocks, and was already working her wrist ropes against it. The job was going faster this time, now that she had the knack of fraying the twisted fibers once she sawed through the woven nylon rope casing.

Vinny started to eat and drink, leaning over from time to time to feed her a morsel of food and grope her chest. Frankly, she didn't care what he did as long as he believed she was at his mercy. He did feed her a bottle of water, which she guzzled gratefully. Her headache abated slightly.

"How did you pull it off? Kidnapping me, I mean?"

"Easy. I followed you from your house, and when you were on a deserted stretch of street, I snuck up behind you and hit you with a brick. Then I dragged you into an alley, tied and gagged you, and covered you with a tarp. I went and got my truck and gave you a shot of dog tranquilizer. That was the tricky part. I didn't want to kill you, but I didn't know how much to give you. I got it right, obviously."

She batted her eyes and tried to look terribly impressed. "That took a lot of planning. I suppose I should be flattered that you went to all this trouble to be alone with me."

He nodded. "You should be flattered."

Jerk. "What is this place? An old sapphire mine? It's really cool."

She tuned out as he launched into a lengthy history of sapphire mining in the region and how old this mine was. She did note that it was in the McMinn Range, though. At least she wasn't too far from civilization and help.

Vinny set aside the plate of sandwiches and sliced apples, and an almost feverish look entered his stare. Here it came. He was going to attack her now. She forced her body to relax, to give away no sign of her intent to fight back. She had to wait for an opening when his guard was down. She sawed even more frantically at her wrists. It would help a ton if she could regain use of her hands. And the rope felt as if she'd almost shredded it through.

If she could just delay him a few more minutes. Then maybe she'd have her hands free. "Tell me more about yourself, Vinny. I feel as if I hardly know you."

"Shut up, Anna. It's time for you to beg."

Brett charged over the hill, and Rico and Zimmerman were already down, their throats slit by an insurgent who was still bending over Zimmerman's corpse, tugging at his assault rifle, which was caught under Zimm's body.

He charged forward and the insurgent fled. Reggie, hovering frantically beside Rico's gutted body, darted forward to block Brett's progress, and let out one short, sharp bark, bodily leaning against Brett, trying desperately to herd him backward. Away from danger.

Reggie had actually knocked him over, he had shoved Brett so hard. Which, of course, saved his life. Brett was falling backward as a satchel charge, hastily hidden under Rico's body by that insurgent, blew up. It had been a big one.

Reggie barked again, and Brett looked up sharply. Montana. Snow. Bright daylight. And Reggie was running back toward him. Brett braced himself for the dog to fling himself at Brett, but instead, Reggie turned in a quick circle and ran back to where he'd just been.

Brett pulled the rifle off his shoulder, and John and Joe did the same. John signaled the ranch hands to stay back and let the three of them go first. Brett took the lead, moving with all the stealth learned in a decade of combat. He approached the outcropping of rock that Reggie was now standing beside, wagging his tail eagerly. He'd nearly reached the dog before he saw the opening. An old mine entrance was carved out of the rock face.

Quietly, he attached a leash to Reggie's collar and passed the leash to John. His father leaned down to cup the dog's nose in his hand and Brett started. He'd forgotten that command. Rico used to do that when they needed Reggie to be quiet and make no noise. His father passed the leash to Hank Mathers, and Reggie sat obediently beside him.

Brett eased into the tunnel with Joe on his heels and John bringing up the rear. Brett moved forward quickly, shielding his small pocket flashlight with his hand as he used it to see the footing.

The tunnel split. He briefly considered going back to get Reggie when he heard a female voice from the larger tunnel, leading to the right.

His entire being clenched. That was Anna, and she had just cried out in pain. Joe's hand landed heavily on his arm, and just in the nick of time. He'd gathered himself to charge headlong down the tunnel to her rescue. Just like he had charged into the ambush.

His men had disobeyed orders and rushed ahead with him when he'd specifically told them to lie down and form a shooting line on top of that pile of rock. As tempted as he was to disobey Joe now, common sense told him to go slow.

In the meantime, the realization that his men had disobeyed his orders roared through his brain. *That* was why they'd all been charging down that pile of rock, right into the blast zone, when the satchel charge blew! He *hadn't* led them into it like he'd feared!

Flashlight off now, he crept down the tunnel carefully, feeling each step before he took it, making sure to move in utter silence. He went about fifty feet when the tunnel turned again. Light shone around the corner.

He signaled Joe to break right into the room and that he would break left. Joe nodded his understanding. John would hang back and cover them both, and he nodded as well. Thank God for military veterans who knew how to do this sort of stuff.

Brett held up three fingers. Folded down one finger. Two. Folded down a second finger. One.

And then he went.

He burst into a small chamber perhaps twenty feet across, lit by a lantern and several candles. Two people were wrestling on the floor. He saw the one on the bottom raise a hand over the head of the one on top and bring an object down hard on the back of the top person's head.

The top person shouted and reared back, arm raised. *Vinny.* Something metal flashed in the man's hand. *Knife.*

Brett identified Anna on the ground beneath him and fired at Vinny. He tapped the trigger twice in fast succession. From his right, two more shots came at almost the exact same time.

Vinny collapsed on top of Anna as Brett raced forward. But before he could get to her, she shoved Vinny off her and clambered to her feet. As she did so, she scooped up the knife and held it in front of her, panting.

Brett pulled up short in front of her. The last thing he needed to do was pull an Eddie and impale himself on a damned knife while she was too panicked to do anything about it.

"Put the knife down, Anna," Joe said calmly from behind him.

It clattered to the stone floor and Brett rushed forward, wrapping her in a crushing embrace. She hung on to him with all her might, her face buried against his neck.

How long they stood there like that, Brett had no idea. But by the time he looked up, John and Miranda and Reggie were rushing into the cave and joined in on the hug.

The dog barked excitedly at Anna, and that finally reached past Brett's weak-kneed relief. "You have to reward him for finding you. He won the game and you have to play with him, now."

Anna laughed and leaned down to scratch Reggie's

ears before dropping a kiss on his nose. "You're the best dog ever, aren't you?"

Reggie licked her back, and everyone laughed.

Anna straightened and looked Brett in the eye. "I knew you'd come for me. I believed in you. I only hoped you would believe in me and know I didn't run away again."

He stared hard at her, hoping against hope that she meant what he thought she did. "I'm here, aren't I? I knew something was wrong as soon as you didn't come home from work on time."

"You were right," she declared.

"About anything in particular?" he asked cautiously.

"I had plenty of time to think about everything you said. I also thought long and hard about what happened the night Eddie died."

"And?"

She glanced over at Joe and then back at him. "The police got it right. I was so panicked that he was going to beat me with his belt that I froze. I panicked. You've seen me panic before, and you know I freeze, right?"

Brett nodded. "Right."

"Once I got past my guilt and self-loathing to think rationally about that night, I realized Eddie was the one at fault. He caused me to panic and he impaled himself on that knife. If he hadn't been blinded by his rage, he would have seen the knife and stopped."

A smile started somewhere inside Brett's chest and started working its way up toward his face as she continued.

"I'll always feel bad about that night. And I'm willing to testify in court about exactly what happened. I'm confident I'll be exonerated from any fault in his death."

John Morgan growled, "You'll have the best lawyer money can buy."

Joe added, "Oh, I imagine when Mona's lawyer sees the police files I got this morning from California, sees Eddie's history of run-ins with the law, and he reads the police report from the night of Eddie's death—which by the way says pretty much the exact same thing you just did, Anna—he won't have any stomach to pursue Mona's claim."

Anna looked around the room, crowded with people who had come roaring to her rescue when she was in trouble, her heart so full she could hardly contain all the feelings in it. "Is this what having a real family is like?" she asked Brett in a small voice.

He grinned at her. "Yup. Get used to it, kid. You'll never have a moment's peace again. They'll be all up in our business all the damned time."

Our business. "As in you and me?" she asked hopefully.

"As in us together forever if you'll have me."

"Are you asking me what I think you are?" she gasped.

He dropped down on one knee to a chorus of cheers. "Anna, will you marry me?"

"Of course I'll marry you, Brett Morgan!" She dragged him to his feet and laid a big, hot kiss on him that promised many more of the same to come. A lifetime more.

Eventually, when his head was swimming with more joy than he could believe, he lifted his head and saw the tears of his parents and broad grins of the ranch hands who were his family. They'd never abandoned him, even though God knew he'd given them plenty of reason to.

He couldn't think of anyone else he would rather share this moment with.

He looked down at Anna and murmured, "Happy?"

"Ecstatic. You're perfect!"

He snorted. "I've got a long ways to go to get there—" he looked over significantly at Willa Mathers "—but I'm willing to do the work. For you."

Willa's eyebrows shot up. "What changed?" she asked.

He shrugged. "I remembered a few things I'd forgotten until I was under enough stress to trigger the memories. I think I'm going to be okay."

Willa shook her head. "Anna, I have *got* to talk to you about how you did it. I've never met a more stubborn, pigheaded man than Brett, and yet you broke through to him when no one else could. What on earth is your secret?"

Anna wrapped her arms around his waist and leaned into him, trusting him to catch her if she fell. Trusting him always to catch her. She looked over at Willa and said warmly, "That's easy. Love is the secret."

* * * * *

WE HOPE YOU ENJOYED THIS BOOK!

HARLEQUIN®

ROMANTIC suspense

Experience the rush of thrilling adventure, captivating mystery and unexpected romance.

Discover four new books every month, available wherever books are sold!

Harlequin.com

HRSHALO2019

#2075 COLTON FAMILY BODYGUARD
The Coltons of Mustang Valley • by Jennifer Morey

After Hazel Hart's daughter witnesses a murder, former navy SEAL Callum Colton saves them from being run down by the murderer's car. But now that the three of them are on the run, Callum's demons are back to haunt him—and he'll have to focus on the present to stop a killer.

#2076 COLTON FIRST RESPONDER
The Coltons of Mustang Valley
by Linda O. Johnston

Savannah Oliver has been arrested for the murder of her ex-husband, Zane, after their ugly divorce—but she doesn't believe he is dead. Grayson Colton believes her, and as Mustang Valley recovers from an earthquake, the two of them have to clear Savannah's name.

#2077 COWBOY'S VOW TO PROTECT
Cowboys of Holiday Ranch • by Carla Cassidy

Flint McCay had no idea what he was getting into when he found Madison Taylor hiding in the hay in his barn. But now they're both in danger and Flint must protect both Madison and his own secrets in order for them to make it out alive...and in love.

#2078 HIS SOLDIER UNDER SIEGE
The Riley Code • by Regan Black

Someone is determined to break Major Grace Ann Riley. After Derek Sayer, a friend with benefits, helps her fight off the attacker, he's determined to help Grace Ann, no matter how independently she tries to handle it. But as their relationship deepens, the attacker is circling closer...

"Flint."

He looked at her once again.

"Flint, kiss me," she said softly.

His eyes flamed as if suddenly shot through with bright neon lights. "Madison, I told you earlier this afternoon that we shouldn't do any more of that."

His slightly husky voice let her know his words meant nothing, that despite what he said, he wouldn't mind kissing her once again. "But why shouldn't we?" She moved a little closer to him, close enough that their thighs touched.

He smelled so good. It was the scent of sunshine and the fragrance of his cologne that had become as familiar to her as her own heartbeat. She wanted to wrap herself up in it and wear it against her naked skin. "Don't you want to kiss me again?"

He drew in an audible breath. "Oh, woman, you're killing me here." His eyes flamed once again and he quickly looked away from her. "Of course I'd like to kiss you again, but you're vulnerable right now, Madison. All of this has you shaken up and you might not really know what you want."

"Well, that's a load of baloney," she scoffed. "Look at me, Flint." She waited until his gaze was once again on her. "I know exactly what I want. I want you to kiss me long and hard."

She knew by the glaze of his eyes and his sudden intake of breath that he was going to do it, and it was going to be amazing.

His mouth took hers in a kiss that seared her to her soul. His hands tangled first in her long hair and then slid down her back to her waist. He tugged her closer to him as she opened her mouth to invite him in.

Don't miss
Cowboy's Vow to Protect *by Carla Cassidy,*
available February 2020 wherever
Harlequin® Romantic Suspense
books and ebooks are sold.

Harlequin.com